T0663978

THE VICTIM AWAKES

"I can't allow you to sit up yet, you've had major surgery performed on your arms, and it's not healed well enough. I'm afraid you might start to bleed." There it was again—skirting around the edges—hinting, touching, and moving away. *Can I say the words?*

"Surgery?" Joanne moaned. "What surgery?... Why... What surgery? Why did you operate on me?"

Tell her, dammit! It's your responsibility...

"You were found in your bedroom with the... the... the surgery already completed."

T34750

CUTUP

WILLIAM CROSS

BERKLEY BOOKS, NEW YORK

PAWNEE PUBLIC LIBRARY
613 DOUGLAS
PAWNEE, IL 62558

If you purchased this book without a cover you should be aware that this book is stolen property. It was reported as "unsold and destroyed" to the publisher and neither the author nor the publisher has received any payment for this "stripped book."

For Ginny

Thanks to good friends:
Judy Boynton and the Mercer Island Group;
Frank Lambirth for patching the potholes.

CUTUP

A Berkley Book / published by arrangement with
the author

PRINTING HISTORY
Berkley edition / March 1993

All rights reserved.
Copyright © 1993 by William E. Cross.
This book may not be reproduced in
whole or in part, by mimeograph or any other
means, without permission. For information
address: The Berkley Publishing Group,
200 Madison Avenue, New York, New York 10016.

ISBN: 0-425-13759-7

A BERKLEY BOOK ®TM 757,375
Berkley Books are published by The Berkley Publishing Group,
200 Madison Avenue, New York, New York 10016.
The name "BERKLEY" and the "B" logo
are trademarks belonging to Berkley Publishing Corporation.

PRINTED IN THE UNITED STATES OF AMERICA

10 9 8 7 6 5 4 3 2 1

chapter//one

He kept to the shadows as he moved along the row of apartment buildings. Shifting a leather bag from his left hand to his right, he studied the siding in the darkness. Building 36. *Where is it?* The fog hugged the grass as he skirted the last structure and looked down a long alleyway of regimentally aligned garage doors. Large block letters on the corner announced—36.

"Bastards," he said under his breath.

People who decide, the ones who run things, always make everything tough to do, tough to find, he thought. His heart pounded; his chest heaved. He'd planned this for months, read every book he could find, practiced over and over and over, and now he was here. The first time. *Gonna do it, now.*

He located apartment 3-B in the one-story building and walked into its enclosed courtyard. It was a tangle of overgrown plants that led up to a dark door and window. Only the muted sound of traffic in the distance broke the hush of the early morning.

His black clothing made him almost invisible in the limited light as he edged along the wall and looked into the bedroom window. The room was unoccupied.

The memory of her walking down the dimly lit hospital corridor flashed across his mind. She was so clean, so beautiful, but so goddamned cold and distant. Her, with her "I'm better than you—you piece of shit" attitude. He had smiled at her a couple of times as she went by, but she looked through him as though he were transparent, of no consequence, or—even worse—something on her shoe to be scraped off on the curb. His stomach churned with the humiliation. He focused back on the room.

1

It was shadowed and only a weak light filtered in from an open hallway door.

Eatin' or takin' her morning bath. He reached up and touched the screen. The window itself was open with just a microthin thickness of fiberglass between him and her bedroom.

Stupid bitch, thinks she knows so much, and doesn't even know about burglars and stuff like that? His knife parted the mesh with a zip, and a hand-sized flap fell away. He unlatched the catch, lifted the screen out, and set it in the planter next to him.

Gentle, gentle ... gotta be quiet. He pushed his head and shoulders in the window, then set the bag on the carpeted floor. As he moved through the opening, his clothing rubbed the sill with a soft hiss. He huddled next to the bag on the plush carpeting and listened. This was the part he loved—the excitement, coiled down with his nerves tingling—his body alive with the ecstasy of anticipation.

From the open hallway door came the barely audible, tinny music from a radio, an occasional gurgle of water, and low nasal humming. He smiled. She had heard nothing. He glanced around the bedroom.

On the back of the closet door hung her nurse's uniform, white and clean even in the dimness of the room, ready for her warm, shapely body. He could picture her during the day as she moved around in it with authority, barking out orders to the women on her shift, changing IVs, doing all the secret things only the doctors and nurses knew anything about. The painful things, the feeling, the cutting ... the surgery ... the magic healing things that made people well, made them live longer. . . .

He shook his head and concentrated. *I'm in a dark room, and I'm here to* . . . Then he looked up at the light from the door and smiled. *Enjoy your bath, bitch. It's the last one you'll ever take, at least without help.*

It was lighter in the courtyard, but the shadows in the room were still deep. He unzipped the bag, withdrew a gun from the yawning interior, then screwed a long gray silencer on the end of it. A glinting scalpel fell to the floor when he withdrew the gun. He cursed silently and carefully jammed the scalpel back into the bag, then stretched a black ski mask over his head and adjusted it so he could see. It covered the top of his head and left only his jaw and mouth exposed. He stood, and as he moved by the unmade bed, he hesitated at the musky smell of her, still emanating from the sheets. The image of her warm, sensuous body snuggled under the blankets flashed in his mind. His loins stirred.

Gotta get to her before she climbs outta the tub, while she's still helpless as possible. . . .

As he started for the door, a shaking fit seized his body from his head to his feet.

He leaned against the wall breathing convulsively. Trying to focus his eyes, he looked at his vibrating hands, then slid to his knees and laid the gun on the carpeting to avoid dropping it. Heat built under the mask so he jerked it off. Sweat ran down his face as he slouched against the wall to keep from fainting. Nodding, his mind drifted away and he was in the muggy death room again, screaming at the top of his lungs.

"No! No! She can't be dead!"

The image of him trying to get to where his dead mother lay on the bed with candles burning on either side thundered full-formed into his mind.

Crying and wailing—

The smells of the dirt floor, the clay walls, and the acrid candle smoke.

The moldering presence of death.

The cloying warmth from the portable kerosene heater—so oppressive, so suffocating.

Flickering light from the candles danced on the bare, rough-hewn walls, adding to the eerie medieval-like gloom. He was young, five years old, struggling against a woman to get to his mother's side—

"No! No! It isn't true!" The mixture of the heat, the raging anguish, and the hopeless feeling overwhelmed him.

"Let me go! Let me go! I have to touch her!" The woman's strong arms held him tightly.

Suddenly he was transported to a sun-bleached, dusty field

where a giant, orange sun filled the sky and grew larger, and larger, and larger—

Then—with a snap—it was black and cold. He could feel his lungs suck for air, but getting slower, slower, and slower.

As his balled-up fists swam into focus, his breathing returned to normal and his shaking abated. Sweat poured from his face and arms. He shivered, reached up, wiped the moisture from his forehead with his sleeve, then pulled the mask back over his head and listened.

The woman still hummed, and the radio still played.

I only imagined the words, he thought with relief. His hand steady again, he picked up the gun and stood.

As he peeked around the edge of the door frame, he could smell the bathroom air—warm, soapy, flowery fragrant and laden with humidity. He shook his head, trying to bring the double images together.

The tub water was thick with bubbles and the long-haired woman leaned back looking at the ceiling. Her head rested on the tub with her arms floating on the surface of the water as she idly played in the foam.

"Bum, bum, bum . . . bum, bum," she hummed an unidentifiable song.

You'll notice me now, bitch! He moved abruptly into the opening, pointed the gun at her, and said in a soft voice, "Don't scream, lady—don't scream—or I'll shoot you."

"Ohh!" she yelled, instantly sat up, then covered her breasts with crossed arms in the same motion. The water sloshed back and forth and ran down the edges of the tub in rivulets of foam.

"Don't make no sound, lady . . . I don't want to kill you, so don't make no sound. . . ."

The woman's eyes were wide with terror as she looked past him into the hall, measuring the distance to the door.

"Don't think about it, lady . . . you can't make it . . . this gun"—he nodded at the weapon—"it don't make no noise. You make a fuss . . . the neighbors, they won't hear it go off . . . don't make no sound," he repeated. "I don't wanna kill you."

"Then what do you want?" she choked out. "I only have twenty dollars in my purse." She shivered even though the bathroom was muggy and warm.

"Lady, I'm not gonna hurt you if you do what I say, you understand?" He pulled his lips back in a thin smile he thought would reassure her.

"Please leave. I won't tell anyone you were here. Take the twenty dollars, it's on the dresser." Her teeth clicked lightly as she talked.

"Lady, you pissing me off now. Twenty dollars? You think I'm stupid?" His smile faded, his voice filled with hate. "Stand up and walk into the bedroom and don't gimme no shit, okay?"

"Oh, God, you're going to rape me, aren't you?"

"Stand up!" he said, firmer this time.

"Oh God oh God oh God," she said absently. Water rained into the tub from her body as she rose, arms still across her breasts. She stepped onto a furry throw rug, grabbed a towel from the wall rack, and hugged it in front of her.

"What do you want?"

"I gotta tell you again? Last time, lady. You go in the bedroom and lie down on the bed. I'm gonna tie you up. You got five seconds to decide. Die here, or do what I say. What's it gonna be?"

"I'll go, I'll go." She took mincing steps toward him while gripping the towel tighter. He smiled again, wider this time. As he backed up and made room for her to walk through the doorway, he kept the gun leveled at her chest. She faced him as she went by, walking into the bedroom backward, her gaze locked on him like a compass needle to a magnetic pole. Edging to the bed, she bumped her calves, then sat. Her fingers were white from clutching the towel in front of her.

"Damn, lady, put your legs up and lay down. I gotta tell you every little thing to do?"

"Oh God, oh God, please don't hurt me," she whimpered softly. She threw her legs up, keeping them locked together, lay back, released one hand, and smoothed the towel on her body.

"Gimme that!" He grabbed the middle of the towel and flung it across the room. She sucked in her breath as her hands flew in front of her, one across her breasts, one shielding her pubic area. "Dammit! You women are so tight-assed!"

He took two pieces of cord from his bag. Holding the gun between his legs, he pulled her right arm over the edge of the bed, tied her wrist, jerked the cord snug, and secured it to the side rails. She mewed as he worked, then cried softly when he yanked her other arm out flat, exposing her body. He tied that one too.

Bending and taking a white rag from his bag, he wadded it up, stuffed it in her mouth, then held the gun against her forehead threateningly when she struggled. She settled instantly. Pulling off one of the pillowcases, he wound it tightly, then tied it around her mouth and chin using both hands to be sure the knot was secure. Satisfied, he walked over and pushed the window down. He lowered the miniblinds and twisted the plastic controller until the slats closed.

He came back, looked at her, and smiled again. Her eyes were large and round with fear. Leaning, he cupped one of her breasts in his hand and bit the nipple hard. Her muffled scream was barely audible. He stood up and chuckled to himself as she moaned.

"Just checking, lady. Relax. Nobody'll hear you with that plug in." He withdrew more cord from his bag, tied her legs at the ankles, and secured them to the bottom of the bed frame. Nodding approval, he switched on the nightstand lamp, and stood over her. She squinted up at him, studying his exposed features.

"Damn, lady. You should take better care of yourself, you know. Too many cheeseburgers?" He reached down and pinched her stomach hard. She groaned again. "I thought your body was better than this." Snickering, he threw the big leather bag up on the bed next to her. Turning to the nightstand, he picked up the clock radio and pictures and laid them on the floor. He unfolded a cloth and draped it on top of the table next to the lamp. After he gently removed the gleaming metal objects from the bag, he spaced them evenly on the cloth with exaggerated care.

She turned her head and watched; her gaze flitting from him to the shiny metal tools on the table and back again. She grunted questioning sounds as he straightened the display with pride. The highly polished scalpels, retractors, hemostats, and saws reflected the harsh light.

"Lady, you and me, we're gonna make history this morning.

Like in the paper and everything, you know?" He said it absently, talking mostly to himself. As he looked from the tools to her, his whole demeanor was different. No longer angry and threatening, his face was soft—transformed to a mask of love and reverence. He reached out and traced the surface of her skin gently with the back of his fingers, then bent over and kissed her on the forehead. She shivered and continued to stare at him as though afraid to look away.

"I wish my mother could be here, you being my first. She'd be proud of me, I know it. I'll do a good job, lady. I know how." His voice choked as he snuffled and cleared his throat. He wiped the corner of his eye.

"It's time, lady. Time for you to go to sleep." He pulled a tin box from his bag, then opened the lid and withdrew a syringe and an ampule that contained a water-clear fluid. He held them up to the light, then took the syringe, poked the needle into the rubbery end, and withdrew most of the liquid. Holding the syringe up, he pressed in the plunger and it squirted a thin fountain of fluid into the air. She struggled wide-eyed against her bonds.

On the fringes of his consciousness, he could see the big orange sun coming . . . coming to fill his sky again. . . .

Before it blotted out his vision, he smiled, then looked down at her.

"Lady—you thought I was goin' to rape you. You was wrong. When you wake up from this in a few hours, you'll wish I *had* raped you. . . .

"Yeah. Compared to this—

"You'll think being raped would of been great—

"Just great!"

chapter//two

"Only an asshole on the absolute bottom of the food chain would ring my doorbell this time of the night!" Chalky Fuchs wore only his shorts when he answered. Leaving the door open, he walked away, rubbing his sleep-heavy eyes. Herb Rosen came in, closed the door, and looked around the apartment. Empty microwave trays sat on the coffee table. The chairs were draped with coats and pants, and dishes covered the counters and the sink.

"When you find your feet, you'll remember you asked me to pick you up—said your car wasn't running or something—remember? It's six-thirty in the morning, like you asked. Working with you is going to be an experience." As Herb talked, he finished inventorying the jumbled room with his trained eye. "Holy mackerel," he mumbled to himself, obviously impressed.

"Stopping by here is the best way to find out what a class guy you're going to be swapping spit with," Chalky said. Herb cringed at that image. Chalky rubbed his hands through his hair as he headed for the bathroom.

"They catch the guys who tossed your apartment?" Herb asked as he continued to look around. He was smiling. "They did a pretty thorough job."

"I'm burglar-proof," Chalky yelled from the bathroom. "My ex-wife has everything of value." Herb cleaned off a spot on the couch and sat with care, as though expecting a discarded piece of pizza to pop up between the cushions. Chalky came hopping into the room with one leg stuck in his pants, sat down, straightened the pant leg, and pulled it over his knee. As he stood, he

9

zipped up his pants and tightened his belt. He rubbed his finger on his teeth, then looked at it. What he decided was unclear.

"So, why do we have to be in early this morning?" Chalky asked as he lifted a shirt from the doorknob and smelled under the sleeves. Choosing to wear it another day, he slid his arms through and buttoned it, then grabbed a tie from a chair and headed back to the mirror in the bathroom.

Herb watched him in fascination, then finally answered. "I don't know. Special meeting or something, I guess." Herb stood and checked his watch and brushed off his immaculately pressed pants even though they were clean. "Aren't you going to shave?" Herb asked when Chalky walked into the room straightening his tie. He was rumpled, but ready to go.

"Don't worry about it. I've got one of those blue razor-things in my side drawer at the office. I can dry shave in a few seconds, it's an art form." He smiled, winced, then rubbed his temple again.

Herb shook his head in wonder. "God, what a masochist. You really gonna wear that coat?"

"What's wrong with this coat?" Chalky asked, looking at the frayed cuffs.

"Nothing, except it isn't 1975 anymore. Why doncha buy some new clothes?" Herb asked.

" 'Cause I don't give a flying fart."

"Everybody cares. You broke?"

"Of course I'm broke! I'm a friggin' cop."

"You gotta worry more about your appearance if you want to get ahead in the department," Herb said as he straightened his immaculate starched cuffs, pulled them down, and smiled.

"I already got a head. Besides, why should I give a rat's ass? My ex-wife, the barracuda, has her fangs in my glutes, my psychotic kid is having a full-time shit fit, I don't have a pot to piss in, and my record in the department is like a rap sheet. I haven't won a pool tournament in six months; and last—but not least—I lost my library card, and some jerkoff used it to get books worth six big ones before I could get it canceled."

"So?"

"So, what do you mean, so? I have to pay for them. Isn't that enough, Herby?"

Herb laughed and opened the door. "Look, I don't mind you having an attitude, but since I'm doing you a favor, don't call me Herby, okay?"

"Fair. I've got to get some coffee before I kill something."

"Fat Phil's?" Herb asked.

"Fuck Fat Phil!"

"Easy for you to say." Herb took one last glance at the room and shut the door.

It was chilly outside as they walked to the car. December was an anything-can-happen month in Seattle and the *Times* had been talking about the likelihood of snow in the higher elevations. An arctic front had moved across Canada and was pushing Alaska's cold air into Washington, making snow a possibility since rain was always on the program.

They climbed in Herb's '66 Mustang and drove to the restaurant. Located a block from the police station, it was unimpressive with its faded sign painted on the storefront window with a menu mounted underneath. The wind gusted through the door behind them as they walked in and found a table. The restaurant was suprisingly busy.

"So why do they call this place Fat Phil's when the sign says *The Regatta*," Herb asked as he pulled back a wooden chair, scraping it on the tile. The din of the other men talking echoed in the room. They both sat and looked around. Most of the customers were uniformed policemen downing a quick breakfast and coffee before they checked in and hit the streets. Cigarette smoke filled the air.

"You haven't met him?" Chalky asked.

"Met who?"

"Phil, the guy who's fat?"

"Only been here once. All I've seen in here are the little quail, waiting on tables, shaking their tushies."

"*Great* tushies," said Chalky with a smile. He admired Giselle as she passed with two loaded trays. Heads turned in admiration as she jiggled expertly between the tables.

"So?" Herb charged ahead.

"So, what?"

"About Phil."

"Oh." Chalky drifted back, still watching Giselle. "Phil

mostly works at night. Odds are you'll never meet him working the day shift." Herb shook his head.

"So. You going to get married again?" Herb asked, trying to breathe life into the conversation.

Chalky watched Giselle bounce by, going the other way with empty trays. She smiled at him. He smiled back.

"I understand she can suck a golf ball through a fifty-foot garden hose," Chalky said absently as he watched her quiver out of sight.

"You going to talk to me or what?"

"I thought I was."

"Forget it. What's good here?"

"Nothing."

"Then why are we here?"

"Tushies, great tushies."

"Gotcha, you son of a bitch!"

Chalky flinched as a penetrating voice boomed in back of him. A uniformed cop closer to seven feet than six smacked him on the shoulder. Chalky looked up and smiled weakly. Chalky was six feet himself, but still felt short next to Rudy.

"Rudy, I've been looking all over for you," Chalky said. "Sit down and have some coffee with us."

"Don't glad-hand me, Fucks. Put it there." Rudy held out his hand and pointed to it with the other one. Chalky smiled and shook his hand. Rudy's face spread in a grin, then said, "Funny. Very funny. Two hundred big ones—right there." He pointed again at his now-empty palm.

"You know we don't get paid 'til Friday. I'll pay you then"—Chalky tried to look sincere—"and, for the tenth time, it's F-u-c-h-s, pronounced Fyooks."

"Whatever," Rudy said with a dismissive wave of his hand. "I'll see you Friday then. Same time and place." He smiled and whacked Chalky's shoulder, this time a little harder. The two men watched him lumber to the register to pay his bill.

"If you've ever doubted we came from the apes, he nails the lid on it," Chalky said, not expecting an answer. Herb looked at Chalky, his face a question mark.

"Pool," Chalky said, answering the unasked question.

"Pool?"

"I play pool a couple times a week. He got lucky at nine ball."

Giselle swooped up and stopped in front of them with a carafe of coffee, pushing a cloud of perfume. They ordered. She poured each of them coffee, smiled, and quivered away in her too short dress, accompanied by the same revolving heads that rotated up, then back, like the wind smoothly fanning shafts of wheat. Chalky thought to himself: It sure beats the hell out of good food.

They talked animatedly for a few more minutes before their breakfast arrived. Herb was Chalky's new partner and they were just getting to know each other. The first few days had been spent in small talk, nothing personal, only weather reports and how are yous. Chalky liked Herb instinctively, but as far as he was concerned, the jury was still out on how they were going to work together.

The food appeared. They made short work of the breakfast and were finishing their coffee when Giselle glided over to the table. She leaned on her tray and pushed up some of what had been jiggling.

"You playing at Maxi's this Friday?" she asked Chalky.

"Does a bear shit in the woods?" He ignored her face and checked out her softwares.

"Understand it's a nine ball tournament. Five hundred bucks top prize."

"Got the flyer tacked beside my mirror."

"You going to win it?"

"If I don't pop an aneurysm before."

"What's an aneurysm?" she asked, frowning. She was the kind of girl who was confused by big words. She liked one-syllable words, words like—what can I buy you, Giselle?—words like that. Short and simple.

"It's something people over thirty get," he said, patting her hand. The condescension missed the top of her head by three feet. She wrinkled her nose, not at the condition but the age.

"You're not over thirty, are you?" The question inferred it was worse than having gonorrhea. Herb spit his coffee out, then choked. Chalky stifled a chuckle.

"No, I'm twenty-nine, honey." He knew being over thirty

was beyond the ken of someone who wasn't even twenty. Herb glanced the other way to keep from losing it. Looking uncomfortable, she smiled and stared at Herb.

"Oh, yeah, they want you on the phone, that's why I came here in the first place." She straightened up and removed the view. Chalky looked at her face.

"The man said it was important."

"Who said it was important?"

"A captain something," she said over her shoulder as she flounced away.

"Screwed again." Chalky slid his chair back and jogged to the phone.

"We've been beeping you for twenty minutes. Where the hell you been?" Captain Stone asked.

"Well, well, my beeper—"

"Your beeper what?"

"Fell in the toilet, off some books on the back of the—"

"Why the blazing hell didn't you report it and get another one?" the captain interrupted.

"Two in the morning last night?"

"Well, get another one, dammit. You know the rules. You're needed now."

"For what?"

"An emergency," the captain said levelly. "That's what the department deals in these days, isn't it?"

"There isn't any need to get testy. I simply meant, like, where? I *will* need to know that." It was quiet for a long time on the other end of the line. Chalky had the feeling he'd better wait, considering the captain's high blood pressure.

"Three thirty-eight Clinton, apartment three-B. This is a weird one, so I naturally thought of you first."

"Anything else you want to tell me about it, sir?"

"See the uniforms at the scene, and get an attitude adjustment. Now!"

Click—

"Dammit! Did the whole world wake up with a hard-on this morning?" Chalky mumbled as he hung up the receiver and walked back to the table. Trying to adjust my attitude last night at Barney's was why my electronic wife did a gainer into the commode anyway. Six tequilas knocks the edge off of being careful. Herb looked up and drained his cup when he saw Chalky's face.

"Trouble?" Herb stood and pushed in his chair.

"Business as usual," Chalky said as he tossed a buck on the table. "Flip for who pays?"

"I never flip with someone who's broke. I'll pay. You can catch me after Friday."

"You're not as dumb as you look," Chalky said as they walked to the cash register.

"How did he know where you were?"

"Home, pool hall, library, or here. He's got my M.O. cold," Chalky answered.

It took them eight minutes to get to the station and pick up their car, twelve more to get to three thirty-eight Clinton.

When Rosen pulled up at the apartment buildings, three black-and-whites with gumballs rotating sat in the alleyway fronting a parade of garage doors. It was an ochre-colored complex of some 150 or more units huddled back in a wooded area at the end of a long, winding drive off Clinton. They climbed out and jogged to the door. Chalky's stomach burned as he thought: This is a hell of a way to get off the dime.

They met a patrolman in an entryway filled with ferns, hanging plants, and froufrou woman stuff. The patrolman's face was white. Chalky recognized the expression. He'd lost his cookies several times in the past himself.

"Rough?" Chalky asked him as he breezed in. The patrolman followed without answering. Three other men were in the apartment, two in the bedroom, one in the bathroom. Their voices and laughter carried into the living room. Chalky extended his hand to the officer and said, "Haven't met you. Name's Chalky F-u-c-h-s, pronounced Fyooks." The snide remark Chalky expected was missing as the patrolman shook his hand. "And that's Rosen." Chalky nodded in Herb's direction.

Herb smiled and looked back from the door. The officer's eyes were blank as he nodded a hello to Chalky, not offering his name, his mind obviously still on what happened.

"You want to tell me about it?" Chalky asked. His tablet was ready. "Take me from the top. Pretend I'm stupid." The officer

was preoccupied or he'd never get that kind of straight line from
Chalky. The patrolman sat. He looked sick, but struggled along
anyway.

"Call came in about fifty minutes ago. I make it, 7:02 A.M.
give or take. They'll have the time at dispatch." Chalky nodded
and sat in the chair opposite him. Herb walked to the bedroom
door, leaned in, and watched the two men finish. Dusting the
room for prints, Chalky guessed.

"The call," Chalky prodded.

"Yeah. A man. Slight accent of some kind. Said there was a
woman in trouble at this location—that we had to hurry—that
he'd leave the door open. Real cooperative. That is, until we
asked his name. Then he hung up."

"And?"

"Jim and me were the first ones here. Others five to eight
minutes later."

"And you are?"

"Sorry. Officer Biggs." He tried to smile, but was unsuccess-
ful. Chalky waited. "Knocked and identified ourselves and got
no answer, so we walked in." Chalky was painfully aware that
he still had no idea what had happened to the woman, but listened patiently. The man was traumatized and needed to tell it
his way.

"Ambulance took her to the hospital ten minutes ago."

"Dead?" Chalky asked.

"Hell no. Stiffs don't bother me like this." Biggs cringed and
rubbed his eyes as if the image had just flashed. "Searched the
place. Nothing. That is 'til we get to the bedroom. She's sitting
up in the bed, big as you please, light on, like she's waiting for
us to arrive. Eyes closed though, sleeping."

"And?"

"And she's sitting up in bed dressed in pajamas, like I said,
hands in her lap, propped up with pillows she was. Bed was
tucked and smoothed, with the sheets folded back just so, as
though she's on display in a hospital bed waiting for inspection,
or company, or something." Biggs was talking faster now, trying to get through it.

"Went over and called to her. Had her name from the address.
A Joanne Pinkers. Lives alone. Thirty-six." He cleared his

throat and looked toward the door. He was paler and appeared to be fighting to keep his gorge down. "I was the one who went around to the other side of the bed when she didn't answer. Looked like she was breathing normally, so I wasn't concerned at first."

"Then?" Chalky leaned farther and farther forward trying to extract the information by pure willpower.

"Then I touched her. Reached over and checked the pulse on her wrist." The patrolman winced again, then gulped. "God!"

"What?"

"Her pulse. Wasn't any. Nothing! No pulse at all!"

"But you said she was breathing normally." Chalky scowled, then glanced up at Herb who had returned and stood at his shoulder.

"She was," Biggs said. "Hand was cold too, like a stiff. Gave me the creeps instantly." Chalky watched him intently, waiting for the punch line.

"What happened?" Herb asked, leaning forward now, getting interested.

"Took both of her hands, going to hold her up so's we could jerk out the pillows and lay her flat. Seemed like the thing to do," Biggs said, as an aside. He dry-heaved once, gripped his stomach, gulped, and swallowed deeply.

"Just breathe deep," Chalky said. "It'll pass." Herb leaned down a little more, hands on his knees now.

"Walked toward the end of the bed holding on to her hands to keep her upright while Jim was goin' to snatch away the pillows—"

"And?" Spit it out! Chalky screamed in his mind, but smiled with feigned patience.

"I went smashing into the wall when I pulled, hit my head and fell in a heap!" Chalky looked at him quizzically.

"You pulled her off the bed?" Chalky asked.

"No dammit! Not her! I was still holding on to her god-damned hands—just her arms! They came off—"

"Her arms came off?" Chalky and Herb yelled in unison.

chapter//three

"You're shitting me!" Chalky exclaimed. He leaned back as though he'd been slapped. He frowned as he looked at Officer Biggs.

"Give me a break," Herb said with a smirk.

"I know, I wouldn't have believed it myself if I hadn't been there. Blew my circuits all to hell!" Biggs's eyes were wide with excitement.

"Came off?" Chalky asked, trying to visualize how that could be possible.

"There I was, lying on the floor, holding hands with two arms that weren't attached to anything. God!" Biggs said again, and shivered.

"How could she be alive?" Chalky asked. "She'd have bled to death before you got here."

"This even gets weirder," Biggs said as he lowered his voice. "If that's possible." He stood up and paced back and forth, breathing deeply, trying to finish without another trip to the porch. "After I got through freaking out, we called the paramedics, then got down to the job of trying to patch this thing together, so to speak." He cringed at his words, then said, "I didn't mean—anything—"

"We know," Chalky reassured him.

"Arms were severed clean as a whistle, like a surgeon shaved them off, right below the shoulders. Real professional." Chalky's neck muscles tensed as the image came clearer, then he unconsciously reached over and rubbed his upper arm.

"The bleeding. Why didn't she buy it?" Chalky asked.

"Our question exactly. We pulled back her pajamas and her

19

arms were—God! I'm going to have to go home—" Biggs
gulped and dry-heaved again. They waited as he came over, sat
down, and wiped the tension perspiration from his forehead.
"Trussed up. Neat, and orderly—like a Thanksgiving turkey,"
Biggs finished.

"Stitches?"

"Yeah. Professional job—like a doctor did it—not even any
blood."

"Had to be some, somewhere."

"Found the original bedding in the closet, soaked red. Also
found what we think to be semen on her and on the bedding.
Lots of it. Really crazy. Can you imagine getting off on that?"
Biggs massaged his throat. "After finishing, this sicko, whoever
he is, obviously washed her upper body thoroughly, put her in
pajamas and cleaned the loose arms of blood. Then, if you can
believe it, he stuck them up the sleeves. Finally, he even
changed the bed, then stage-set the room . . . like he knew what
we'd do." Biggs got up, excused himself, and headed out the
front door. From the opening, Chalky and Herb could hear the
hacking sound of his retching. They looked at each other in silence.

"So, what do you think?" Herb asked.

"I should have been a dermatologist," Chalky said.

"Dermatologist?"

"Yeah. No emergencies, but lots of money."

When Chalky and Herb went into the bedroom, the other men
had finished dusting and filed out. One man said, "It's all yours.
Prints looked pretty smudged. Guy must have rubbed the sur-
faces with a bloody rag. Don't know how much good they'll
be." Chalky said great, then they spent a half hour crawling
around on their hands and knees looking for a clue of any kind
they could use that the perp might have missed. This Joanne
was a crackerjack housekeeper and the bad guy had left nothing.

"Who could hate someone that much?" Herb asked.

"Doubt if he even knew her." Chalky stood and brushed his
hands and pants.

"How so?"

"Doesn't compute. You don't say: Boy, she really pissed me off, I'll show her. I'll drop by and cut off her arms. No. This guy's a looney tune with a blown head gasket. When this Pinkers comes to, she'd be able to ID him if she knows him. I can't see that happening."

"Yeah, well, I don't see anything in here that's going to help us," Herb said, waving at the room. "You?"

"Nothing solid, except—" Chalky bent and snapped his finger against the bed. "What does this tell you?"

"I give up, what?" Herb brushed his fingers over the bedding, then said, "Tight."

"Exactamundo! There's hope for you yet. And that means—"

"The military, or a nurse. Orderly maybe."

"Maybe. Anyone who can make up a bed this tight almost has to be trained in something," Chalky mused as he rubbed his chin. His own unmade bed at home flashed in his mind.

"A doctor with a military record?"

"A crazy doctor with a military record—maybe." Chalky walked out of the room. Herb followed. It was drizzling and overcast as they ran to their tired Plymouth. *Just what I need,* Chalky thought.

"Where now?" Herb asked as they reached the car.

"The hospital."

"You think this is a one-shot deal?" Herb asked. Chalky shook his head no as they climbed in.

"That's the way I read it too."

The wipers clicked in the quiet car all the way to the hospital. They had a lot to think about.

"Come on in, Carrie, you know you don't have to knock," Dr. Margaret Chandler said to Dr. Carrie Frost as she walked into a small office and sat in a leather chair opposite her desk. Dr. Chandler looked up from a lab report she had been reading as Carrie sighed and stretched.

"Sounds like you're carrying the weight of the world, Carrie," Dr. Chandler continued as she smiled and laid the report aside.

"Not really. Just a little tired. Thought I'd come in and see what's bothering you, Pegs. Saw you counting the tiles on the floor as you walked by about an hour ago." Carrie was Dr. Chandler's friend and the only one who used her nickname at the hospital.

"Sorry. It's only that I . . . I thought I was immune."

"Immune to what? Men?" Carrie asked, then smiled.

"No. Immune to being shocked. I thought I had seen everything in the last six years . . . that nothing could upset me."

"Bad one, Pegs?"

"Unbelievably bad. Worse than bad. Awful!"

"You're talking about the lady on the third floor who had her arms amputated?"

"Yeah, how did you know already?"

"Are you kidding? Ten minutes after she was brought in she was the topic of conversation throughout the hospital. You handling her?" Carrie leaned forward and her bright eyes shone with interest. "What's your guess on what happened?"

"Yes, I'm taking care of her. May have to clean up those sutures. But not much to guess on what happened. Why and who are the big questions in this." She stood, walked over to the narrow window, and stared out as though the answers were somewhere off in the distance on the grounds among the trees and the rain. Her white coat hung loosely on her tall, curved frame. "Someone did a semiprofessional job of removing them. Used triple-O nylon to put her back together."

"Bleeding?" Carrie asked.

"We're watching her blood pressure. It's a little unstable. Might have a couple of minor leaks. Gave her two units of red cells for backup. Figured she had to lose at least that much or more in the procedure."

"She awake yet?"

"Starting to stir occasionally. I'm going up there in a half hour or so. I thought I'd keep her sedated for a while, but I'm nervous about it because I don't know what she's had. She had to be anesthetized for that kind of surgery." Peggy bit her lower lip as she considered it.

"Has to wake up sometime," Carrie said simply.

"God, Carrie, can you imagine?"

"What?"

"Imagine what it would be like to be injected with something, then wake up with no arms for the rest of your life. Especially this lady. She was a head nurse on the night shift right here at Crosier. A woman who works with her hands all day long. God!"

Carrie shivered and hugged her arms even though it was warm in the office. She shook her head slowly and stared at the wall. Words were inadequate.

"I've already called Ed Fortsam in psych to meet me up there," Peggy said. "Aside from the residual pain, I can't imagine what this is going to do to her mentally when she wakes up and realizes what's happened. You want to go up with me? I could use the moral support."

"Sorry to bail out on you, Pegs, but I have rounds. Can I call you tonight? Maybe we could grab a pizza and I could talk you down."

"Thanks. I'll be home late but I'll phone you if I get in before eight. If it's later than that, I'll be too bushed to worry about food anyway."

Carrie got up, looked back and smiled when she reached the door, then closed it behind her. Peggy stared at the folder, but her eyes were unfocused. All she could see was someone cutting into that woman's healthy arms and watching them fall away. Arms that had guided her through life, held books, caressed lovers, sewed on buttons. Now, they were useless pieces of detached flesh. Cold. Unmoving.

Wrapped in plastic in the morgue.

Herb and Chalky parked the Plymouth in the rear lot of the hospital. Chalky could wait to do this interview. He'd questioned his share of out-of-control women in his time, but this was justifiably going to be the granddaddy of emotional scenes. Trying to come up with the right approach to question this poor woman was almost impossible.

He played with the words: I'm really sorry someone cut off your arms, but could you put that awful thing aside for a moment and answer these few questions, please. No, that wasn't it. I'll have to play it by ear, he thought. Have to allow her condition to dictate the course of the interview.

The two detectives went into the reception area and asked to talk to the doctor who was handling the case. The nurse called a number, said a few words into the phone, and hung up. She swiveled in her chair and pointed to the elevators.

"See Dr. Chandler in 233, waiting for you," she said cryptically, then returned to her work. The men hurried to the bank of elevators and the door was closing on one that was full. Another one dinged, slid open, but it was crowded also. They shook their heads in unison, then impatiently headed for the stairs next to the elevators.

"I hate the smell of hospitals," Chalky said as they rounded the first landing, his voice echoing in the stairwell. "Reminds me of the time I had my tonsils out when I was about seven or eight. That awful ether crap. Heaved for three days. Terrible! And the antiseptic smells . . ."

"Makes me nervous as hell too," Herb said. "I've never been sick, but every time I've visited a hospital as an adult, someone in my family has died."

Chalky stopped in front of the fire door and asked, "How many times you been?"

"Once. My uncle Marvin." Chalky shook his head and opened the door. They proceeded down the hall and found 233. Chalky sucked in a deep breath and opened the door.

An attractive woman stood at a filing cabinet putting folders away when he walked in. A white coat hung on the coatrack by the door. Chalky took in her casual but elegant street clothes. She smiled warmly when she looked up.

"Girly, we're in a hurry," Chalky said. "Is the doctor coming back in a minute?"

The woman hesitated for a second, then answered in a low voice, "What doctor are you looking for?"

"How many doctors could you have in this postage-stamp office? Chandler. The name on the door."

"And you are?" Chalky sighed, pulled his badge from his corduroy coat, and flopped it open as though it were magic. He would rather have been somewhere else and the questioning put him off.

"Your name is—badge?" she asked with a smirk.

"Sergeant F-u-c-h-s, pronounced Fyooks, Seattle Police Department. Is that official enough for you?"

"If you could have a seat, I'll see what I can do for you. I have to take this to the lab"—she indicated the folder she was holding—"then I'll be right back." She stood and glided through the door before he could respond. Chalky collapsed into the seat and rubbed his forehead. What a day, he thought.

The two men sat impatiently for ten minutes as they exchanged horror stories about what had happened to friends who had gone to the hospital for minor services and had ended up with long stays or dying. Chalky had a flash of déjà vu. It was like sitting around a campfire as a kid telling ghost stories. The whopper about the guy with the severed arm popped into his mind. Finally, Chalky got up and paced around the room, anxious to get moving.

The door opened and the woman came back in. She smiled at them, went to the coatrack, and put on the white coat. Chalky frowned. Pulling out her wire-rimmed glasses, she adjusted them, then sat behind her desk and folded her hands in front of her.

"Now, what can I do to help you, gentlemen?"

"You. You're Dr. Chandler?" Chalky asked.

"Of course."

"Then why did you make us wait?"

"I always make people wait when they talk to me in a condescending manner. I have exactly five minutes before I must leave. We can spend it discussing your manners or whatever you came to talk about. Which do you prefer?" She continued to smile. Chalky rubbed his brow. His head hurt again.

"Oh, this is Sergeant Rosen," Chalky said and nodded. Herb smiled. "This Pinkers—Miss Pinkers. I understand you're treating her, the lady with the arm problem?" He wondered: Why me, God, why do I always get the ball busters?

"Arm problem?" She scowled with irritation. She hesitated, then took off her glasses and stared at him intently, unsmiling. "What precisely do you want to know, Officer?"

"Mostly, when can we question her. Is she conscious yet? We're in limbo on this investigation until we get some feedback from her. She may know the guy who did this." Beautiful gray eyes for such a cold broad. Nice figure too, he thought.

"I really don't expect her to be in any condition to be questioned right away. This may be difficult for you to understand, but Miss Pinkers is going to be in shock when she wakes up."

"Unlike the opinion most people have of us, we do have the ability to empathize." Bet you didn't think I knew that word, sweetheart. "But it's still important we talk to her as soon as possible. The nut case who did this may be considering it for a new hobby, you get my meaning?"

Tiring of the repartee, Peggy said, "I understand completely. I can see why you'd be concerned. As soon as she's coherent, we'll ask her permission to call you in. Where can you be reached?" As she spoke, Chalky withdrew a bent card from his well-worn wallet and laid it in front of her. She continued, "If I were you, I wouldn't expect too much. It's entirely possible, considering the circumstances, she may remember nothing. She could blank out the entire incident."

"Let's hope not. Call anytime, day or night, preferably sooner than later." Chalky hesitated, then asked, "One last, quick question?" She nodded. "Her arms. You couldn't put them back on. Reattach them?"

"Too much time had passed. And even if we could have, they would have been useless to her. She'll do better with prosthetics."

"Pros-the-tics?" He stumbled over the word.

"Artificial arms." She leaned and offered her hand as she stood. "You'll have our complete cooperation, Sergeant—"

"F-u-c-h-s, pronounced Fyooks," he said as he rose and shook her hand. Soft, feminine, bedroom eyes, he observed as he took in a whiff of her quiet, tasteful perfume. She returned his smile openly. Her gray eyes crinkled in the corners, the animosity gone.

As Chalky and Herb walked down the hall, Chalky glanced over his shoulder and watched her walk in the opposite direction. Herb looked at him questioningly, then shook his head as they proceeded to the stairs.

They clanked down the steps and out into the rain. "You're not thinking what I think you're thinking, are you?" Herb asked as they walked to the car.

Chalky just smiled.

chapter//four

Joanne Pinkers crouched in the corner as the roaring of the beast came closer and closer. She'd been running for hours and she was too weak to go any farther. If she could just hide here—

The door flexed in as the monster crashed against it! The horror was on the other side now, panting, desperately trying to get to her. The heavy animal odor penetrated the room. In the dim light, the doorknob rattled, then turned.

Her eyes riveted on it—

Smash! The door splintered open and the beast was there, in front of her. No place to hide, no place to run! The huge, black form took one step toward her, then another.

It reached out—

Then she had the sensation of flying up and away from the bottom of the pit into the sky, away from the nightmare torturing her.

The first thing she was aware of was the bright light on her eyelids. She tried to open them a crack, but her lids quivered feebly and stuck together.

Finally, one lid popped up enough to see an out-of-focus green color. She moved her mouth. It was dry and her tongue felt large and rough. Strange taste, she thought. Medicine? She could feel her brow mechanically furrow as she pondered that. Her mind worked in a slow and plodding manner, struggling from one thought to another, as though examining a single idea at a time was all it was capable of doing.

Sounds? A metallic clang came from the distance. What could that be? Then, the click of heels on a hard surface. Someone walking. Smells? Like medicine. Cleanser? No. Antiseptic?

What was it? Like when I skinned my knee as a child. Iodine? And the feelings? She tried to lift her head, but her neck muscles only trembled. She thought: My hair fell against my ear—so I must have moved.

A hospital? She was suddenly able to assemble all the input. What am I doing in a hospital? With a flash, the vision of the man in the ski mask in her bedroom was in front of her again. It jarred her and brought her up to another level of consciousness. Her other eye flickered open, and with an effort, she leaned her head forward.

She was in a brightly lit hospital room, gray-green. A private room. The door was ajar and steps came toward her. She dropped her head back to the pillow. Her vision spun for a moment, then righted itself. The slight movement brought wave after wave of searing pain from her arms and hands.

She tried to move her right arm, to bring her hand up and look at it, but it failed to budge. Must be under a tight sheet, she thought. That's it. Through the pain, she could feel pressure against both of her arms. She groaned out loud and her voice sounded alien in the small room. How tight could these sheets be? She pushed her right arm against it harder, and when she did, the agony became so blinding she had to close her eyes. Someone screamed next to her—assaulting her ears—then she realized it was her own voice. She struggled to sit up, but could only wiggle back and forth, causing a tidal wave of suffering each time.

"Don't, don't," she heard, then jumped when something warm touched her forehead. A hand. Continuing to groan, she opened her eyes. A woman. A doctor.

"What—what am I doing here?" Her voice sounded strange and distant, vibrating inside her head like an echo chamber.

"You're going to be okay, you're going to be fine," the voice came back, soft and caring.

"Untie me so I can move. Ohhh! Ohhh! Why do my arms hurt so much? Mouth is so dry."

"Try to relax." The voice again—then a sharp sticking pain in her bottom.

"Help me, help me—" Her tongue got warm and heavy as the pain receded. "Who are you?"

"I'm your doctor," she heard. Then the voice blended into a high-pitched ringing as a cloud of well-being carried her back into the blackness.

"Is there anything else you'll need, Doctor?" The nurse looked at Peggy Chandler as she stared down at Joanne Pinkers. Peggy shook her head without turning and the nurse squeaked out of the room. She laid the hypodermic on the nightstand, then walked around to the other side of the bed to adjust the flow on the IV that trailed to the woman's ankle.

"She awake?" Peggy looked up. Dr. Fortsam stood in the doorway. He approached the bed. His glasses hung from a chain around his neck and his pliable features showed concern. His paunch strained against his belt as he bent forward and looked at the woman.

"I sedated her, Ed. Her pain was unbearable." Peggy looked back at the woman.

"Putting it off?" He smirked.

"Maybe that too," she answered, then sighed. "I feel it's better she sleep through the night. We can do it in the morning, if that's okay with you."

"No problem. Whatever you think's best." He patted her arm, then went to the door. "Call me about an hour before you need me. I'll get here as soon as possible. She's going to need as much help as possible."

"I know, I know." He left and shut the door behind him. She walked to the foot of the bed and made a notation on the clipboard attached to the end of it, then looked down at Joanne. The small figure on the bed lost focus as tears leaked from Peggy's eyes. She took a Kleenex tissue and wiped them dry.

"Sleep and rest," Peggy said softly. She stared at the sides of Joanne's body where her arms should have been.

"Dear God, how am I going to tell you? How?" She looked up at the window. The rain tapped on the window as the wind picked up. The room darkened as storm clouds assembling overhead mirrored Peggy's somber mood.

"Sleep and rest. Tomorrow is going to be just awful for both of us." She reached down and brushed a lock of hair from the still figure's unlined face. "Just awful," Peggy said, then dimmed the lights and walked out.

A massive fireball of a sun beat down on the small Mexican village. Dust devils joined the children at play as they kicked a small can in an open yard in front of a tin-metal shack. Laddering up the Tijuana hills, hundreds of similar shacks looked down. Dirty and disheveled, the children played, unmindful of the squalid conditions. Next to their yard, an open sewer ran in and around discarded tires, the stench long since ignored by the children. They screamed and yelled in crisp, high-pitched Spanish, blocking out the sound of the woman who called from the door.

"Hijo!" she called. "Hijo." Her voice was thready as she leaned against the doorjamb for support. Carlos Martinez was running, kicking a ball. He looked back when he heard the pathetic sound of his mother's voice. He froze and stared at the shack. Five years old, the only clothing he wore was a tattered too large pair of pants rolled up to the knees. Orange dust lined with sweat streaks powdered his face and body, and his long hair was wild and matted.

"Mama! Mama!" he screamed as he ran toward her. When he got to the door, his mother was gone, vanished back into its depths. Inside, she lay on a stained and torn mattress on the dirt floor. The heat and smell of decay overwhelmed him. The corrugated metal hut absorbed the relentless sun and had raised the interior temperature to over 120 degrees.

His mother looked up at him through rheumy eyes, her right upper arm discolored and swollen to three times its normal size. The repugnant smell of the infection crowded the small room.

Carlos and his mother were the remnants of the Martinez family. Carlos, his father, mother, and sister had come north from Guadalajara with nothing but their clothes and the dream of getting to the United States, the land of opportunity. On the way, bandits knifed his father and he died under a bridge culvert. His mother and Maria, his older sister, were both raped while Carlos screamed and watched helplessly. When the bandits left, they took Maria and he never saw her again. His mother had a minor knife wound in her upper arm, but had trudged with him to this shack where the two of them lived on handouts, hoping to get a chance to make it across the border. The knife nick in her arm festered and grew continually worse. Her body was burning with fever, but she could only lie there, waiting to die or to get better. Each hour, her strength and will to live ebbed away.

She closed her eyes and drifted into unconsciousness as Carlos pulled on her dress for her to get up. He screamed relentlessly in the ovenlike cubicle, "Mama! Mama!"

She remained motionless.

In his dingy bedroom, the now-grown Carlos Martinez lay on his bed, mumbling incoherently as the last of the vision faded slowly. He thrashed, groaned, and called out occasionally to the unseen force that tortured his fevered mind.

The small two-room apartment looked gray and dingy in the light filtering in the grime-covered windows. The cell-like bedroom, where he lay, had only an unfinished wooden dresser in addition to the bed. A crammed, single-doored closet was wedged open with boxes. On the dresser was a picture in a thin, gilded frame, centered carefully on a clean handkerchief, from which the smiling face of Carlos's long-dead young mother surveyed the room. On either side of it, a candle burned. Above, a crucifix glistened in the light of the candles, the plastic body of the anguished Jesus echoing Carlos's tortured vision.

In the larger room, the sitting area contained a portable television with bent rabbit ears on a spindly legged coffee table. Dirty blankets covered a chair and couch while stuffing protruded here and there. A sink hung on the wall by a couple of screws and legerdemain, a cracked frameless mirror above it, and a wire-backed dinette set with two chairs completed his furnishings. Against the wall was a bench, a weight set with a long bar and two dumbbells.

In the bedroom, Carlos leapt to his feet as though energized by an electrical current and looked around the room with the glazed eyes of someone who expected an attack. He wore only his pants, no shirt, shoes, or socks. His well-muscled, twenty-six-year-old body was smooth-skinned and dripped with sweat.

He charged out the bedroom door, ran down the dark hall

with his bare feet flopping on the aged wooden planks, banged through the front door, onto the porch, to the sidewalk, and ran blindly. His sweaty arms and legs pumped like pistons, his mind unaware it was overcast, forty-eight degrees, and raining. His out-of-focus eyes stared vacantly at the fireball that burned down on the tin metal shack in the hazy distance.

He had to get there . . . had to hurry . . . his mother needed help.

After Carlos regained control of himself, he wandered around in the rain for an hour or so, then, exhausted, found his way back to his apartment. Cold and shivering, he fell into an instant, almost drugged sleep. He dreamed. Images of heat, violence, and terror filled his consciousness. Voices whispered and unseen hands grasped at him. The one recurring vision was about his mother and the day she died. When awake, he tried to consign it to some dark corner of his mind, but it was always there, pushing and fighting to get to the surface. While sleeping, he had no control. As a result, he never slept soundly. He continually tossed and turned as the ugly visions became real. They retreated only when the gray overcast leeched the light from his windows.

"So what do you think? You want to take a break for a sandwich? It's only three-thirty," Herb said with a touch of sarcasm as he looked at his watch. He and Chalky were sitting in their unmarked car on a side street.

"You do the other group of apartments to the south?" Chalky asked.

"Yeah, my dogs are killing me."

"Wimp. Anybody see anything out of the ordinary?"

"Well, there's one old lady over there, upstairs unit, who says she saw a man sneak in the next door apartment after the husband left for work. Left with a smile this wide. She even gave me the guy's name."

"How about we cruise Parker Street to the north?"

"We already covered that area. Same results."

"Had three not-at-homes," Chalky said. "Come on, it's on the way."

"You really love this crap, don't you? What's the odds on this guy doing this gig, then walking two blocks to his car? And why would he park that far away? Doesn't make any sense." Herb grimaced and rubbed the calves of his legs.

"Look, Petunia, you can sit in the car. I'll door-knock, you just keep the jalopy in shouting range, okay?" Chalky laughed and pulled away from the curb. Amazingly, when they drove by, neighbors still milled about the lawn of the apartment building they'd taken Joanne Pinkers from that morning. Local hardware and sporting goods stores will do a landhouse business in guns and locks the next few days, Chalky thought.

After Chalky knocked at the last door and returned to his unmarked car, he sat for a minute, then leaned forward and squinted into the distance.

Herb bent, looked out the windshield and followed the direction of his gaze, then turned and asked, "What? What are you looking at?"

"Never end a sentence with a preposition," Chalky said as he continued to stare. He reached down, started the engine, and cruised up to the entrance of a private road that disappeared back into a stand of cedar trees that grew so close together moss covered the trunks from the lack of sunlight.

"Good-bye lunch," Herb said as Chalky bounced onto the dirt drive and drove between the trees. The road was narrow and the branches and undergrowth raked the sides of the car as they idled past. Herb shook his head as he thought about the scratches he'd have to explain when they turned the car in that night.

"There," Chalky said as the car rocked to a halt. In front of them sat a small house, circa 1930s, with bushes and brambles creeping up over the porch threatening to return it to nature. A red chimney with bricks missing around the top emitted a thin ribbon of white smoke from wood that was probably still green. "Deductive reasoning. Where there's smoke—"

"There's a house," Herb finished with a sigh.

"Shall we?" Chalky mused, still smiling.

"Why not, maybe they'll invite us to lunch." Herb followed Chalky up to the porch. Boards were missing from the porch and Chalky wondered idly if the tenant was burning the house in his fireplace, piece by piece. Chalky knocked—

"Git off'n my porch, or I'll blow yer balls off!" a thin, reedy voice screeched from the dark interior.

"Police!" shouted Chalky through the rusty, holey screen door. He held his badge up with one hand and instinctively held the other palm up to show he had no harmful intent. "Want to ask you a question."

"What's 'at you're hollen up?"

"It's my badge," Chalky said. He peered into the dark interior to no avail.

"How the hell I know it's a badge, you peckerwood! Don't you be makin' no sudden moves!" The voice sounded high, falsetto. A woman? he wondered. "Stick it in 'at 'ere hole inna screen." Chalky bent and pushed his badge and wallet next to the handle.

"Inna hole, shitheel!"

This is some kind of joke, right? he thought. Chalky shrugged his shoulders, reached down, and pushed his wallet into the hole, glanced back at Herb—

And it disappeared from his hand.

"Hey, goddammit! Give me that!" Chalky shouted. He felt foolish, negotiating through a hole in a screen. He heard a clasp unsnap, and the door creaked open. What looked in the dark like a tiny child came out from behind the door and pushed it wide. It was a short, incredibly short, old woman, in her eighties, four feet ten at most.

"Why didn't you say you was a cop right off?" she grumbled and hobbled into the dark living room. Herb smiled and followed Chalky in.

"I said I was a cop," Chalky said weakly as he bent and picked up his wallet and badge from a table where she had dropped it. She sat lightly in a rocker and proceeded to nudge herself back and forth and stare at them through small eyes in deep-set sockets, her face framed in a spray of thin, white baby hair. Sitting had changed her height only a couple of inches; Chalky found that amusing. The chair complained with a squeak each time she pushed.

"Whataya want?" she asked, making it two words. She

worked her mouth in a circular motion, much as a cow would chew its cud. Chalky wondered what she had in her mouth.

"It's against the law to threaten a police officer with a gun, ma'am," Chalky said. "You got a gun?"

"You're not too bright fer a cop. You see a gun? You must not be very good at your job." She glared at him. Herb tried to keep the chuckle in, but it escaped. Chalky frowned at him.

Chalky decided he'd lost this one, but he charged ahead anyway. "Were you out of your house this morning between five A.M. and eight A.M.?"

She leaned to the side as though considering it, then spat onto the floor. In the dim light, Chalky could see several thicknesses of newspaper spread on the rug where it landed. Big, brown spots on the paper indicated it had been well used. Chalky's stomach roiled, then he looked away for a moment when he realized she was chewing snuff.

"You remin' me of my grandson, Elmer, the one 'at still lives in Chattanooga, he's a nice fella too, but not too bright, you get my meanin'. You want a cup of tea?" the tiny woman asked, lightening a little. Chalky glanced up at the sink where two cats picked through the remains of the prior meal still on the drainboard.

"Thanks, nice of you to ask, but we have to get back to the station."

"Fell off'n the barn, middle of the winter, never made much sense after that, but smiles a lot." She shifted the cud to the other side of her jaw.

That was it. Herb bent over in mirth, giving up any attempt to control it. He got up, still laughing, excused himself, and went outside to wait. Chalky could hear him giggling in the yard.

"Did you see anybody in the neighborhood who didn't belong while you were out this morning?" Chalky persisted. In spite of trying to be serious, he found himself smiling at the woman.

"Yep."

"Where and who?"

"Apartment building, white one with all them flowers in front." Chalky nodded. It was a couple blocks away. "Dark-lookin' man, comes along 'bout seven-thirty, thereabouts, walkin' from the south like he's got a bee in his bonnet, gets in a white truck, and takes off like a bat outta hell."

"Truck? What kind of truck?"

"One of them with no winders and what has them slidy doors."

"Winders? Oh—windows. You mean a van?" She nodded and continued to ruminate. "Anything unusual about him?" Chalky asked eagerly, knowing the man came from the direction of the crime scene.

"Sure you don't hanker for some tea?" The lady smiled now, revealing a brown picket fence of random teeth.

"Thanks, we really have to go," Chalky said as his stomach twinged again. "What did the man look like?" He withdrew a small tablet and pencil and wrote furiously as they talked. The rocker squeaked faster.

"Twenty-five to thirty years old, dark. Like that Pancho Villa guy, 'cept'n' no mustache, you know. Carryin' a satchel of some kind—the kind them ole-time doctors used—like in the cowboy movies and such when they made house calls." Chalky was excited but tried not to show it.

"How tall would you say he was?"

"Taller'n me." The picket fence appeared again. "Shorter'n you."

"The van. You say it was white. You know the make?"

She shook her head no, then brightened. "But it had some flowers on the side, like the kin' of thing they have on a truck that delivers 'em."

"A florist truck?"

She said yes, then turned serious.

"There a name on the truck?" Chalky asked.

She shook her head no.

"This guy do something bad?"

"If it's the man we want, yeah, he did something real bad." She worked her mouth faster. "Could you identify this man if you saw him again?" A yes was too much to hope for.

"You mean, like from one of them lineup things?" This time she showed even her back teeth. She leaned. Chalky cringed, but she held her fire.

"Could be," he said.

"Damn tootin'." She slapped her knee. One of the cats dropped to the floor and rubbed against her leg as she moved rhythmically. Nervous as a cat in a roomful of rocking chairs flitted through Chalky's mind as he kept an eye on its tail.

"May I have your name, please?" Chalky filled a page, then flipped over to a clean one.

"Ida. Ida May Thornton."

Chalky asked for a phone number, but she had none. She asked again if he'd have a cup of tea, and he guiltily refused the third time and thanked her profusely for her help. His stomach bubbled with excitement. He'd forgotten he was hungry. He petted her cat, thanked her again, then went out the door and onto the porch. She followed. Herb was sitting in the car, smiling up at him through the windshield.

"I din't have no gun," she said softly and winked. The paper-thin skin wrinkled around her eyes as she stood on the porch. Her housedress hung straight down from her gnomelike body as the cats circled her feet. Chalky bent at the waist, kissed her on the forehead, and her smile increased by twenty watts.

"Ain't too bright, but I figur'd that," he said, imitating her speech pattern in an affectionate way. He turned and walked to the car.

chapter//five

The tired pickup truck bounced along Perry Avenue then turned onto a narrow street of old apartment buildings. A young black man named Cooper moved energetically back and forth, keeping time to the rap music pounding from the dash speakers. He peered out the side windows, slowing down and speeding up after he checked each number on the old structures.

"Yeah," he said when he recognized the number and slid to a stop. He continued to *boom-chicka-boom* through his pursed lips as he walked up onto the wood porch of the apartment building. Cooper went to the exterior door, looked inside, then opened it hesitantly and entered a long, dark hallway.

Instinctively stopping the rhythmic sound, he felt uncomfortable in the gloomy, dark hall. The corridor had a bare wood floor and the closed-in odor of old, moist wood and dusty carpeting. He tried to whistle softly to fill the quiet, but his mouth suddenly went dry. As he walked along, he had to lean close to each door in order to see the door's identifying letter. They were alphabetical; he was looking for "E."

The letter "E" was missing from the door in front of him and only the faded outline remained. He rapped lightly, and the sound echoed through the corridor. Farther away, he heard a woman yell, but the words were indistinguishable, then a baby cried somewhere above on the second floor. He tapped a bit harder with his index knuckle and leaned his head against the door to listen for stirring from inside.

The door squeaked open at his touch.

It was black inside. He stuck his head in tentatively and looked around.

"Carlos?" he whispered. "Carlos? You here?" A low, muffled mumbling came from the dark interior. He stepped into the room and stood by the door, letting his eyes adjust to the gloom. Inside, the heavy, warm air smelled of sweat and something burning. "How'd I get into this?" he muttered under his breath. "Carlos? I'm here," he said a bit louder. The mumbling sound was audible now, but still unclear. It was coming from a partially opened door on the other side of the room. From the crack, a dim light flickered. A candle? he wondered. "Hey, Carlos, you ready to go?" He used a normal voice, but it seemed unnaturally loud in the darkness. The guttural mumbling continued. It was a man's voice. "Shit," Cooper whispered and edged across the room toward the door. The sensible thing to do was to get the hell out of here, but he'd promised Carlos a ride and he always kept his promises.

A few feet from the door, his foot caught on something hard. It clattered and he stumbled, smashed into the door, and knocked it wide. Falling hard through the opening onto the floor, he hit his head on the metal corner of a bed. Lights flashed in his consciousness, then he was aware he was lying on his back looking up at the ceiling where light from burning candles danced. He leaned forward on one elbow.

In the dim light Carlos sat on his knees with his head on the table in front of a picture of a woman. He was naked, and his brown body glistened with moisture. On either side of the picture, a candle sputtered.

"Then . . . when I was . . . the first time . . . I cut . . . there was blood . . . then it wasn't me . . . mama . . . I can . . . can see you . . ." Carlos muttered disconnectedly. Cooper started to say something, then realized if Carlos was oblivious to the noise he made when he fell, hearing his voice was impossible.

Cooper got up on his hands and knees. Taking one last look at Carlos, he crawled out the door. Carlos's litany continued unabated. Cooper's skin crawled. Carlos was a loner who acted strange in the hospital, but this was too much—too fucking much! Cooper's only goal was to get the hell out of here and not come back. He crawled as silently as he could through the door and bumped what he had tripped over, a dumbbell from a weight set. He stood and tiptoed toward the door, when suddenly—

A light snapped on and blinded him.

"What the hell you doin', man?" came Carlos's voice from behind him. Cooper froze in place and turned slowly. He smiled weakly at Carlos who stood with his hand on the light switch. Carlos was either unaware, or it was of no importance to him, that he had no clothes on.

"Just come to get you, man?" Cooper said. He was really frightened, but had no idea why. He had the vague feeling he had interrupted some kind of bizarre ceremony, a ritual that was private.

"Whatcha doin', sneakin' 'round in the dark?" Carlos looked at him quizzically, then reached up and rubbed his forehead as though trying to clear his mind. "Why didn't you knock on the damned door?"

"I did. You didn't answer, so I walked in. I didn't mean no offense. Tripped on this thing." He pointed to the weight on the floor. Carlos glanced at it, then back at him.

"Shouldna been sneakin' around, man," Carlos continued, unmindful of what Cooper had said. "Lemme put my clothes on, I'll be right out." Carlos walked into the bedroom and closed the door. Cooper sighed, walked over, and stood by the front door.

"Weird shit," he said to himself. Drawers opened and slammed shut and hangers jingled from the bedroom as Carlos sorted through them as he dressed. "Weird shit," Cooper repeated as he looked at his watch. He hated to pick up someone to ride with him to the hospital, but Carlos had asked and offered to buy some gas, and what the hell, money was short. He wondered how in the world he was going to get out of this in the future without a scene.

What kind of heavy dope is this guy playin' with if he couldn't hear me fall on the floor like that? he wondered. People in the hospital screwin' with drugs was everyday stuff, but he wanted no part of it, him being on parole and all. He should walk away and not look back, but pissing off somebody who was playing with half a deck was a double bad idea. Double bad.

"Weird shit," he whispered again.

• • •

Carlos slumped sullenly in the truck most of the way to the hospital. Something had happened at the apartment when he was unconscious, but asking Cooper was out. He was distant and watched Cooper out of the corner of his eye. Cooper was acting strange—nervous. When the visions had cleared, he heard the sounds from the other room. He found Cooper tiptoeing toward the door—he wondered how long Cooper had been there and what he'd heard. This kind of thing would have to stop. In the future, he'd have to lock his door.

Carlos worked the night shift because he got to the point where he had trouble sleeping at night. He'd tried working during the day like most people, but he lived in such terror of the visions that came to him after dark that he'd stay up, roaming around until dawn. The only solution was working during the night. Unfortunately, in the last few months, the visions had started to come in the daytime too.

Miss Jackson, the night supervisor at Crosier Community Hospital, had caught him two or three times, hiding in the housekeeping closet on the third floor, trying to control those hated visions. He'd used that room because the small room in maintenance was too far away. He tried to cover it up each time by telling her he had the flu and was lying there until his dizziness passed. It was unlikely she believed him, but good housekeeping help was hard to get, and that made firing him extremely remote.

Screw her! I have to get the paper and find out about the lady. See whether she's alive . . . see what they say, the reporters, the doctors . . . whether they believe a man could do that by himself, without any help.

When he operated on the nurse, his hands had moved like precision instruments, cutting, tying off, sewing—fast and effortless, just like he had seen it done at the operating amphitheater at the hospital. While he worked, he imagined being in a surgical room with an attending surgeon and nurses watching him in almost reverent admiration. He could hear the thunderous applause when he snipped the last stitch. He winced at the unbelievably erotic pleasure he'd gotten when he sliced into her flesh. No drug high could even be close to that.

"You okay, Carlos? You don't look too good," Cooper's voice interrupted.

"Why shouldn't I be?" Carlos glared at him, and Cooper looked back at the road. Carlos wondered again what Cooper'd heard in the room. Cooper looked straight ahead and bit his lip, obviously uncomfortable. It was silent in the cab again.

First thing, I have to get a paper to make sure the lady is still alive—then if she is—when I get to work, I'll try to sneak up to her room during a break and catch a glimpse of her, he thought as he smiled. *It'll be like what the doctors call rounds. Yeah, that's it . . . I'll make my rounds.* His body tingled with pleasure at the anticipation.

"You read the front page of the paper?" Carlos asked.

"Wha . . . what?"

"The paper, the fucking paper! You read it this morning?" *Stupid son of a bitch. I should kill him, not take a chance,* Carlos thought. *Maybe I said something about the woman and he heard it . . . maybe . . .*

"Paper? Front page? I never read that crap, man. Only the sports and comics, man. Anything else depresses me," Cooper stuttered, then smiled as though he had all the important categories covered.

Carlos shook his head and looked off into the distance again.

"You bring the damned thing with you?" Carlos asked. His words were cutting, but Cooper continued driving without changing expression.

"No. I'd go back and get it, but it's too far. You 'spectin' to win the Lotto or something?"

"Stop at the stand on Jefferson," Carlos ordered. He looked away and was silent again. He hated the company of Cooper because he kissed up to those damned doctors and nurses like everyone else in housekeeping. *Please rub my face in the dirt . . . sir! Yes, sir! No, ma'am! Always kissin' ass like we're less than human.* He glared over at Cooper. *Shouldn't take a chance—he could have heard something back there.* His fingers twitched as he felt Cooper's flesh separate under his scalpels. *Maybe later. . . .*

Cooper stopped dutifully. Carlos jumped out, bought his paper, and folded it on his lap when he got in the truck. He pointedly ignored it to avoid having Cooper ask some stupid question or notice what he was reading. When he read about the woman he wanted to be alone, to savor every detail. It was not to share.

They arrived at the hospital at ten until seven and punched their cards at a time clock. Cooper appeared relieved to be there and scurried off in a different direction with only a quick good-bye.

"Bastards!" Carlos exclaimed. He hated the ritual of punching in. It always underlined that he was a nobody, a nothing. The nurses and doctors never punched in . . . only people like him. Just the people who cleaned up, did the scut work—the crap that nobody else wanted to dirty their hands with. Not the high and mighty bitches and bastards he had to kiss up to when he met them in the halls.

Yessir, no, ma'am! Fuck you! All of you! Only us Mexicans, blacks, Filipinos, and a smattering of whites to clean up your shit! Fuck 'em all! He spat on the floor in violation of all the rules as he walked up the hall. *If they saw him, so what. Fuck 'em!*

Laughter and talk filled the busy cafeteria, typical shift change banter. Across the room, a hand raised as his eyes swept the room. Maria Lopez tried to flag him down, but he ignored her and jogged into the hall.

He had fifteen minutes before someone tried to find him. Looking around to make sure no one was watching, he opened the door to a small room in maintenance he'd discovered weeks ago. It smelled of hot oil and thrummed from the machinery that kept the hospital alive, but here he was free of the annoyance of dealing with other people. He snapped on the low wattage bulb.

In the sparse light, he opened the paper to the first page. He read: tanker truck turned over, blocks traffic, with picture. Russian rebellion in the Baltics, call for food from Poland, state of the economy, real estate, and then the sports.

Nothing on the woman.

"Bastards, bastards!" he spat out as he finally reached the classifieds with no mention of it. "Must have been too late to get in." The door opened.

"What the hell you doin' hiding in here, Carlos? I seen you

duck in here." It was the shift foreman, Miss Jackson, a heavy-set black woman. From the door, she said, "You best be getting your skinny ass up to the second floor and get them beds changed."

"Chengando puta," Carlos said through his smile. His mind translated it to "fucking whore" in English. She smiled back, not understanding Spanish. Telling these vermin what he thought of them in his native tongue gave him a measure of pleasure.

"I hope that means, yes, ma'am, I'm on my way. 'Cause my phones been ringing off the hook. That what it means?"

"Por supuesto, pendeja!" (Of course, stupid.) She smiled again as he moved quickly along the corridor to the laundry to pick up his cart of linens. She followed, keeping pace.

"Y'all hear about that woman in 314, got her arms cut off by some crazy dude?"

"No. She alive?" He stopped, eyes flashing.

"Now what the hell she be doin' in 314 if she be dead?" She shook her head. "They don't put no dead people up there," she said as she walked away. Carlos smiled. He'd have to get up there as soon as possible—as soon as he finished the bulk of his job on the second floor.

Maybe I can hear them say something, about how good the job was. Then they'll all know how great I am . . . they'll have to let me in medical school—treat me as an equal. Yeah, then I won't have to punch no more time clocks, he thought.

Carlos picked up his load of linens and headed for the elevators wearing a thin smile. He felt like a doctor going on his rounds—almost. *Yes, Doctor*—he could hear the nurses saying—*it's a magnificent job and will be written up in the journals. You're the finest doctor in the hospital. Imagine, a double amputation without assistance and no infusion of blood, almost a miracle, almost as good as—*

The elevator door opened. Two nurses were talking and giggling. They glanced right by him as though he were nonexistent. The image in his mind evaporated.

Peggy found herself preoccupied the whole day with the problem of how to handle Joanne Pinkers the following morning. In surgery that afternoon, she'd performed a gall bladder removal and an emergency appendectomy. The surgeries had been routine, and she found her mind drifting back to Joanne Pinkers while she worked.

The closest incident to Joanne's was a man who'd had his legs severed in a railroad accident and he had no memory of it when he woke up. While Peggy pondered that, she snapped at a surgical resident a couple of times and apologized later. A male surgeon could be preoccupied or moody, while she was expected to contain her emotions or be branded a bitch. The double standard annoyed her, but it was part of the macho profession she had wanted to be part of so she had to accept their rules.

At eight-thirty she went by Joanne's room once more before she left for the evening. Mrs. Howard, the head nurse, was leaving the room just as Peggy approached. The nurse glanced up from her clipboard and smiled when she saw Peggy.

"Doctor, glad you're here."

"Nice that somebody's glad to see me."

The nurse said, "Her blood pressure has been 110 over 75 for the last two hours and her color looks excellent now."

"Febrile?"

"Not a hint."

"Well, at least the crazy washed his hands."

"They catch him yet?" The nurse's brow furrowed as she hugged her clipboard.

"I have no way of knowing. I've been in surgery. How's she been sleeping?" Peggy walked to the door.

"We're dripping Demerol as you directed. We'll take her off at seven o'clock tomorrow morning. She should start to come around sometime after nine A.M." Peggy knew the unasked question was, will you be here? She guessed that dealing with the woman themselves was something the nurses wanted to avoid if possible. The way she felt, it was hard to find fault with that attitude.

"I'll be here around eight-thirty in the morning," Peggy said.

"Doctor, may I ask you a question?"

"Of course." Peggy stopped in the doorway and leaned on the molding. "Always."

"I looked at the stumps of her arms." Peggy waited. "That wasn't performed by a doctor, was it?"

"You're very observant. No, I don't think so. At least, not a practicing doctor. Whoever did it knew the procedure, but the flaps and the suturing are ragged and unprofessional."

A loud, clattering sound came from their left. They both jumped and turned. A dark-complexioned young man dressed in green had knocked a tray off the housekeeping cart he'd been straightening. On his knees, he fumbled around on the floor retrieving the tray and the linen with embarrassed urgency.

"Sorry," he muttered as he rose and picked up the tray. He kept his head lowered and looked at the floor as he pushed the cart down the corridor.

Peggy watched him walk away for a moment, wondered what he had been doing there, then turned back to the nurse and asked, "Is he new? I haven't seen him before."

"Him? No. That's Carlos. He's worked here for several months now." Peggy looked up as the man disappeared into an open elevator.

She had the distinct feeling he'd been listening to their conversation.

Carlos could feel the heat rise in his face from his anger as the floor numbers of the elevator counted down. His hand shook on the handle of the cart, and his body felt cold. This was playing out differently than the fantasy in his mind had these last few months. It was wrong! This was supposed to be like his dream. The general public would be horrified, but he expected nothing less than admiration from the doctors in the hospital. And she had said—

The door opened and he shoved the cart into the long hall toward the laundry. The heavy air was laden with moisture, heat, and the smell of disinfectant. As he passed the coffee room he heard a voice call to him. He concentrated on the cart and ignored it.

"Carlos? Why didn't you answer me?" The sound of steps behind him. Maria Lopez caught up to him as he turned the corner into the drying room. "What's the matter?" she asked. He turned to face her, then slammed the cart against the wall where it collided with several other unloaded ones. The temperature in the room was oppressive. Two black women worked on the folding tables with their backs to them, their arms shiny with sweat.

Carlos was dizzy and his pulse raced. *I have to get out of here.* In the recesses of his mind he could feel the visions stir, forcing their way to the surface. A soft ringing echoed in the distance, but it would soon get louder. Lately, it had been harder to keep the visions buried. Many times, after they had gone, he had no memories of what he had done. He would look up at the clock when his head cleared and sometimes an hour would have passed.

It was almost okay when the visions had intruded for only seconds, but now? What would happen if they came and never left? If he was stuck there? Living and reliving those same scenes, over and over? Would he die? Maybe that was what his hell was going to be.

He shook his head and focused in on Maria's flawless face and long, straight black hair. As she studied him with her large brown eyes, her concern made him even more uncomfortable.

"I don't feel too good," he said weakly. The sweat peppered his skin, not from the heat, but from what was coming. He had to get away.

"How come you always shut me out when I want to be your friend?" she asked. Carlos felt cornered and looked around furtively for a way to escape.

"I tol' you before . . . don' bother me," he said. His Spanish accent became heavier as he got weaker. She put her hand on his forearm. He jerked away as though burned, then backed into the cart he'd just parked and the row racketed as they dominoed against each other. His breathing was heavier, his eyes hotter. He bolted for the door. As he ran through the opening, he jostled another black woman who was coming in, then he disappeared down the tunnel.

"Mercy me, what's wrong with that man?" the woman said as Carlos's steps echoed in the distance. Maria walked to the door with tears in her eyes and stood with the black woman. They watched him disappear around the corner of the basement hall. The woman turned to Maria and said, "You okay, child?"

"Why do you suppose he acts the way he does, Mavis?"

"I reckon only God knows the answer to that question," Mavis answered. She put her hand on Maria's shoulder and drew her close, dwarfing Maria's petite figure with her own. She'd been watching Maria's infatuation with Carlos for months.

"I only want to be his friend. Every time I get close to him, he acts as though I've got the plague or something." Maria wiped tears from the corner of her eyes and cleared her throat.

" 'Pears to me he has his own devils chasin' him all the time. I reckon he don't even know what it is that's botherin' him."

"But if he'd just talk to me . . . I know I could help him—be his friend."

"You're setting yourself up for some bad times, girl, if you want to be friends with that boy. He's good-lookin', but he's got miseries."

"But he seems so unhappy."

"I know, I know. His eyes stare right through you as though he's a-lookin' somewhere else, at another world. I can't see no happiness for a pretty girl like you with a mixed-up boy like that." Maria nodded and walked back into the laundry. Mavis shook her head. Giving advice to a young girl who had her cap set for a man was a waste of time.

Carlos banged into the small janitorial room. Not bothering to turn on the light, he rushed to the far wall and felt for the cabinets. He found them, then stepped around behind them and knelt. The space between them and the wall was about twenty inches wide. Back in the blackness, a pile of sheets covered the floor. His hiding place.

He pulled himself into the depths, then lay down. Moisture soaked his clothes, hair, and body. His eyes were still unfocused. The ringing in his ears grew louder as he wiped his forehead with a corner of the sheets. They smelled sour from past use. He'd made it just in time.

His biggest fear was that he'd have one of these visions in front of other people, then they'd take him away to someplace awful. He thought of all the medicines they'd given him in California to try to control them, but none of them had worked. His mind flitted around, trying to find something to concentrate on, hoping the awful vision would go away, but it came closer.

Maria. Why did she keep bothering him? Why? What did she want from him? Then . . . there was something, something he had to do, but the memory was vague and unformed . . . what? He groaned.

The blazing sun appeared in the corner of his peripheral vision again and grew larger. His teeth chattered as he stared blankly at the almost-black ceiling. There was nothing he could do . . . he'd have to give himself up to the vision and let it carry him away.

He groaned with the inevitability. Rocking back and forth, he shivered. Suddenly the room was hotter and his skin tingled.

"No, no!" he shouted, but he knew it was no use. This was the hated one, the vision that rended him apart, and it was coming . . . coming. . . .

As his consciousness leeched away, the sound of his mother screaming and thrashing around filled the room. Hot, fetid, suffocating—it was a black hell with no escape. A hell with the air reeking of the stink of decay and infection.

He was back in Tijuana in the middle of the night. It was pitch-black in the tin shack. A child again, he was afraid to go to his mother because she was becoming increasingly violent and had lost the ability to recognize him when she woke from her fevered coma.

At only five years old, his thoughts were the pure emotion of terror. If he left the shelter again for help, no one would come. Besides, he had no place to go. The other people in the surrounding shacks moved in and out in the night, but nobody bothered with or cared about anyone else. They were all on the edge of survival.

His stomach seethed with the need to throw up. The smell from his mother's infected arm was oppressive. He crept over near the wall and looked for his last three wooden matches. He had guarded them and kept them wrapped in an oily rag. His only possessions were a battered, smelly kerosene lantern and the filthy mattress left by the previous tenant.

Crawling on his hands and knees, Carlos felt for the lantern, which he remembered as being a few feet from where his mother now lay shrieking and crying. She scuffled around looking for something in the dark. His heart pounded in his chest as he reached into the blackness and felt for the lantern.

Finally, his short fingers scraped its hard surface. The lantern still radiated the heat from the relentless sun that had shone during the day. The heat had lain like a blanket on the shacks and nothing had moved since morning. His mother suffered in a fevered coma all day and had awakened only a couple of times for short periods. Now that it was dark, she had regained consciousness and moved about, screaming almost continually.

He had tried to give her water earlier, but she had choked on it and batted him back against the wall. His mother—the tender woman who loved him—had slowly disappeared and this insane, unreasoning creature had taken her place. He lay still and shook with fear. It had been too hot for the children to go outside that day and even the scrawny dogs that constantly combed the trash piles for scraps were intimidated to shelter.

"Mama?" he asked in a whisper. Her screams and curses had ceased; she just groaned and cried. As usual, his mother failed to recognize him or respond. He scratched one of the stick matches on the lantern. It blazed with a shooshing sound, filling the small tin shack with a flickering glow. With quivering fingers, he turned the knob on the lantern. It was down to the last inch of kerosene.

It emitted a soft hiss, then gradually glowed brighter and filled the dark with its sputtering light and the penetrating smell of the burning fuel. He pulled the globe over the wavering flame and leaned away from it. Spots danced in front of his eyes for a second, then—

He saw her.

Leaning against the wall, eyes open, rolling back and forth, she breathed in deep, racking sobs—almost like heavy panting. Her infected arm lolled from under the blankets she'd wrapped herself in. Her upper arm was now the size of her thigh, and in the undulating light of the lantern, the tight skin glistened yellowish-red from the pressure of the infection.

He crept closer, trying to make out what she was doing with

her other hand in the shadows of the blankets. Something flashed. The blade of a knife?

Drawing away, he was confused about what she intended to do. This shell of a woman was his mother, but he could no longer approach her for fear she would hurt him in her agony much as an injured dog would viciously bite anyone who touched it.

She raised the knife in front of her and tried to focus on the wide blade. Time ticked by slowly as she moaned and studied it as though seeing it for the first time. Carlos crawled within two feet of her, but was afraid to get any closer. The disconnected sounds she uttered were senseless.

"Mama?" he whimpered, his voice tentative, his hands up to his mouth. Her fevered eyes continued to study the knife with an intensity that indicated she was mulling a decision.

She screeched—

He jumped—

The knife slashed down on the offending arm and carved a smiling arc across the swollen part. The distended skin exploded like a water balloon and spewed blood and yellow pus into Carlos's face. He sat shocked for a moment, then began to squeal and choke as hot blood and gore dripped from his eyes, hair, nose, and chin.

Standing, he stumbled blindly outside onto the still-burning sand, fell, and rolled while howling like a wounded animal. Then the retching began. After many minutes, with sand and gore stuck to his face and chest, he stumbled off into the night. He had to get away from this nightmare—away from this crazed thing that used to be his mother.

They found him the next day in a junkyard; sitting, staring, dehydrated, and near death. They brought him back to the camp and found his mother.

She had died during the night from loss of blood and was now lying in state in a mud hut on the border of the village. Two men took him into a candle-lit room to view her body.

After that evening he was mute for weeks. He would simply sit and stare at the visions in his head—visions of the shack, of the hot fields, and of the huge fireball of a sun. He watched his delirious mother and the flashing knife coming down, then recoiled from the hot, wet putrescence slamming into him, washing over him, burning into his skin.

The horrific vision projected vividly in his mind, like an endless motion picture . . . over, and over, and over. . . .

chapter//six

When Carlos finished work at four in the morning, he punched out, then waited by the exit doors used by the rest of the employees. It had been a busy shift. With three people missing, he had worked fast and sullenly through the whole evening and had to retreat to his room only once when the vision of the sun intruded. That one had lasted a scant fifteen minutes.

As he waited by the doors, he clenched his hands into fists and kept running over and over in his mind what the lady doctor had said: *"Ragged . . . unprofessional . . . wasn't done by a doctor. . . ."*

The words tore at him, made him want to break something, hurt somebody. Hurt her. *What does she know, she's just a fucking* puta, *probably worked her way into her job by fucking everybody in sight—yeah, that's it.* When he worked in the laundry, the sheets he folded became the doctor's neck, and he pressed so hard he could feel her skin parting.

"Carlos?" Maria's voice interrupted the image. He jerked alert, suddenly embarrassed because the fantasy of her skin parting had made him hard. Maria came through the doors alone as usual. He tried to smile but failed, so he just stared at her. "Are you all right?" she asked.

He'd never had a relationship with a girl or a woman. How he was supposed to act or what he should say was a mystery to him. His only sexual release had been in his dreams when he would cut into living flesh, made somebody well, then sewed them up. He'd also reached orgasm a few times when he practiced with his tools, and when he cut into that woman two days ago, the nurse. That was the best. The real thing. Maria waited patiently and watched him compassionately with her large doe eyes. He glanced at her small, perfect body and firm breasts and wondered why she failed to excite him.

"You wanna have something, coffee maybe?" he heard himself say. The cloud in front of her eyes disappeared and Maria brightened. She took him by the arm and led him toward the coffee shop near the hospital without answering. On the opposite corner, the restaurant did a brisk business. He had to talk to himself to keep from lashing out to get away. His arm burned where she touched him with her dirty hands.

The coffee shop was warm and noisy. Maria walked ahead and selected a booth in the corner, a couple of seats away from anyone else. Maria sat and motioned for him to join her. He was silent as Maria chattered about how glad she was that he finally talked to her and how much she liked him.

Her voice grated on his consciousness and he picked up only a word here and there: "—went over to . . . the cat jumped off the windowsill, and then . . . we're having a party . . . Janis said . . . how was your evening, I saw you—"

"I want the doctor's address," he said, cutting through the nonsense sounds.

Maria sat for a moment, frowning, trying to associate that with what she'd been talking about, then asked, "What do you mean?"

"You know girls in administration, don't you?" He again attempted to fight a smile to the surface—to make his voice sound casual. His face remained uncooperative.

"Yeah?"

"I saw her name on the door . . . Dr. Margaret Chandler. She's a surgeon, I think." Sweat trickled down his back. He'd never talked to a girl his own age before . . . not in a social setting. As his tension built, the walls seemed to close in.

"You want me to get this woman's address?" she asked dumbly. He nodded and clenched and unclenched his fists under the table. His ears rang.

"I know a girl . . . sure I could . . . I guess I could. But why do you want it?" She stared at him innocently.

God, she was stupid. Why didn't she just do what I want—

why did people always make things so hard. Bastards! he thought.

"It's important!" he snapped, not successful at modulating his voice. "I need it right now." Maria frowned and appeared to search for words. He stood up. "I have to go. Can you get it for me?"

"Yeah, I guess, if it's important," she said in a confused tone. He nodded, leapt up, and ran toward the door. She reached out helplessly, her mouth open, as he banged through the door into the darkness away from her eyes.

It was black out and the overcast obscured the stars as Carlos made his way to the hospital instead of going home. His ears rang, and the sun crept into his peripheral vision again. He knew he would just have time to make it back to the little room before he drifted away. If someone found him here on the sidewalk, they'd know something was wrong with him and he'd lose his job. He had to hurry. . . .

This was going to be a long one, he could tell.

Maria sat in the restaurant and sipped her coffee after Carlos had left, trying to understand what that was all about. She'd watched him for weeks, hoping for a chance to talk to him. He excited her with his dark, brooding good looks, but he was so strange. Was he shy? And why would he want the address of a doctor, especially a woman doctor? Was he interested in the doctor? No, that couldn't be it. She was too old . . . in her thirties at least. Why did he want it? If he'd only explained it to her. She knew it would be a cinch to get it from Dianne in administration, but also knew that it broke all the rules. Mother of God, I could lose my job or something if anyone found out, she thought. But, it's my chance . . . my chance to get to know him better . . . and maybe . . .

"Look, fella, I've got enough problems right now, okay?" Chalky checked his image in the mirror. An occasional chat with himself while he shaved seemed to put things in order. It was six in the morning and the bathroom was steamy from his shower.

"But I say she's pretty with a great body, well, almost great.

Definitely above average." There it was. Sex raising its ugly head again.

"You've looked stupid before, but this could be the grand-daddy of all rejections." He made an O with his mouth and slid the razor smoothly from his ear to his Adam's apple. The razor collected a long ribbon of foam, and he cleaned it under the stream of water. He'd lain awake a couple of hours during the night thinking about the lady doctor with the gray eyes and the crinkly smile. Hell, she could be married for all he knew, but she'd touched something in him, something warm and fuzzy, something he'd tried to bury after his disastrous marriage. Did he see interest in the doctor's eyes, or was she just nice to everyone?

"Nice? You've got to be kidding. She treated you like a putz, making you wait.

"I deserved it. I *acted* like a putz, played the big city cop, a regular Dickhead Tracy.

"Well, you're going to see her again today. You going to have the courage to ask her for a date?

"Courage? Who needs courage when I'm this good-looking?" He smiled at his now clean-shaven face, bent, splashed water onto his cheeks, and toweled it dry. He inspected his previously brushed teeth, then smiled again. "Damn right I'm scared, partner. My AA degree looks pretty pathetic compared to her umpty-do degrees. Christ! How long and how much school does it take to be a friggin' surgeon.

"Yeah, but your raw sex appeal has to count for something." He flexed his chest and arm muscles approvingly, then exhaled and shook his head as though changing his mind.

"Forget it, slack jaw. I'm going to have to learn to breathe through my nose before a broad with that much class is going to buy into my program. I can see her, drinking beer and cheering while I play pool, hanging loose with my scum-bag friends." The telephone rang and interrupted him. He was relieved because the direction of this internal dialogue was the pits. Grabbing his pants off the doorknob, he stepped into them, then swore when he saw the wet spots appear on the pant legs because he was still wet. His dripping feet made puddles in the hall leading to the kitchen. Have to put a couple more extensions in, he thought.

"Tabby?" he asked when he picked up the phone.

His daughter Tabitha was crying into the receiver. He waited a minute for her to stop. She was fourteen and her hormones were driving him and her mother up the wall. Lately this had been a typical call.

"What's wrong, baby?" he asked as he sat down at the dinette table next to the phone. His daughter cried louder. "I'm freezing, babe. I'm going to put on a shirt, be right back." He stood and walked into the bathroom, ran his fingers through his hair, pulled on a shirt that he'd had hanging on a hanger from the towel rack, struggled socks over his still-wet feet, and asked, "Why me, God? It was such a nice day."

He dropped back into the dinette chair and put on the shoes he'd been carrying. When he picked up the phone and listened, she was sniffing and blowing her nose, unaware that he'd been gone.

"Mom said you wouldn't want me," she said without a prelude. He wondered why everything she poured out sounded like an indictment. Must be genetic.

"I'd love to have you here, babe, it's just that I have to work and need to know beforehand when you're coming." He stood, stuffed his shirt into his pants, and tightened his belt. "You want to come up for a long visit? I can arrange my time."

"I want to come to live with you."

"Great with me, babe, but does your mom know anything about this? Of course she doesn't," he said, answering his own question. "I suppose, why would be a nice place to start. You having trouble?"

"She's off for the weekend on one of her retreats. I'm staying with Judy 'til Sunday. As far as Mom, the why is because she's a bitch!" she spat.

He fought back the temptation to say, Yeah I know. Instead, he said, "Don't use that kind of language about your mother. She's been good to you. Don't tell me, she won't let you do something that you want to do, right?"

"It isn't that simple."

"So, tell me, I've got time." He glanced at his watch. Herb would be here any minute.

"Can I live with you, yes or no?"

Great, just what I need—an ultimatum from an emotional fourteen-year-old girl at six in the morning, he thought, then sighed.

"Honey, you know I'd have you here in a flash if your mother would go for it. But right now, I'm working on a murder case, well, almost . . ."

She snuffled deeply. "Mom was right, right? You don't want me," she cried.

"No, that's not right . . . but what I wanted never seemed to have a whole lot to do with it, kid. The court made that decision ten years ago. What's going on down there in Centralia with your mom? I'm waiting."

"She doesn't understand me."

"That's supposed to be my line." He sat and supported his chin with his hands, elbows on his knees. Somehow this conversation was taking on the same characteristics as the one with Biggs yesterday, slow and convoluted.

"She won't let me do nothing."

"Translated?"

"Dating."

"Aha! We have it. Boys, right?"

"So? I'm old enough."

The doorbell rang. Saved . . . it had to be Herb. He yelled through the door and Herb walked in.

"Honey, I want to talk to you, but I have to go to work."

"Daaad," she whined, drawing it out into three syllables.

"Come hell or high water, I'll get down to see you this week, maybe go bowling . . . you like that? We can talk about this dating thing then, okay?"

The last few times he'd seen her, he felt as though he were fumbling around for something to keep her entertained. Now that she was growing up, he had trouble understanding what pushed her buttons. Conversation, a show, and dinner didn't seem to get the job done anymore. He'd tried to get her to share his interest in books, but that was a definite no sale. Hell, grown-up women were a mystery—how the hell could you

hope to understand them when you threw in the raging hormones of pubescence. He promised her he'd come by next
Wednesday and she hung up.

Chalky went in and put on his coat. He and Herb walked out
into the overcast morning and climbed into Herb's car.

"What's the program this morning, Chief?" Rosen asked.

"After we take care of some things at the station, we go to the
hospital again. See if we can get in and see that Pinkers. I've got
a bad feeling about that though. My guess is this lady is going to
give us next to nothing, even when and if we do get to her."

"How so?"

"Call it professional instinct if you want. This whole thing is
so weird, I can't see anything going smoothly, doesn't work that
way." They drove along in silence for a few minutes, then
Chalky asked, "What do you think of that good-looking lady
doctor?"

Herb smiled. "You mean professionally or physically?"

Chalky chuckled. "Maybe both."

"Professionally, she seems to be able to kick ass and take
names—physically—who knows? Since I married Beth, I don't
look at other women that way anymore."

"Sure, and I can run the hundred in eight seconds flat,"
Chalky said.

"Honestly. That's your problem, you just haven't met the
right lady yet."

"You've never met my ex-wife Violet. The thought of getting
involved with any woman again after that marriage makes my
blood run a little cold."

"Give me a break, she couldn't have been that bad."

"Look, I hate jerks who rag on their ex-wives, so don't get
me started, okay? Let's say that we were seriously incompatible
. . . her with her gurus, chanting, incense, humming, and complete lack of affection. Dammit! I told you not to get me
started."

They were silent for a couple more miles, then Herb said,
"Hey, it wasn't a total loss . . . you told me about your daughter.
She must be a great kid." Chalky reflected on how much trouble
he'd had over the years with Tabby, in school and out, and how

she'd bounced back and forth, using first Vi, then him to get what she wanted.

"Alligators have the right idea," Chalky said.

"How's that?"

"Kids give them any crap, they eat them."

chapter//seven

Peggy got up in the morning after a restless night. She'd considered taking a sleeping pill before going to bed, then dismissed the idea because she knew that being lethargic in the morning would only add to her problems. As she lay awake in bed the previous night listening to the hum of the electric clock, she ran the scene of her meeting with Joanne Pinkers over in her mind. With a couple of exceptions, this was going to be the most emotionally draining thing she'd ever done. Even telling a family that someone had died during surgery seemed to be easier by comparison. When that happened, it was usually not unexpected, and it had a finality that gave them a handle to emotionally deal with it.

With Joanne Pinkers, this would be the beginning of a long nightmare for her; a nightmare that would last the rest of her life. It seemed impossible that anyone could ever completely adjust to . . . make a real mental peace with this kind of a mutilation.

When she pulled into the hospital parking lot a little after eight A.M., the fog hung like a blue-green icy blanket in the treetops. It seemed to be an omen of what kind of day it was going to be.

She walked in the rear door, and as she entered, the familiar disinfectant aroma comforted her. It smelled like her second home after years of twelve-to-sixteen-hour days in that environment. Before she had left her condo this morning she'd placed a call to Fortsam's service and recorded a message for him to meet her at Joanne's room at nine if possible. She had no verification that he'd be there, but she was going ahead anyway. Putting it off any longer was impossible. It had to be done, ready or not.

As she walked down the hall to the elevator, the man that the nurse had identified as Carlos walked toward her. She wondered idly what he was doing there since she knew he worked the night shift. She glanced at him and nodded good morning. His eyes were flat and red, and he looked disoriented. He stared at her without acknowledging her presence—simply walked by with his eyes locked on hers in a fixed gaze. After she passed, she felt a chill and turned. He still stared over his shoulder and watched her, even as he disappeared around the hallway corner.

She tried to remember where she'd seen eyes like that before, then remembered. Sharks. Sharks at the aquarium. Flat, black orbs with no depth or feeling, no indication of any humanity or pity lurking inside.

Just my imagination, she thought as she pushed the button for the second floor. As the doors closed, she heard her name being paged. Ed Fortsam. Please let it be him.

She picked up the phone in her office and the operator put her through. Ed was talking from an extension somewhere in the hospital.

"Can you make it at nine?" Peggy asked, not bothering with preliminaries.

"Wouldn't miss it." His voice was cheerful and animated and the tension drained from her body.

"Thank God, I wasn't looking forward to facing this alone," she said.

"Of course, you'll have to have dinner with me tonight to compensate me for my professional expertise."

"Don't you ever give up? Besides, it isn't fair, asking me when I need you to take the pressure off."

"I have no pride."

"I'll think about it," she said and hung up. She knew that he was asking her for a date, not to a business dinner. He'd made it plain for the better part of the last year that he was interested, but she'd been able to parry his advances to this point. She also knew that once she conceded to one date, that would be the beginning of something that she had no intention of pursuing.

Like a large percentage of psychiatrists, Ed came to his profession with a closetful of personal baggage that he still carried around. Beside that problem, she was certain she had no male-female attraction to him at all. Aside from his physical appearance, he was too calculating and self-serving about everything he did.

Peggy had buried her needs as a woman these last few years to focus on what had become the centerpiece of her life—surgery. Now that she'd achieved a modicum of success in that, flipping the switches back was going to take some doing.

"Penny for your thoughts," Carrie said from the doorway of the office. Peggy brightened.

"What are you doing here so early?" Peggy asked.

"Checked with the floor nurse. I understand you're going to talk to 314 this morning. Thought you might need some moral support. I've got about an hour."

"Are you kidding? I'll put you in my will." Peggy beamed with relief.

"It's eight-fifteen. When are you going up?"

"Let's do it shortly and get it over with."

"How about Mr. Personality, Fortsam? He going to rattle his bones and pontificate his nineteenth-century voodoo?"

"He'll be there at nine, or a little before. Besides, he's got conditions attached to it. Wants to go to dinner in payment."

"What a butt! You're not, are you? That makes you fifteenth on his list." She plopped heavily into the seat across from Peggy's desk. "He's tried to date everyone including the damned candy stripers." Carrie took a pack of cigarettes from her pocket and lit one with a flourish.

"You're kidding," Peggy said.

"Wish I were. He even winked at me a couple of times—can you imagine? Even when he knows what I think of him." Carrie continued with her diatribe about Ed Fortsam as Peggy sat and allowed her mind to drift.

Peggy could hear her mother's voice echo through her head: "Remember, Pegs, if you want something really bad, the way to get it is to concentrate on that one thing to the exclusion of everything else. Don't let *anything* sidetrack you." Peggy had been studying for an exam in her room when her mother had found her crying, came in, and sat down beside her.

"Mom, I don't know whether I can make it or not. It's just too hard, too hard. . . ." Her mother leaned forward, put her arm around Peggy, and rubbed her daughter's forehead with the palm of her hand.

"Pegs, the only way you can fail is if you decide to fail. Have you decided to fail?"

Peggy sniffed and looked up at her mother. "No, but it takes so many hours, and it seems to come so easy for the other students, especially the guys."

"Don't believe it. Everyone has his own demons to kill, some simply hide it better than others," her mother had said. "The hotshots you think are so self-confident have the same insecurities that you do, maybe more." Peggy had repeated this conversation with her mother in different forms, when she first attended college, then medical school.

". . . and then he finally called Teresa. Pegs? Are you listening to me?" Carrie sat forward and raised her voice slightly.

Caught dreaming, Peggy jerked alert and answered, "Of course! I was only reflecting on what you were talking about."

Carrie smiled and stubbed out her cigarette. "Sure, sure you were. I'm ready—let's do it." They rose, walked into the hall, and headed toward the elevators, Peggy still thinking about how much she owed her mother.

"You have any surgeries scheduled today?" Carrie asked as they waited for the doors to open.

"No, thank God. I have to make rounds, then I think I'm going to go home early. Tomorrow's going to be a long one." The doors slid open, and the two women stood quietly as they were whisked to the third floor. The machine dinged, and the door opened. They walked to the nurses' station and picked up Joanne Pinkers's file.

The nurses were congregated in the back room. They stopped chatting and looked in their direction, obviously very interested in what the doctors planned to do. The conversations in the halls that morning had centered on the lady with the missing arms. Nurse Howard came to the desk and nodded a greeting.

"She awake yet?" asked Peggy. The nurse knew who she was asking about.

"Moving a little. Made a few sounds, but not fully awake."

"You ready?" Peggy asked Carrie.

"Hell no, but let's go," Carrie answered. Peggy turned and went into 314. Carrie followed and shut the door on the prying eyes. The room was in low light, the rheostat turned down to provide just enough illumination to see where they stepped. Peggy turned it to half-on. Joanne's eyes fluttered, and a frown creased her forehead.

"It's eight twenty-five. We going to wait for Fortsam?" Carrie asked in a hushed voice. She walked around to the other side of the bed. Peggy went to the left, released the rail, and slid it down. Joanne stirred.

"No, I can't see any reason to. He's usually late anyway, and I don't want to wait that long. I have to get this over with," Peggy said. "The tension is driving me crazy."

Joanne was strapped loosely in the bed to keep her from moving and injuring herself while she slept. Peggy sat on the edge and studied her face, then let her gaze slip down to the bandaged stumps of her arms protruding from the white hospital gown. The nurses had changed her dressings just before they took her off medication and the sleeves were still rolled up. Peggy shivered.

"Who . . . who are you?" Joanne's voice shocked Peggy and she jumped. She was unaware that Joanne's eyes had opened while she was inspecting the bandages.

"I'm Dr. Chandler . . . I'm taking care of you," Peggy said uncertainly. Damn, maybe I should have waited for Fortsam, she thought. She glanced toward the door hoping he'd walk in.

"Oohh!" Joanne groaned when she shifted her weight on the bed. Peggy reached out, put her hand on Joanne's head, and brushed a lock of hair away from her face.

"I know it's hard, but try not to move right now, if you can."

"Water, can . . . can I have some water," Joanne asked weakly. Her voice had the dry, restricted sound typical of some-one who'd been under sedation for a long time. Peggy poured a half glass of water, took a flexible straw, inserted it, then sat on the edge of the bed and held it up to Joanne's mouth. Joanne took a couple of deep sips, then, exhausted by the effort, let her head fall to the side. After a moment, her eyes opened again and she asked, "That man . . . who was he? . . . Did they catch him?"

"What man?" Peggy asked. Joanne's gaze shifted between Carrie and Peggy, then settled on Peggy.

"The man in my apartment, the man who . . . who . . ." Her eyes grew wider and wider, then she made a choking sound as though strangling on something.

"Relax, relax," Peggy said. "You're safe now. Whoever he is, he can't bother you here." Joanne stopped gagging, and her breathing slowly returned to normal.

"Oohhh!" Joanne's voice came back, saturated with pain as she struggled to move. Peggy could imagine all the courseways of severed nerves leading to her brain flashing alternating waves of pain and confusion. Peggy glanced over to Carrie, then down to Joanne.

Joanne was a beautiful woman with long auburn tresses that shone with highlights even in this half-light. Joanne asked, "Why do you have me strapped in and the sheet so tight? It's so tight I can't move my arms."

Peggy's heart jumped and speeded up. It was out in the open—the subject she'd dreaded.

"We have to keep you from moving. To keep you from injuring yourself," Peggy heard herself say. She could feel herself being drawn in, edging closer and closer to the horror that she was ultimately going to be forced to reveal.

He cut off your arms! The words screamed and reverberated in Peggy's mind, but she dreaded saying them. The dampness under Peggy's hair and on her neck was uncomfortable, and she knew the tension was causing it.

"Unstrap me, so I can sit up," Joanne said, then groaned again, more softly this time. "Why do my hands, arms, and shoulders ache so much?" she cried, her voice raised slightly as her concern grew. Her voice broke, either from the pain or the emotion.

Peggy glanced up at Carrie. Carrie's eyes were locked on Joanne and glistened in the half-light. Carrie met Peggy's eyes with a helpless expression and shrugged.

In a soft and compassionate tone, Peggy said, "I can't allow you to sit up yet, you've had major surgery performed on your arms, and it's not healed well enough. I'm afraid you might start to bleed." There it was again—skirting around the edges—hinting, touching, and moving away. Can I say the words? she wondered.

"Surgery? Oohhh!" Joanne moaned when she jerked toward Peggy. "What surgery? . . . Why . . . What surgery? Why did you operate on me?"

Peggy felt the box around her get smaller. She looked up. Fortsam was still not there. She admonished herself: To hell with Fortsam! Tell her, dammit! It's your responsibility. Fortsam's supposed to help her after the fact.

"I didn't operate on you," Peggy said. "You were found in your bedroom with . . . the . . . the . . . the surgery . . . already completed." Peggy's voice was lower and less forceful. She wanted to run out of the room, but her obligation kept her leaning over the bed. She could feel her mother's hand in the middle of her back, pushing her forward, making her stay, forcing her to do her duty as usual.

Joanne moved her head back and forth in a rhythmic motion as if trying to escape the words and the pain at the same time. She stopped suddenly and her eyes bore into Peggy. The silence in the room was so complete Peggy could count her own heartbeats.

"What surgery?" Joanne half whispered in a fear-filled voice.

It was here. All the hours of apprehension had been condensed down to this one moment in time.

"Your arms have been amputated," Peggy whispered, matching the huskiness of Joanne's voice. "Both of them, just below the shoulders. He amputated your arms."

She wanted to say something inane, like: But you're going to be okay, you're going to live, you can get into another profession and have a happy, productive life even with that handicap. . . .

"Amputated," Joanne repeated as though the word had no meaning. "Amputated?"

"He removed them just below your shoulders," Peggy continued. Peggy started to say something more, but was interrupted by a low keening sound from deep within Joanne's chest that sounded too alien to be human. A chill went up Peggy's back as the ungodly sound echoed from wall to wall. Peggy's heart raced as she desperately tried to think of some way to help, to maintain control, but the words were out—out into the air like an uncaged animal and could never be taken back.

Joanne's body was rigid as her head tilted to the side. The unearthly scream slowly changed in tenor until it seemed to vibrate from the center of the earth and scorch a lightning streak into the heavens. Peggy and Carrie stumbled away as Joanne's shrieks degenerated into an out-of-control, throaty wail. The door slammed open behind them.

"Let me take over!" Ed Fortsam pushed by Peggy to the bed and glanced down at Joanne, now completely unaware of who was in the room as she continued her vibrato screams. He looked up at the two women, then signaled for them to leave. They both stood hypnotized for a moment, until the word "Go!" slapped them in the face.

They found themselves in the hallway walking rapidly away from the room. In the background, the penetrating howling was more muffled behind the closed door. Peggy knew it would be months, if not years, before that tortured voice disappeared from her dreams.

chapter//eight

Chalky and Herb finished breakfast, then went to the station and brought the paperwork in their other files up-to-date. Paperwork. The bane of a policeman's existence. They discussed where to start their investigation of hospital personnel and decided that since Joanne Pinkers lived and worked close to Crosier Hospital, why not start there?

At 10:30 A.M. Chalky and Herb jogged up the stairs of the hospital. When they had walked across the lot, they noticed a white van with the words "TV News/team" lettered on the side. It was parked in front, taking up a section of the no-parking space.

"Somebody ought to give this guy a ticket," Chalky said. He had a thing about newspeople anyway. Pushy, shovey, invade-your-space kind of people. Something like hyenas around another animal's kill; smelling, sniffing, always trying to get something that belonged to someone else. And with about the same amount of sensitivity. Screw the victim; screw the family. As long as they got the story first. Jerks. Only met a few that he liked.

Back into the smell. The antiseptic, the too-clean-for-words atmosphere. The hospital buzzed with activity and made Chalky wonder if they were having a two-for-one sale or something. Take out your appendix with a gall bladder special—free crutches with every foot surgery—choice of fabrics on your free cushions after a hemorrhoid operation— He was really getting into it when they arrived at the glass door that led into the administrative section.

"Officer Fuchs!"

As he held the handle to the door, Chalky was stunned to hear his name pronounced correctly for a change. He turned. Dr. Chandler walked up and smiled, her hands deep in her coat pockets. God, she's good-looking, he thought. And those eyes. Knockouts. Long eyelashes. He felt his stomach shift.

"You want to try to see Miss Pinkers?" Peggy asked. "I'm going back up there right now. Can't guarantee anything because she was very upset earlier, but we can try." She smiled wider. Wow, he observed. Even her teeth are perfect. Bet she never had a cavity. "When we get there," she continued, "I'll go in first. If she can handle it, I can give you five minutes with her."

Herb said, "Look, why don't you go and try to talk to her, I can handle the director, no big deal." Chalky stood immobile, staring at Peggy, trying to decide what to do next. Making a decision while he stared into those beautiful eyes had his mind slowed to a crawl. She turned to Herb when the silence got too long.

"We can both go with you," Herb said, breaking the uncomfortable pause. "Won't take that long, then we can come down here."

"Great," she said as she turned and walked away. They followed. Chalky lagged behind.

"Sorry," Chalky whispered to Herb as they followed several steps behind her, "just had a few brain cells check out and go south on me back there." She moved in her no-nonsense stride as they struggled to keep up. He watched her slender legs weave a pattern on the tile floor in front of them, and he could almost feel the warm wake she left in the air, tinged with her delicate perfume.

"I'm losing a little respect for you, partner. Thought I was going to have to locate some oxygen to kick-start you," Herb whispered back and finished with a chuckle.

"Leave me alone," Chalky grumbled. He could feel the heat in his cheeks. Jesus! When's the last time I did that? he wondered. He loosened his collar. High school. No. Grade school? Shit. Nobody noticed that blush. He glanced at Herb and was amused that he was smirking and checking out her legs too. The elevator door was open. They walked in and she tapped the button.

"I should call Dr. Fortsam's service to make sure, but I know how important this is," she said.

"Sure is," Chalky said.

"One of the nurses called me and told me that Miss Pinkers's mother arrived only a half hour ago. That might be a stabilizing influence, and it might be a good time to try to talk to her," she said. She looked at Chalky, smiled, and her eyes crinkled again. Chalky searched for something more profound to say as the elevator dinged and the door slid open.

Screams and shouts echoed in the hall. Two nurses ran by the open door. The noise came from the end of the hall, in the direction of the room that Chalky and Herb knew they were headed for. 314. Chalky's adrenaline pumped, and he was first to the door. Two nurses stood outside.

Loud, urgent voices from inside the room overlaid the ringing screams that echoed off the tiled hallway. Several pajama-clad patients watched from their doorways.

"All we want to know—just sit down—don't get excited—" The voices of two men. Chalky shouldered by the nurses and was shocked at what he saw.

Two newsmen, one with a camera, were questioning Joanne's mother while Joanne continued to squeal and struggle against her restraints.

"Police! In the hall, now!" Chalky said, trying to keep his voice under control to not add to the confusion.

Joanne's heavyset mother looked up from the seat where they had her cornered and cried in a thin, tired voice, "Please, make them leave us alone, please."

The man with the mike in his hand turned, recognized Chalky, and said, "Officer Fuchs, give me five more minutes, and I'm out of here."

"Mark Butler, should have known it was you," Chalky growled. "You've got five seconds, or I'll carry you out." Peggy came in, pushed by Chalky, and elbowed her way past the cameraman to get to Joanne whose shrieking was lower but still insistent. As she passed the cameraman, he whipped the camera back toward the writhing Joanne and the lens accidentally slashed across Peggy's brow. She fell heavily against the bed and held her hand to her forehead where a thin trickle of blood showed immediately.

"That's it!" Chalky yelled as he grabbed the cameraman and sent him reeling into Herb who took him by the arm and threw him into the hall. The camera clattered onto the hard tile floor. Chalky seized Mark Butler by the arm, walked him tiptoe into the hall, and slammed him against the far wall. Mark's hawkish face grimaced in pain. The nurses went into the room, and the door closed behind them.

"Officer Chalky Fuchs just smashed me into the wall without provo—"

"Shut up!" Chalky yelled through clenched teeth, interrupting Mark's monologue into his mike. In the background, the clamor from the room had died down as the nurses took charge, calming the situation. From the elevators, two security guards rushed up to them. The hall was lined with more patients and nurses watching the excitement.

"We've got a legal right to—"

"You kissed off your rights, Mark—y! If anyone in that room is injured, you may be a patient here!" Chalky kept his voice low, leaned into him to control him, and squeezed his arm harder. Mark cowered from the pain.

"Ladies and gentlemen, you heard it . . . if that isn't police brutality, then I—" Mark's voice was high and squeaky as he screeched into his microphone.

"Come on, let's get these animals away from here," Chalky said to Herb. The cameraman was silent, but remained against the wall taping the conversation with the Camcorder he'd picked up. Herb took him by the arm and hustled him toward the elevator. The cameraman followed meekly, but kept rolling the tape. "We've got it," Chalky said to the two security men who stood on the perimeter, anxious to be of help. "Best thing you can do right now is not let anyone in that room." The two men nodded and stood by the door.

Chalky and Herb pushed the newsmen into an empty elevator, got in behind them, and punched the ground-floor button. Herb and Chalky faced the newsmen as they cringed against the back wall. Mark still held the mike of his tape recorder in his hand.

"And now, ladies and gentlemen, we're being illegally detained and are confined—" His voice broke in midsentence as Chalky pushed the emergency stop button, and the elevator rocked to a halt.

"What the fuck are you doing?" Mark's narrow eyes were wider with fear. Chalky noticed that the mike button was off.

"All your tapes, now!" Chalky roared.

"Haven't you ever heard of free speech, you Neanderthal! We refuse to be—" Before he finished the sentence, he found his face jammed into the wall with his arm up behind him in Chalky's steel grip. A drop of blood ran down his upper lip.

"Jesus Christ, you fascist . . . you broke my nose!"

"That's a good place to start, you little putz! Every time I think you maggots couldn't possibly get any lower, I'm proven wrong. That poor woman in there is damned near dead with the weight of the world on her back, and you jerks—"

"Oww! Dammit—let me go!" Mark threatened, complained, and ragged at Chalky about his constitutional rights, but Chalky ignored him. Chalky took his free hand and popped open Mark's recorder, removed the tape, then pocketed it. When Chalky finished, he released him and looked at the cameraman. The cameraman smiled and ejected his tape and handed it to Chalky.

"You don't want to complain about your constitutional rights?" Chalky asked the cameraman.

"I just spent three grand getting my nose shaped. I like it the way it is," he said, continuing to smile through his even teeth. A pragmatist.

"Smart boy," Chalky said. He released the button, and the elevator shuddered back into motion. When they got to the ground floor, another security guard was waiting. Chalky asked where his office was, then took the two newsmen into a small retaining room and seated them at a table.

After a few minutes of intensive questioning, Mark admitted that one of the night-shift nurses was related to his wife, and had called her the night before about the woman with no arms. Mark was known in the industry for always searching for the sensa-

tional. It had made a name for him in the Seattle area. Mark
knew it would make hot copy, especially if he had pictures of
the mutilated woman.

The cameraman sat quietly, but Mark continued to argue
about their rights and their tapes. He demanded to use a telephone to call his company lawyer.

"No problem, soon's I find out if any of those people upstairs
are going to press charges," Chalky said as he slid a metal
wastebasket over in front of him. He removed a Swiss Army
knife from his pocket and opened it. He then took the two tapes
and pried the cases open with the end of the blade.

"Don't you dare! I'll have your job!" Mark was a slow
learner; his nose still dripped red.

"You couldn't do my job, maggot," Chalky said as he pulled
the tape from the first cartridge. "You people assaulted them
and invaded their privacy and have no right to these pictures."
The two newsmen watched silently, then groaned, as Chalky
systematically cut the extracted tapes into smaller and smaller
pieces with his knife and dropped them into the trash basket. So
much for their fantastic no-arms-lady story.

"Shit," Mark said under his breath, all the fight gone out of
him.

They glared at the basket as Chalky said to Herb, "You hold
them here. I'll go back upstairs and see if anyone wants to pros-
ecute." Herb nodded. The two newsmen screamed at Chalky as
he left the office, something about attorneys and crap like that.
If he had a dime for every time some bozo had threatened him
with an attorney, he'd be able to open his own business somewhere. It was right up there with—I'm a taxpayer, you work for
me.

These lice were not important; he was worried about the
good-looking doctor and whether she was hurt. As he approached 314, gray eyes walked from the doorway with a nurse
and a doughy, pasty-faced sort of guy with thinning hair. They
talked low and animatedly, and gray eyes looked pale.

Her hair was askew where she'd washed the blood from her
forehead, and she wore an oversize Band-Aid. The bleeding had
stopped. One of the security men still stood guard at the door. It
was quiet inside.

"*There* you are," the doughy guy said. "I'm Dr. Fortsam. You're a cop, aren't you? What are you going to do to keep things like this from happening?"

"I'm not a cop, I'm a sergeant in the police department. And we can't stop people from doing stupid things any more than we can stop people from asking stupid questions." The nurse next to Peggy smiled slightly.

The doughy man was about to say something more when Peggy leaned against the wall and held her hand to her forehead. Chalky took her arm and supported her to keep her from sliding down the wall.

"Where can I take her to sit and rest?" Chalky said.

"Doctors' lounge four doors on the right," the nurse said. "Let me help you." She went to Peggy's other side and held her arm. They walked to the room. The doughy man stood in the door for a moment with his mouth working, then he slammed back into Joanne Pinkers's room. Chalky knew he'd hear more from him. He had the "I'm a doctor and therefore superior to you" attitude Chalky'd confronted several times before. Small potatoes. Right now he was worried about the lady with the gray eyes.

"Shouldn't she go down and get checked out?" Chalky asked of the nurse. They entered the room. It was unoccupied. The fragrant odor of coffee came from a setup on the far wall and masked the smell of stale cigarette smoke. The fact that doctors smoked always was a wonderment to Chalky. Even he knew it was bad.

"I'm fine, just a little dizzy," Peggy said as they lowered her into an upholstered chair. "Think it's mostly from a cold I've been trying to beat off." The nurse shrugged her shoulders and gave Chalky a look that said it all. From past experience, he knew doctors were the hardest to convince that they had anything wrong with them. Chalky assumed she'd already refused aid.

Peggy rubbed her forehead and leaned back. "Five minutes, and I'll be fine," she said. "You have other things to do, please don't bother with me."

"How about some coffee?" Chalky asked, reluctant to leave her. "Black?" She nodded. He looked up as the nurse left, then poured Peggy's coffee into a china cup, took it to her, and sat down in an adjacent chair. She drank the coffee in delicate sips, then sighed.

"Thanks, that helps."

He made a forget-it gesture, then asked, "You still have my card?" Peggy patted her coat pocket and smiled. Chalky felt his stomach shift again. Damn. She looks like a little girl swallowed up in the chair. A damned pretty little girl, he thought. "Well, I'll be very mad if you have any trouble of any kind and you don't call me personally."

"Oh?" She took another sip of coffee and grinned at him coyly. "Is that standard procedure, Sergeant?"

"It is, if you're damned good-looking with gray eyes." She smiled wider. He felt warmer, then squirmed. He stood up and searched for something to say that would make his leaving sound graceful and assured.

"I'll call if I have a problem," Peggy said through her smile as she glanced up from her steaming coffee.

"And by the way," Chalky added. "If you'd write a letter of complaint to the department, about the way those two newsmen manhandled your patient and her mother . . . not counting what they did to you, it might make my life a little easier."

"I'm way ahead of you, Sergeant. I'd already planned to do that. Why? What could they do? They were in the wrong."

"We both know that, but the department always has to respond to complaints and they intend to register one about me and Herb."

"You're kidding. That's ridiculous. I'll write it before I leave today."

"Thanks. Oh—" Chalky said as he remembered something else. "We have information right now—I don't know how reliable it is—the man we're looking for is a young male with dark skin, Latin of some kind. Not for publication, of course, at least 'til we're sure."

"You have his name?"

He shook his head and continued: "There's a one in a hundred possibility that this loose cannon might drop by here to check out his handiwork, so . . ."

"So, if I see anyone fitting that description . . ." She patted her pocket and beamed again. He found himself smiling back. Her smile was like an on-off button for his own. His automatically came on when hers did.

His smile disappeared, and he said, "I don't have to tell you how dangerous this guy is."

"I have no desire to be a hero, Officer."

"I'd be grateful if you'd call me Chalky."

"Chalky's not your given name, is it?"

"Well, the name on my certificate is . . . Jerry. . . ." He said it with disdain. "But please call me Chalky, I wouldn't know who you were talking to if you called me . . . that name." He grimaced.

She smiled more broadly. "Thanks again . . . Sergeant . . . Chalky."

Beautiful—musical, he thought. He'd never really heard his name said that like before. Mumbling something awkward, he left the room. Standing at the elevator, still entranced, he remembered why he'd come to this floor, then smiled. When he went back in, Peggy was gazing out the window.

No. She chose not to press charges, simply wanted them out of the hospital. He left and went to 314. Joanne Pinkers' mother said pretty much the same thing. He found her outside the door, eyes still red, blowing into a well-used handkerchief. Chalky asked her if she knew whether her daughter had any enemies or knew of anyone who had threatened her. Her mother said she knew nothing about her daughter's personal life and never talked about it. That took care of any follow-up questions. She said that the doctor had sedated her daughter. The doughy man was still inside with her. He knew Joanne's condition would prevent her from answering any questions even if she were awake, so he thanked her mother and went downstairs.

The two newsmen still stared sullenly at the floor. Herb got up when he came in.

"And?" Herb asked.

"They wanted to press charges and asked us to take these two roaches in, but I talked them out of it on one condition." The two men glanced at each other. "Said if we make sure they don't come back, they'll let it slide . . . for now." He emphasized the "for now," to let them know they could still be charged at a later date. "Two minutes to get your asses out of here," Chalky said as he glared at the men. They got up and left without a word, not a grumble. They would stay away, Chalky was sure of that. Just as sure as he knew that he'd hear a lot more from them or their company attorney.

"You think these security guys have the smarts to keep out the riffraff?" Herb asked as they headed for the administration office.

"No, but I don't know what the hell we can do about it," Chalky answered. "With our budget, there's no chance we're going to break a uniform loose to baby-sit." He knew the security men the hospital hired were only a cut above mall rent-a-cops. They were a combination of short, skinny kids wearing outsized uniforms with loose-fitting leather gear; and old, paunchy guys with florid complexions, whose idea of exercise was going from the sofa to the refrigerator for a beer.

Miss Perry in administration was a sweetheart. Late forties maybe, with a rail-thin body and watermelon-sized hooters she kept jacked up under her chin. A marvel in engineering. False eyelashes, way too much makeup, and soaked in perfume that hit Chalky out in the hall.

Divorced probably, trying to look twenty-nine, and not even close to pulling it off. Jesus. Life could be a kick in the groin for an aging woman if she didn't accept it gracefully, he thought.

When they asked for information on hospital personnel, she fluttered around the room and finally selected a phone in the adjacent office. To probably run the request by whoever paid the light bills, Chalky guessed.

Five minutes later, she came back in. Her fluttering had ceased, and she showed her caps. She zeroed in on Chalky as the single guy, then blinked and batted her way through a couple more minutes of explaining why she was not supposed to do this, but considering the seriousness of the situation she was permitted to do it this once, but they had to treat all information with the utmost confidentiality. As she talked, Chalky wondered what she really looked like under her makeup.

It took a half hour for her to make copies of the personnel status on all of the files. She reluctantly gave him the pictures accompanying each one with the promise that he had to be sure to return them within a week. He promised. She smiled, put her hand on his wrist, and rubbed her breast against his arm while they stood at the copy machine. When Chalky glanced at her, he noticed that she had pulled in her stomach a bit to make her treasure chest more noticeable. God, I wonder if she plays tennis, he thought.

He beat a quick retreat with lots of thank yous, smiles, and promises to bring back the pictures quick as a bunny. As far as the files were concerned, he decided that they'd probably have to duplicate them and return the originals because this case had the smell of complications. She seemed disappointed as he backed out, as though she wanted to say something else, but just smiled instead.

"I think you have a friend," Herb chided as they walked toward the car.

"Ten minutes more of that perfume and I'd of lost consciousness."

"If you had, I think you'd have awakened with a smile on your face."

"You caught that?" Chalky asked.

"You kidding? Say, you think those are real?"

"I'll never know," Chalky said as he slammed the door and started the engine. "I'll never know."

Peggy locked the door to her private office. She had given instructions to the switchboard that she'd be tied up for about forty-five minutes and to hold all of her calls. Carrie had nagged her to go into emergency for an X ray, but she'd finally assured Carrie that she was okay. This Pinkers thing along with the cold creeping up on her were using up her reserve energy. She knew that what she needed was a hot shower, and she needed it now. Even though she had one in her private bath, she'd never used it because her schedule was always too tight. It took her seconds to undress and step into the stall.

The hot water felt good as it beat down on her enervated body. I could spend the rest of the day here, she thought. She wanted to go numb, to unhinge her mind and drift away from her problems. To forget her obligations and what had happened today.

Damn this profession. Damn it all to hell. No time of my own . . . no time to have fun like other people . . . but could I do it? Have fun. Have I forgotten how? she wondered.

She rubbed her hands down her water-slick breasts. Her stomach stirred, and she was reminded of the yawning desire that she had to repress constantly. The desire for a man. Not any man, but someone who'd be gentle, tender, and love her. Her diplomas and kudos in the operating room had failed to warm her the way a man could.

Brad, you creep, she thought. Polished but with a rough edge, Brad Ingstrom had been her last serious love. Two years ago. Then she learned from Carrie that he had been dating other women. All the time he'd been talking marriage and using her. She twinged with the embarrassment. She'd tried to bury the memory, but it kept resurfacing. He was married now. Poor girl, whoever she is, Peggy thought.

Peggy'd been so hurt that no one had been able to get through her armor, until now. And a cop? You're kidding me, she could hear her mother saying. She was expected to marry a famous attorney, captain of industry. Her mother had planned it, engineered it, like everything else in her life. Arranged surprises of single men at dinner parties, chance meetings. Since Peggy's father had died two years ago, her mother'd concentrated on it almost to the exclusion of everything else.

As the stinging spray beat down on her shoulders and breasts, she rubbed her hands across her nipples. They were firm, and the inside of her thighs ached as her interior heat increased. She thought of Chalky's long blond hair, blue eyes, and his thin, muscular body. "Chalky. What kind of name is that? Chalky," she said again, softer.

Not so bad, she thought. The way he handled those reporters, so firm, so hard, yet so gentle when he touched her. Damn! She could feel tears well up again. Taking the washcloth, she rubbed her body roughly as though trying to wipe away the hunger she felt, then rinsed and dressed hurriedly.

"Dark complexion, that's what he said," she mumbled and forced herself to think about other things. She tried to imagine what this crazy person would look like. Swarthy, furtive, and have . . . eyes that would . . . strange eyes. . . .

She shook her head. Trying to visualize anyone who could do anything that heinous was impossible. Peggy's thoughts drifted back to Joanne Pinkers.

Peggy's step was springier as she went down the hall. She headed for the elevator to go up and see Joanne again. How lonely she must feel. What Peggy could do for her clinically was minimal, but she knew that just being there when she woke up was important.

chapter//nine

Chalky and Herb got back to the station about four o'clock after pounding the pavement in the area of the crime looking for other leads. No one had seen anything. When Chalky went in and checked the message board, he had a note to talk with Captain Stone as soon as possible about a complaint filed by the newsmen that morning. No surprises there. He decided that as soon as possible would be sometime tomorrow and stuffed the note in his pocket. Being yelled at was more than he could handle right now. It would screw up his Friday afternoon and evening. Just when he thought he had that worked out, his phone rang and Captain Stone told him to come to his office. He sighed, stood, and trudged in.

"You know about this complaint, of course," the captain began.

"They said they were going to, so it's no big surprise," Chalky said as he slumped into the wooden chair.

"Tell me about it." The captain leaned back and lit his pipe. He was quiet as Chalky filled him in on exactly what had happened.

"You say this doctor is going to write a letter of complaint about their activities?"

"Today, she said."

"Good. Sounds like you might have been a little heavy-handed, but given the same situation, I might have done the same thing." The captain leaned forward and tapped his pipe. "Chalky, regarding this case—the Pinkers woman." Chalky nodded. "I'm reassigning your and Herb's caseload. You're working full-time on it, effective now." He stood and paced.

85

"I'm already getting calls from upstairs on this. If you've been watching the news, it's become a hot potato. We need this joker off the street as soon as possible. You have any leads?"

"One. Sounds plausible. We're following it up."

"Good. Now, get out of here and keep me informed on your progress."

Chalky made his way to his desk. That had been a lot easier than anticipated.

He hung his coat on a peg on the wall. He told Herb about their reassignment. Herb was relieved because he realized how important this case was.

"You think this is bad now, just wait 'til this crazy does another one," Chalky said.

"Damn! This is a heavy responsibility," Herb grumbled. He scowled and went back to his paperwork.

"Welcome to the fire."

Chalky sat and attacked the job of filling in his report. This was the part of the job he hated. If he belched, he had to write it down. Herb whistled behind Chalky as he sorted through the files they'd picked up at the hospital. After forty-five minutes, Chalky signed the report, sighed, and leaned back. He dropped it on Herb's desk for him to read.

Herb glanced up and asked, "You want to go over these people I've weeded out?"

"Find anybody with 'I did it' tattooed on their forehead?" Herb chuckled as Chalky picked up the first pile and idly scanned them.

"Those are housekeeping people, sorted by young male, dark complexion, Latin type," Herb said. "There were more than a hundred fifty people altogether."

"Housekeeping?"

"Yeah, that's what they call the people that make the beds, clean up, all that sort of thing. Seemed the logical place to start."

Chalky nodded and said, "Twenty-four," as he finished the count. "How about the medical personnel?"

"I haven't gone through those yet, but if we're going to follow up on that old lady's lead, the guy would be comparatively young. Most of the medical staff are old cockers, some are women, plus a few yuppie-looking white males."

"That lead she gave us is thinner than my shorts, but it's the only thing we've got right now. Makes sense to chase it down until something better comes along. Nothing pans out here, we'll dig deeper into the files, then we'll consider hitting the surrounding hospitals."

"How about the truck?" Herb asked.

"Take the people you've pulled and run them for vehicles in the morning. Who knows, we might get lucky. Odds are it's stolen though. We don't know the make or year, or what the flowers looked like, or even if the whole damn thing means anything at all. Can't do squat with the truck until we get more. Can't even issue a be-on-the-lookout unless we can tie one of those people to it." Herb straightened the piles as Chalky watched.

Chalky bit his lip, then asked, "You really think I should ask that doctor for a date?"

"Where'd that come from, left field?" Herb laughed. "How the hell can you be so certain of other things and so whipped about her?"

"I'm not whipped," Chalky bristled. "Just not sure she's for me—a guy like me—her being a doctor."

"What the hell's wrong with a guy like you? I think you're a real sweetheart." Herb ducked the pencil that rifled by his head. "So ask her already, so we can get on with our lives."

"You think I should?"

"I think you should."

Chalky smiled, leaned back, and put his hands behind his head, thinking.

"You're the point man on this case," Herb said as he gestured toward the piles. "What's next on the program?"

"First thing tomorrow, we call the hospital. You talk to the balloon-smuggler and get how many of these studs were on duty during the crime. We take the pile that's left, split them, and hoof it." Chalky stood and put on his coat.

"Sounds like fun. What's on your dance card for tonight?"

"First I have to cash my paycheck, then round up the jolly blue giant and drop two hundred bucks on him . . . do supper . . .

then, voilà! Show time! The pool tournament." Chalky smiled
and straightened his tie.

Herb stacked the files into orderly piles, then asked Chalky as
he was leaving, "You think this guy is going to strike soon?"

"Like to be wrong, but I'd bet my three-piece pool cue on it,"
Chalky answered. "Could be anytime . . . but a cold feeling in
my gut is saying maybe tonight."

Carlos had slept fitfully during the day, waking up several
times, getting drinks of water, going to the bathroom, sitting
and staring, then back to bed. After seven hours in the apartment, he had only two hours of solid sleep. His body was
charged with electricity. He had to do something, had to get the
doctor's address, do something, hurt her, find Maria, do
something—anything.

"*. . . the surgery wasn't done by a doctor . . . ragged,
unprofessional . . .*" He'd tried to hide from it, but it played and
replayed in his mind, "*Ragged, unprofessional . . .*"

"Bitch!" he screamed as he threw his shoe against the wall.
"Got to get out of here!" He leapt up, dressed feverishly, and
slammed out of the apartment. It was only five o'clock in the
evening and he still had two hours before he was supposed to be
at work. As he jogged along the sidewalk he felt renewed by the
cold, stinging air. The sky was overcast and scattered with a thin
layer of cumulus clouds. He ran faster and faster until his lungs
burned with the need for more oxygen and from the icy cold air.
Clouds of steam billowed from his mouth as he crossed the road
at the corner and turned down Hempstead, a long avenue of
small homes with spacious lawns that swept back from the
street.

As he loped along, dogs barked and the muffled sounds of
television laugh tracks echoed from the rectangular slivers of
yellow light peeking between the trees. Because of the overcast,
most of the cars that passed had their headlights on. The noises
faded from his consciousness and all he could hear was
"*Ragged, unprofessional, ragged, unprofessional. . . .*"

He trotted on until he came to a narrow, two-lane street that
was even darker because it was shaded by the tall cedars that
lined each side. It was too early for the streetlights to be on.

Pinecones, needles, and small branches littered the dirt path, and the randomly spaced houses sat farther back. He slowed, turned, and walked down the road for a couple hundred yards, then angled more by instinct than by sight into a dirt driveway that meandered among a stand of trees.

Carlos came to a burned-out house with a free-standing garage next to it. The only evidence of the fire on the garage was a blackened side and two windows cracked from the heat.

He turned to the remnants of the house, lowered himself through one of the daylight basement windows to the collapsed interior, then picked his way through the fallen timbers to a cavity in the wall. He reached up with a practiced touch, withdrew a leather bag, then gingerly made his way back the way he'd come. Carlos easily levered himself out the window after pushing the bag onto the ground at eye level.

The garage door was unlocked, and he swung the large barn-door-type doors wide. The white van sat in the almost-black interior. Carlos climbed in, laid his bag on the seat, started it, and slowly backed out the driveway without turning on the lights. He stepped down lightly and swung the garage doors shut. He got back in and clicked the car door closed softly. He had to keep his aunt from hearing the sound from her house. She lived about fifty yards away, and this was her truck she'd used in a now-defunct floral business. She owned the burned-out house and stored the truck in the still-functional garage. Her children's cars overflowed the garage at her house and lined her driveway, so there was no room to park it there.

It was perfect for him. Carlos could borrow it anytime he wanted to without her knowing it. Just fill it with gas, and keep it in running order—a little oil, a little gas, that's all it took.

The evening traffic was heavy. Carlos made his way directly to the hospital and entered the lot from the rear. He cruised near the emergency entrance. The doctors' parking area was adjacent to it.

It's here, he thought. The red Jeep Cherokee. Dr. Chandler's car. He'd seen her leaving the lot a couple of times in it. *The bitch!*

He pulled into the visitors' lot and selected a parking spot that had a good view of her car, then idled in and turned off the motor. He could wait.

And Maria. Fuck her! I don't need her. I'll wait and follow the doctor. If I'm lucky, in a half hour I'll know where she lives.

He stretched and leaned back, more relaxed now, his annoyance and indecision replaced by the peace of resignation.

He knew what he had to do.

The wind ripped across the lot in gusts as Peggy made her way to her car at 6:30 in the evening. A fine mist of rain made the wind that much more cutting. She dreaded the drive home on the I-90 freeway, across the floating bridge, past Mercer Island, and through Bellevue. Then on some five more miles to the small bedroom community of Issaquah. In this weather, she knew the traffic would be bumper to bumper.

She'd bought an upscale condo there a year ago because she wanted to live away from the hustle and bustle of Seattle. She called it a condo, but had been told by someone that it was a townhome. The difference between the two had always escaped her.

When she pulled out of the lot, she was disturbed because the lights from a van in back of her glared into the rearview mirror. She had to click her mirror to dark, so she could see.

The entire day seemed like a nightmare, from what had happened with Joanne Pinkers in the morning to those damned newsmen. The emergency appendectomy was a nice touch too. A young girl had lied to her mother about a pain in her side because she was afraid. She had self-medicated herself with a laxative the night before thinking the pain she felt was constipation. This morning her appendix had burst, spreading poison through her system. Peritonitis. Stupid kids. Like playing Russian roulette with a loaded gun. They brought the girl to the hospital in an ambulance because of the pain. Peggy had to put a drain in and load the girl with antibiotics. In two or three days she'd have to go back in and remove the drain and the appendix, provided she could keep the infection under control.

And then there was Fortsam. He had come to her office after she'd finished with Joanne Pinkers and did everything except chase her around the office, trying to put his pudgy hands on

her. What a creep! She was quietly furious with him for forcing
her to avoid him, and angry with herself openly after he left for
not having the strength of character to tell him to take a hike.
Damn! Her mother had always taught her to keep her feelings
bottled up. Just once she'd like to punch a guy like that in the
face for making her feel so intimidated, so violated. After what
had happened today, she knew that fencing with him and trying
to avoid him was going to fail. She'd have to tell him no and
make him understand it.

It took her about an hour to get to her condo. Normally it
would have taken about a half hour, but a truck had turned over
on the Lake Washington Bridge going the other way. Of course
commuters had to slow down to visually supervise the clearing
of the obstruction as they went by. Hoping to see a dead body
she assumed.

The wind blew harder and rain whipped in sheets across her
driveway as she drove into her garage. The area she lived in was
still under construction with only three of the eighteen condos
in her complex occupied. She'd commented to Carrie that she'd
feel a lot more comfortable when she had more neighbors. She
felt so isolated, with most of the buildings blackout empty
around her. She felt it might be a while however, because few
people who wanted to live in condos could afford one of the
2100-square-foot units she had bought. The condo was a tad
pricy, especially in a bedroom community like Issaquah.

Sidney, her overweight tiger-stripe cat, met her at the door
and immediately told her loudly and insistently how abused he
felt. While she petted him, she once again felt guilty about not
putting him on a diet. It was tough because he complained bit-
terly if his food was cut back.

"Sidney, give me a break, will you? I've had a tough day."
Appealing to his sense of fairness was a flop as usual, so she
had to spend a few minutes scratching and pampering him until
he got over feeling neglected.

Outside, the wind picked up and whistled by the windows
carrying the rain in waves, hard against the glass. Suddenly
chilled, she dropped the cat to the floor, went into the living
room, and built a roaring fire in the fireplace. Peggy selected
four split logs to make sure it would give off enough heat. It was

nights like this she felt nervous about the lack of neighbors because the darkness made her feel as though she lived in the woods by herself.

She went around the ground floor and turned on all the lights with the exception of the den. She'd never bothered to put a bulb in the lamp in there because she never used the room . . . even kept the door closed and the vent turned off to save heating it. She was usually at the hospital or home in bed. The lights and the blazing fire made her feel a bit more comfortable.

As she sat in front of the fire, she rubbed her hands together and started to feel sleepy. Then she heard it.

A noise from the den.

Something scraped.

Instantly alerted, she looked at the telephone wondering if she should call 911.

"Don't be a coward, go in and check," she said to herself in a sotto voice. A chill went up her back. Sidney rubbed her leg, unmindful of any disturbance or intruders. Intruders? Don't be so melodramatic, she thought. Carrie had nagged her to buy a gun for protection, but she was more afraid of a gun than she was of any threat.

Peggy rose from the chair and stared into the hall. Even with the lights on, it seemed threatening. Her body tensed as she listened for any sound.

Scree . . . A sound again, like something scratching on glass. Inside? Outside? It was difficult to tell. She looked at her purse and thought of the card of that detective.

Ridiculous. What can he do? she thought. It took me an hour to get here, it would take him the same amount of time. God! Stop being a coward and go check it out. In the background, thunder rumbled as a counterpoint to the wind whipping the windows.

Tick, scrape. . .

She froze. That noise definitely came from the den, but it sounded as though it came from inside the room, not something scraping the house or window.

Out! Have to get the hell out of here. She tried to control the panic growing inside her. Just get your coat, get in your car, and drive away. Don't be an idiot and go in and check, for God's sake, she thought.

She edged across the kitchen picking up her coat as she moved. It was silent in the room now, but she was almost paralyzed with fear. *Why didn't I take Carrie's advice and buy a gun?* She stepped lightly as though sudden movement might cause whatever was in the room to leap into instant action and smash through the door. Her nerves were piano-wire taut as she crossed the kitchen toward the door.

The cat screeched—

And jumped away—

"Damn!" Peggy screamed as the cat scurried up the stairs out of sight.

Her heart raced as she grabbed the handle of the door to the garage and flung it open—

A dark figure blocked the doorway—

She shrieked and fell backward—

It was Chalky.

"Police," Chalky said from force of habit. She had stopped on the other side of the kitchen and splayed against the refrigerator. "Jesus, I didn't mean to scare you—you left your garage door open, and I . . . well, I . . ."

Peggy giggled nervously, then breathed deeply in an attempt to control her voice. Gasping in deep gulps of air, her hand to her chest, she walked over to a kitchen chair and laid her coat on the back of it.

"Come in quickly and close the door—I've got a problem." Her voice quivered.

"Sorry," he said sheepishly as he came in and shut the door. He laid his long flashlight on the counter. "What's wrong? You left your garage door open, so I walked in and —"

"You have a gun?" she interrupted.

He frowned. "Always."

"Before we talk, I heard a noise in my den and was leaving because I was frightened. Will you go in the room and look, please? Hurry, okay?" She pointed at the hall and the closed door. He nodded, pulled out his automatic, and walked softly toward the room.

"God, am I going to feel foolish," she mumbled as she

peeked around the steps and watched him open the door. She could hear him walking and poking around in the room. She moved to the door to the kitchen, ready to spring through the garage door if anything happened. He walked from the room and smiled as he holstered his weapon.

"Nothing," he said. "No bulb in the light, but it's a small room. Checked everywhere." He nodded to the stairs and said, "Upstairs? Have you checked there?" She shook her head no. He took the steps two at a time and was gone another five minutes. Her face flushed when she thought of the panty hose she had left lying on the curtain rod in the master bath. Since Brad, no man had been in her bedroom.

"Not a thing, except for the cat under a bed up there," he said as he skipped down the stairs. "A very fat cat."

"I wondered where he went," she said.

"Let me take a look around outside, be right back." He grabbed his flashlight and was out the door before she could answer. Amazing how having a man around can make you feel so safe, she thought. He was gone ten minutes this time, then knocked gently on the front door.

"Hi," he said when she answered. "Where were we?" He smiled broadly.

He has the same rugged good looks that Brad had, but he seemed softer somehow, and not mean-spirited like him, she mused.

"You're probably wondering what I'm doing here," he continued matter-of-factly. "I thought about what I was going to say on the way over, because I figured you'd be too smart to accept a phony-baloney story."

"Let's just say I'm glad you came, regardless of what the reason is." She could tell he was uncomfortable and tried to give him a little slack. "Why don't you sit down. Would you care for a glass of wine?"

"No thanks. Look, I'm sorry to bother you, I wanted to ask you something, then I'll go." He took the offered seat to the left of the fire.

She sat opposite him, entwined her hands in front of her, and waited. He was going to ask her for a date, she knew it, and she was undecided how to respond. The vision of her mother shaking her head no flashed in her mind. She forced it to evaporate and smiled. He cleared his throat and stared into the fire.

"How is your head?"

"That's the question you drove twenty-five miles through the rain to ask me?" She kept her voice soft so as not to sound critical. "I'm sorry," she said. "It's nice of you to ask. It's fine." She rubbed the adhesive bandage. "How'd you know where I lived?"

He cleared his throat again and stared into her eyes this time. "Records." He matched her low tone. "Wasn't any phone number, or I wouldn't have bothered you in person. Figured your number was unlisted . . . so I drove over . . . I guess. . . ." His voice drifted off and he swallowed.

The fire popped and hissed, and one of the logs collapsed. They both watched it as though they had all the time in the world. Peggy knew he'd wanted to ask her something else when he came in. He stood decisively, as though making up his mind about something.

"It's not anything that can't wait until tomorrow during business hours, I'll call you then." He headed for the door. Confused, she stood and watched him from her chair by the fire as he walked out the door. He leaned back in and said, "Lock this behind me," and disappeared.

She was still looking at the door when she heard his car start in front. "Men," Peggy said absently. She shook her head and locked the door.

Deciding she would have said yes if he had asked, Peggy went into the kitchen and poured a glass of Chablis. After she took it into the living room, she sat and stared into the fire for a minute. Sidney came padding down the stairs and rattled a greeting low in his chest to indicate that he had forgiven her. She felt very alone suddenly, and the sound of the wind reminded her of her earlier fright. She hugged herself, then took a sip of wine.

"Before I enjoy this wine, I'd better make sure that window is locked," she said to the cat. She stood, went into the kitchen, and got a light bulb from an upper cabinet. When she walked to the den, she hesitated at the door, then strode across the room, screwed the bulb in, and snapped on the light. She walked to the window and checked the lock.

It was unlatched—

She wondered if Chalky had unlocked it, then assumed she must have left it open that morning. But there wasn't anyone in the room, so no harm done, right? she reasoned. She had a vague feeling of discomfort, then decided that she was going to call that security alarm company tomorrow that had sent her a brochure.

She turned to switch off the light when she saw it—

Drops of water and mud on the windowsill.

She shivered with instant realization. Thunder rolled in the distance and the pane rattled.

The window had been opened earlier.

Someone had been here.

In this room.

chapter//ten

Chalky talked to himself as he drove away from Peggy's condo. It had been a lot of years since he had felt so tongue-tied. High school maybe. He kicked around what he had said, compared with what he had intended to say.

Embarrassing. Face it, flatfoot, he thought. The future isn't going to include you and that doctor, not in a romantic relationship anyway. Idiot!

He had left a little early for the pool tournament. It was being held in the city of Renton, which was a driver and a three-iron from Issaquah, the city where the gray-eyed doctor lived. It had seemed like the thing to do. Just stop by, be his normal breezy self, inquire about her head injury to show her what a nice guy he was . . . hell, he *was* concerned, then suavely ask the big question. Dinner? A little vino with a splash of romance?

Then, the garage door was open and he had reverted to his Mr. Cop persona.

Running around inside and out kind of took the edge off the moment, he thought. I would have asked her, but it didn't seem to be the right time. . . .

Bull! Admit it, Bunky . . . you chickened out. He banged the steering wheel with his palm.

That's not it, besides, the lady offered me a glass of wine, didn't she?

No. She was being nice to you . . . appreciative of what you did, he decided.

This conversation was a dead end, so he dismissed it and tried to concentrate on the tournament, but somehow, it had faded in importance.

He stopped his car on a dark street, clicked off his radio, and listened to the wind-whipped rain hammer on the windows and roof of the car.

I should go back and ask her. What have I got to lose? The worst thing that could happen is she'd say no.

No—that's not the worst. She could laugh . . . that would be the worst.

You? A cop? You want to date me, a doctor? You've got to be kidding—

Screw the pool tournament! Screw pool in general. Screw everything. I'm going home.

He started his car and drove silently through the night mesmerized by the clicking wipers. When he got to his apartment, he paced for a while, then surprised himself by cleaning up his kitchen. That done, he felt better. He snapped on the dishwasher, then straightened the living room.

Even he was appalled at how long some of the items had been lying around. Socks, shoes, shirts, coats, and pants that had become part of the decor. He turned on his disc player and listened to an oldies reprise while he vacuumed. "Vacuuming on a Friday night, what a bon vivant! Should be out on the town like any respectable single guy, trying to get my brains screwed out," he grumbled.

His last semisteady girlfriend had been Patty Mullens who worked in dispatch. Nimble and nice he called her. Her strong point was the fact that she could touch her nose with her tongue. What a gift. She could do everything with it. Everything.

Their twice-a-week romps in the hay had degenerated to once a week, then once every other week, then the relationship had just lurched to a halt from lack of motivation on both their parts. Sort of canceled for lack of interest. He heard that she was dating some low-life number-cruncher down at city hall. He had felt nothing when he learned that, only kind of wondered why they had dated each other in the first place. Who you kidding? he thought when he remembered her gift.

After an hour of working intensely, he felt marginally better and had stopped punishing himself for being such a washout with the doctor. He knew he should be thinking about the case, but the doctor had crowded it out.

The apartment. At least *that* was a problem that he could do something about. A home should be cleaned every six months whether it needed it or not.

Carlos sat in the van behind one of the vacant condos for a half hour after the man had left. He had been waiting in the den on the other side of the door when he heard voices in the kitchen.

Fortunately, the window was silent when he closed it and leapt back into the rain. He had made it out only a few seconds before the man had come into the room.

He slowly inched his van onto the street in front of her condo, then to the main street, where he turned on his lights and moved away.

Stupid! I should have shot him, then I could have taken my time with the doctor. The bitch! There isn't anyone around her . . . nobody would have heard even if she had screamed. I'd return, but I don't know whether he's still in the area . . . maybe coming back . . . to fuck the bitch.

"*Ragged . . . unprofessional . . . ragged . . . unprofessional. . . .*" For the past few hours, thoughts of her had crowded out everything else. What she said in the hospital had stung and burned into his consciousness. His skin was hot and fevered, and he had trouble focusing his thoughts. *What does she know, a* puta *that had to fuck her way into her job.* He could feel his loins ache, and he got hard when he thought about cutting into her flesh. Her skin would be soft and would fold away smoothly under his scalpel. The warm rich blood would well up, and then he would—

A horn sounded, and he jumped. The light was green. He dropped the van into first gear and accelerated off into the darkness and rain with no clear idea of where he was going.

He thought about the surgery on the doctor as he drove. The streets were a blur through the wet windshield. Hypnotized by the hum of the engine, he suddenly realized that he was parked on a dark side street with his lights out, his motor idling. Looking around confused, he got his bearings, then recognized the street.

This was Madison, several blocks from the hospital. He'd

walked by here many times at night and in the early mornings. He remembered the one night he'd seen the young woman in the window of the small, one-story home on this street. The one with the picket fence all around. His excitement rose. *Maybe she lives alone.* Turning off the engine, he picked up his bag, stepped into the dark, and moved off hurriedly in the direction of her house.

It was a perfect night to do almost anything undetected.

Carlos came crashing into his apartment at eleven o'clock in the evening. With one arm he struggled to hold a heavy weight wrapped in a cumbersome blanket and carried his satchel of surgical tools in his other. He was soaked, and his hair hung down in long strings. He dropped the blanket heavily onto the dinette table, his satchel on the chair, then went into the bathroom and stripped off all his clothes.

Unmindful of the fact that he was naked, he walked to the front door and opened it. He ripped off the piece of paper that was tacked to the door, then slammed the door in anger. It was a note from Cooper:

> *Came by to get you. You wasn't hear.*
> *Can't pick you up no more,*
> *car's not running good enuff.*
> *Sorry. See you at work. —Cooper*

He yelled unintelligibly and ripped the paper into smaller and smaller pieces. Finally, releasing the anger with a shout, he tossed them against the wall. "Just one less problem to worry about." This night had been one frustration after another.

When he had arrived at the young woman's house, he had opened the gate and snuck around to the side of the house. Standing by a window, he could hear laughter and music coming from inside. The blinds were open a crack, and he could see that there were at least five people inside. He had slid down onto the grass, gnashing his teeth, and was staring up into the rain trying to decide what to do when he heard a sound. A flapping sound. Then he saw a dark form move toward him through the rain.

Laughter beyond his walls returned him to his apartment and the present. He shook his head. He had a job to do and he had to do it quickly, then get in to work for the balance of his shift. His ears rang, and he could feel himself being drawn into the vortex of a vision again, but he fought it. He had to finish this, get it done, dispose of the parts, then take the truck back.

He laid his tools on the table next to the mounds in the blanket, then carefully unrolled it. The blanket was soaked, but was warm from the bodies.

"I'll take the Seahawks and fourteen," the tall, thin man said to the heavy man who drove the disposal truck. The long rays of early morning light cut diagonals across their windshield.

"Against San Francisco? Bull crap. I'll give you ten." They closed in on the line of trash cans and Dumpsters in the rear of an apartment complex. The rain had stopped and a light wind blew stray pieces of paper across the alleyway.

"You're such an asshole. You don't want a bet unless it's a sure thing."

The fat man chuckled, then said in a singsong, "That's why I be a drivin'—an' you be a Dumpster divin'!" His stomach shook as he laughed.

Since that was about the thirtieth time he'd heard that, the tall, thin man could only work up a grin, then said, "Twelve points."

"You're on," the fat man said. The truck slowed, and the wet brakes screeched in protest as they jerked to a stop. "Now, get your skinny ass down and feed the kitty."

The thin man jumped to the ground and emptied the loose trash cans into the giant bucket. The powerful hydraulic arms raised the trash with a metallic whine to the top of the truck, swallowed it up, then quickly returned. The fat man backed up to the first Dumpster with the thin man guiding him.

The thin man was about ready to tell him to lift the Dumpster when he yelled, "Wait! Wait!"

The fat man dropped to the ground, walked to the rear of the truck, and said, "What's the matter? What do you mean, wait? We've got to get this load back to the—"

"I heard something . . . in there," the thin man said, gesturing to the Dumpster.

"Just rats, ain't you ever heard—" He stopped when a low, crying sound came from the Dumpster. Looking at the thin man, he said, "That ain't no rat."

"Jesus, don't I know it." The wind changed, and blue smoke from the diesel truck drifted across where they stood. "You gonna look?" the thin man asked.

"You're the diver . . . you look," the fat man said.

The thin man walked over to the Dumpster, pulled up the lid, leaned it against the wall, then peeked into the Dumpster. His face went white.

"Holy shit!" he yelled. "I think I'm gonna throw up." He looked away.

"What is it," the fat man asked, not venturing closer.

The thin man walked away from the barrel, leaned against the wall, and said, "Call dispatch from the truck and have them call the police . . .

"We need a cop out here—NOW!"

chapter//eleven

Breakfast dishes and glassware tinkled. The deep male voices were especially loud and boisterous in Fat Phil's restaurant as Chalky and Herb scraped out their chairs and sat down. The odor of cigarette smoke blending with the smell of eggs and toast was heavy in the air.

"Where the hell were you?" had greeted Chalky from several tables the minute he had walked in the door.

"Girl," said Chalky each time the question was asked. That ended the confusion because it was a given that getting laid took precedence over a pool tournament—in fact, just about anything, except maybe a good football game or the Superbowl. When he said it, the asker would nod knowingly and smile—then Chalky would reflect on the image of him vacuuming and cleaning into the wee hours.

If they only knew, he thought. But then, technically, he had opted not to go because of a girl, so it was pretty much the truth. The only thing that pissed him off was the fact that the jolly blue giant had won the five hundred bucks. That would be good for several spine-dislocating backslaps in the days to come.

"Girl?" Herb asked through a thin grin, waiting for the response.

"If I tell you, you won't tell a soul?" Herb shook his head and inched closer. "It was the doctor," Chalky whispered.

Herb blinked, leaned back, and said, "You're kidding?" Chalky reluctantly told him what had happened the night before. Herb listened and nodded in all the right places. He was a good listener too—not offering unneeded advice or jumping on him for being such a jerk. Chalky was getting to like him more each day. Yeah. He'll do, he decided.

"Jesus, that's why you were standing on the curb waiting for me this morning . . . you didn't want me to see your apartment." Herb chuckled. Chalky could feel his face get a little warm. "Having a clean apartment isn't like having a social disease, you know," Herb added.

"It would be if this blue-crew knew about it." Chalky gestured at the boiling activity around them. A table across the room erupted in laughter. "Damn, this is like eating breakfast in a high school cafeteria."

"Like your new sport coat," Herb said. "Didn't recognize you at first without the corduroy."

"It's been in the back of my closet. Been saving it for a special occasion."

"Like going in to work on Saturday?"

"Give me some slack, okay. I've got dishpan hands."

Herb smiled. "You know, if you want to impress anyone, anyone female that is . . . I'd suggest you remove the price tag from the sleeve."

"You're kidding." Chalky reached down, self-consciously removed the tag, and smiled. "Thanks," he added.

Herb asked, "You want to talk about the case?" He knew when the subject needed to be changed too. Chalky nodded, then Herb pulled a bent file folder out of his inside coat pocket. "Took it home and studied it last night." Herb seemed embarrassed by putting in the extra effort.

Giselle laid their breakfasts down, smirked, and watched Chalky closely. Her face reflected that she expected a comment. Disappointed, she jiggled away. Chalky looked at his food. Herb looked at him questioningly, then said, "You *are* preoccupied."

"Anything interesting in the files?" Chalky asked, not wanting to talk about Giselle.

"Well, for one thing, I took a map and did a one-mile radius. Figured the place to start would be the guys who lived the closest."

"Sounds reasonable. And?"

"Found five guys in the circle," Herb said, tapping the file.

"That's assuming it was random. If he *picked* her, it could be anybody."

"It's a place to start," Herb said as he shoveled in a forkful of hash browns. Chalky fingered through the five, all Spanish surnames. Gomez, Martinez, Rodriquez, Guerra, and another Martinez. He wondered if the two Martinezes were related. All the right age profile and similar in appearance except for the one with the mustache. All had thick, black hair. God, Mexicans really had the genes to grow good-looking hair, he thought. The mug shots from the hospital files looked like police photos. Just for ID, no care taken. He wondered if the buxom sweetheart had taken them.

"When they going to have the DMVs on these people for us?" Chalky asked.

"One or two o'clock Patti said."

"Since these guys all work the night shift, I suppose we ought to wait until late afternoon to door-knock." Herb nodded.

"You call the garage about your car?" Herb asked. "Not that I mind giving you a ride."

"They finally got the rear end fixed, took it for a test drive, and the transmission went tits-up. Another three days, another twelve hundred bucks."

Herb shook his head in disbelief at Chalky's luck. Giselle walked up to the table, glanced at Chalky, and posed with her hip jutted to one side as she energetically worked on her gum.

"I figured you were going to take me out with that first-place prize money last night," she said, "and you didn't even show." Instead of waiting for an answer, she simply tossed a comment over her shoulder as she walked away: "You're wanted on the phone, again—same guy."

It was the captain with his usual shorts-too-tight attitude. Chalky listened for a couple of minutes, hung up, then came back to the table. He gulped his coffee standing up. Herb took the hint and gathered the sheets into the file and stood.

"Gotta go to the lab first thing," Chalky said. "You have strong elastic on your socks?"

"Why," Herb asked, smiling.

"Because if you don't, what you're going to see will knock you out of them."

● ● ●

The gusty winds had blown the rain clouds from the previous night inland, and patches of blue threatened a reasonable sort of day. Any day without rain was on the plus side of the ledger in the Puget Sound area. Natives expected rain and considered it a bonus if it was dry. Any other philosophy weather-wise would drive the faint-hearted to fairer climes.

They entered the 3rd Street building. A brunette waited by the elevator in a raincoat.

"Chalky Fuchs, you sexy son of a bitch."

"Jeanette," Chalky said. "This is Herb Rosen, my new partner in crime. Jeanette Patterson—lady detective par-excellence—works vice on the night shift." Herb shook her hand. She talked enthusiastically as they got in the elevator, then waved good-bye when the two men got out on the second floor, the floor the lab was on. "We dated, couple years ago," Chalky said cryptically. "Married now, some guy in the front office."

They entered a frosted glass door with "Forensics" neatly lettered at eye level and walked up to the desk. "He's expecting you," the Japanese girl at the desk said. "Mr. Parker told me to tell you to walk in, he's finishing up."

"Thanks, Yoko," Chalky said. He hesitated for a moment and introduced Herb to her. Yoko was the only thing about this office that Chalky liked. Tall and thin with the chest of a twelve-year-old boy and a million-dollar personality, Yoko kept everything humming on schedule in the office and always had a hundred-tooth smile. He wondered why she stayed with Parker-the-Prick. The name had been earned and used by others in the department before Chalky ever met him.

Chalky had filled Herb in on the past head-to-heads he'd had with Parker. His first name was a blank to Chalky, but it was of no importance. Parker's nickname was perfect. His always-at-the-ready condescending attitude and short answers had brought them to the point of blows on several occasions. As a consequence, Chalky suspected that anything he personally worked on always ended up on the back burner. If he were pragmatic, he would have kissed Parker's ass and made up with the little bald-headed creep, but there were some things in life that made him want to upchuck, and Parker was definitely on the list.

When they walked into the lab, a group of men were working around a large, flat table in the rear. Flashes of white light illuminated the walls as pictures were being taken. The men talked in low tones. "Turn her this way—that's far enough," they heard as they approached, then the lights again. Chalky heard a soft whimpering sound.

"Oh, it's you," Parker said in his usual through-his-nose tone as he noticed Chalky and Herb approach. He stepped toward them, away from the table.

"Two more pictures, then we're out of here," the photographers said in the background. Chalky nodded hello, then reluctantly introduced Herb. Using his name without "the-prick" attached was awkward, but Chalky managed it. He knew it was only a question of time until he slipped.

The lights flashed a couple more times, then the men walked by and out the door. Herb tried to look around them as they passed to see what was on the table. He'd been patient, but now his curiosity was winning.

"Hear you found them in a Dumpster this morning early," Chalky said. They approached the table.

Two small dogs lay on the table, one on its back unmoving, the other on its stomach. It wiggled and tried to crawl in spite of the fact that its rear legs were gone.

"Goddamn!" Herb exclaimed. The dog that was not moving was obviously dead. It had been shaved up to its hips, legs removed, and the stumps had been neatly sutured. The small dog that whimpered and struggled was sewn up too.

"My God," Chalky said in a choked-up voice. He knew what to expect, but still found it appalling. He reached down, picked up the small black and white long-haired dog that was wiggling. It cried softly when he rolled it over. "Sshhh, shhh," he whispered, trying to calm the animal. He rubbed its fat belly. It lay still and peered up at him with trusting eyes, eyes that were confused and in pain. "Son of a bitch," he mumbled as he fought back the lump in his throat. "What kind of a crazy bastard would do this?" No answer. "The legs, they were in the Dumpster too?"

"They searched through the trash. Both animals' severed legs were gone," Parker said.

"Crazy, crazy!" Chalky muttered as he petted the animal gently and checked out her small body. He fluffed the baby-fine fur away from the nipples on her belly. "What's this?" he asked. A barely visible series of numbers was tattooed on her stomach.

"Beats me, I hate dogs," Parker said.

Figures, Chalky thought as he took a pad and copied the number, then turned the animal back on her stomach.

"That has to be a young dog, wouldn't you say? What kind is that?" Chalky asked.

"Shih Tzu," Herb offered. "My sister has one like it. Pedigree as long as your arm. Damned expensive little ankle-biter."

"Is it going to live?" Chalky asked of Parker. Chalky picked up the dog and held it gently in his arms. It settled and quieted.

"Probably. It's not shocky, but it doesn't matter," Parker said matter-of-factly.

"What the hell do you mean, it doesn't matter," Chalky asked heatedly.

Parker glared at him. "Just what I said. If we find the owner—which I doubt—whoever it is won't want a maimed animal back. And if we don't find them within a couple of days, I'll have to put it to sleep, anyway. Either way, you see, it doesn't matter."

Chalky hated that euphemism almost as much as he hated Parker. Put it to sleep. People should say what they really meant—kill it, destroy its life. Parker'd probably enjoy it. The puppy closed its eyes, obviously exhausted from the struggling and the loss of blood.

"I want this dog kept alive," Chalky said. "It's evidence in another crime."

"You expect to get a description from the dog?" Parker said smugly. Chalky fought down the urge to push his pinched face through the wall. "Two days, no more, no less. I'm not running a kennel here," Parker finished.

Chalky bit his tongue, laid the puppy gently on the table, then turned and walked away. Herb nodded to Parker, then followed. Chalky stifled what he was really thinking because if Parker re-

alized how pissed he was, the gnome would probably off the
dog just to frost him. He *was* a prick.

A few minutes later, they pulled into the station. Saturday
morning. Normally they'd have been doing the weekend thing,
but they both wanted to put a period after this case. The message board had a note from the captain. It was punctuated by
"Now!"

"Give me five minutes, I'll massage the captain and be right
back." Chalky walked to the captain's office, but he was gone. A
reprieve. Chalky took out his pad when he got to his desk, wrote
the seven numbers down again, and thought about them. "Stupid," he said. "Has to be a phone number." The dash was missing after the first three numbers, but that had to be it, a phone
number.

He dialed. The telephone rang and was picked up on the
fourth ring by a woman who sounded as though she'd just
dragged her butt out of bed. Chalky identified himself and could
hear her snap to attention. Her name was Verig. She worked at
the library.

"You missing a dog?"

"Did you steal them?" she asked aggressively.

"Yes or no, please." The whole world was on the prod. Saying, did you steal them, pretty well capped it, but he wanted to
hear the words. It was silent for a moment.

"I had two dogs, they're both gone," she said weakly.

"I'm sorry, when did you miss them?"

"Last night, between six-thirty and eight. Do you have
them?"

"Can you describe them for me, please," he continued un-
daunted. She did. They were hers. The second dog, the one that
was dead, was a terrier named Trixie. The one that lived was a
seven-month-old puppy she had named Princess. He got her address for the record. Her house was about four miles away from
where they had been dumped. He heard her breath intake when
he told her where they had been found and what had happened
to them. She moaned and started crying. Shit! He felt like doing
it himself.

"You want to pick up your puppy?"

"Look," she said steadying her voice, "I just got her and

haven't had her long enough to be attached to her or anything like that." Never a yes or no, always a tap dance. He waited. "No rear legs, my God!" She cried again. "Poor Trixie," she wailed, referring to the dead dog. Save your tears for the live dog. Trixie wasn't feeling any pain, he thought.

"You going to pick her up?" Chalky wanted an answer.

"What will they do with her if I don't?"

"After two days from this morning, she'll be killed," he said, intentionally not softening it.

"Do it." She hung up before he could say anything else. He wanted to call her back and ask her if she'd have her children murdered if they were injured, then thought better of it. All it would accomplish would be to make him feel better. If it's not perfect, throw it out—shitcan it. I don't like people very much this morning, he thought as he slammed down the receiver.

Chalky sat at his desk for a long time and stared at the clock on the wall. The papers this morning were full of the Joanne Pinkers case and Chalky knew that this was the type of sensationalist copy that would be picked up by the wire services within a day or two. This case had notoriety written all over it.

You could kill ten people, slice and dice them, machine gun them, blow them up, kill them in any way, and it was business as usual. But cut someone's arms off with no intention of killing them . . . well now, that was hot copy. It piqued the morbid imagination of the masses. "We've got to get this guy fast before this thing becomes a circus," he grumbled.

Herb was down having copies of some of the pictures made. Chalky picked up the map from his desk, then located the address of the woman who owned the dogs. He drew a point. It was a quarter of an inch from a dot that Herb had made. Walking distance. It was lettered "H." He looked up H on Herb's list. Gomez. Roberto Gomez. Christ, could it be? Could it be that easy? It was too much to hope for, but he felt a twinge of excitement.

Herb came back in with the photos in a folder, sat at his desk, and filed them. Chalky pointed to the dot on the map and told him what it was. Chalky grabbed a handful of pictures, including Gomez's picture.

"You feel lucky?" he asked Herb. "Get your coat."

Herb grabbed his coat, then asked, "Where to?" as he followed Chalky out the door.

"We're going for the brass ring. If we get lucky, we'll have next weekend off."

Ida May Thornton. What a kick in the drawers, Chalky thought as they closed on her house. Herb cringed as they scratched the new car on the tree limbs making their way down her drive.

Anybody Ida's age who'd threaten to blow your balls off had some real class, Chalky thought, then smiled. Spunk, that's what she has. Not many people had it these days. Too many people were willing to compromise, go along, not make waves.

"The big question is, are her eyes dependable?" Chalky said out loud as they rocked to a stop. They went up the tired steps. It might have been Chalky's imagination, but it seemed more of the boards were missing from the porch. They knocked and waited.

"Git off'n my porch or I'll turn my dogs loose on you!" a thin voice came through a crack in the door.

"It's me, Ida May . . . the policeman . . . Chalky . . . remember!" Dogs. Couple of attack cats was more like it. He chuckled.

"I got all the Bibles I need! Now move!" The door squeaked open a couple more inches behind the screen door. This was beginning to look less promising to Chalky.

"Police! Police!" he yelled, holding up his badge to the crack. He laughed, then Herb joined in. There was a comedy routine in here somewhere.

"Stop your yellin', I can hear you, dammit!" The screen door unlatched and popped open. "Git in here, yer lettin' out the heat." Chalky and Herb made their way into the now-familiar living room. The cats were nowhere in sight. As usual, it took seconds for their eyes to adjust to the dark. A fire burned furiously in the fireplace fueled by what appeared to be sawed boards. She disappeared into the kitchen, brought in a plate of cookies, and laid them on the coffee table.

"Knew you'd be back, considerin' what I told you," she said. "Figured it was important stuff. Been listenin' to the radio, 'bout what happened to the woman down the street." She sat and rocked. "Have a cookie. Can't offer you any milk, the cats ate it."

"We have some pictures, we'd like you to look at them," Chalky said.

"No lineup?" she whined, obviously disappointed.

"Maybe later, honey," Chalky said. "How about it, you up to it?" He pulled out the pile of pictures. She reached up and snapped on the bulb of the floor lamp next to her rocker. The glaring light filled the room with deep shadows and revealed how worn everything was. Her face was skeletal in the penetrating light. Must be two hundred watts, he thought as he squinted.

"Well, let's get to it," she said, "electricity costs money." Chalky walked over, bent forward, and handed her the pile of pictures. He had selected ten in all. Not wanting to hover, he returned to his chair.

"We suspect one of these men," he said. "We want you to go through these carefully and try to pick out the man you saw the other morning. The one who got in the van." Chalky would have crossed his fingers if he thought it would help.

"Son of a bitch gonna get the chair?" she asked. Her mouth worked to and fro. Chalky had forgotten about the snuff. He glanced down. The paper was positioned and already inaugurated.

She looked carefully at each picture, shifting it back and forth, in and out, from one gnarled hand to the other, trying to focus her eyes in the glaring light. After each one, she'd just say, "Mmmmmph," drop it, then pick up the next. Chalky's enthusiasm sank. This would have been too easy, he thought.

"This one!" she said accusingly, jabbing her bony finger at a picture. Chalky popped up, walked over, and took it from her outstretched hand. He stared at the photo, then handed it to Herb with a smile.

Roberto Gomez. Bingo!

chapter//twelve

The hilltop area where Gomez lived had degenerated to a combination of old houses, laundromats, used furniture stores, porno shops, and dark, smoky bars. The few houses in the neighborhood were weighed down with decades of rain, and their exteriors were neglected in a climate where maintenance was necessary to survive.

Chalky and Herb sat silently and stared out through the windshield as they moved along the gray streets. Shadows lengthened and the gravity of what they had seen in the last couple of days was affecting them.

"What do you think makes this guy tick," Herb said.

Chalky shook his head when he thought about the little dogs at the lab, then said in a subdued voice: "Damned if I know. I try to understand these people, but I've given up trying to put labels on them. Why does a man beat his wife and kids; another gives up on life and decides to steal for a living; and somebody else kills a person?" He breathed deeply, then sighed. "At least you can put a tag on those. Drinks too much, bad health, drugs, caught his wife cheating—take your choice. But this type of thing? Who knows. Has to have a little gray matter rearranged, or just missing. The funny thing is, when we catch the nut, they'll put him away for a lot of years, but he'll get three squares a day, a nice bed, and they'll teach him to play tennis or volleyball, to make breadboards or something. And the people he screwed up? They'll never know either, they'll simply blame us for not catching him sooner. Go figure."

Gomez lived in a large rooming house that had two sets of concrete steps on two levels leading to the front door. It was so steep that one side had a wobbly handrail of rusty metal plumbing pipe for support. Since Gomez worked nights, this was their best shot at finding him home. With a little luck, he'd be sleeping, and taking him into custody would be quick and easy. Theoretically.

Inside the dark hall, the first door to the left had a faded hand-lettered sign that read: Maniger. Close, but no cigar, mused Chalky. The smell of mildewed carpeting was stifling. They went up and down the halls on the first floor, then the second. The doors bore no names, only the hollow sound of televisions playing behind most of them.

Buy a book—get a life, he thought. Seventy percent of the doors had bulky outside latches and padlocks. What could people living in these rooms have to steal except their televisions?

They went back downstairs to the "Maniger's" door and knocked. From inside came the sound of movement. A cat yowled, a woman swore, then heavy thumping came toward the door.

The door swung open. A huge woman imitating a walking pear squinted through slits for eyes and asked what they wanted in a tone that told them to make it fast. They were probably upsetting her eating and television-watching schedule. A wave of sour-smelling body odor wafted into the hall. They winced, held their ground, and said they were policemen and had Gomez's house number, but needed his room number. They showed their identification when she glared at them suspiciously and said they only wanted to ask a question or two, then smiled.

"He's in 2C. That's the second floor, but you're wasting your time."

"Why are we wasting our time," Chalky asked wearily. Why do people always make you ask? Never give it to you straight out.

"Knocked on my door early this morning, said he was goin' to be gone for a day or two, and would I feed his cat." Chalky was fascinated at the way her neck jiggled when she talked.

"Cat?" Chalky said in a surprised voice, then asked, "Say where he was going?"

"Ain't none of my business." She shut and latched the door. They were dismissed.

Chalky knocked on the door again. Steps thudded back to the door and vibrated its frame. She opened it a crack and peered out with one eye this time. Chalky explained that if she saw Gomez before they did, it was important that she not tell him that they had come by. The door banged harder.

She was right, knocking on 2C was a waste of time. They made their way down the cracked concrete steps to the street and climbed in their car.

"Cat?" Herb asked. "Why would a guy who maims animals have a cat?"

"Why does a guy maim people?" Chalky added.

When they got to the station, Captain Stone called Chalky into his office and queried him about the case. Chalky brought him up-to-date, then returned to his desk. He pulled out the telephone book, fingered through the yellow pages, then dialed a number. He ordered a half cord of firewood and said he'd mail them a check. The delivery address he gave was Ida May Thornton's. He told them to pile it by her porch and not to tell her where it came from. After he hung up, he thought: Now, maybe there'll be something left of that house the next time we go back. He figured she was unable to cut her own wood and too proud to ask anyone for help.

"Softy," Herb said from behind him.

"Give me a break, will you?"

Herb stood and clapped him on the shoulder and went upstairs to get the DMV reports. While he was gone, Chalky called the lab about the fingerprints. All the viable ones were from the hands of the victim. Pretty much what he expected from the looks of the scene.

Herb returned and sat heavily at his desk. He leaned back and thumbed through the sheath of papers he'd brought with him.

"Where's the rest of them?" Chalky asked, referring to the reports Herb was fondling. Herb had only six.

"Believe it or not, eight of these guys don't even own a car, none on record anyway. Making beds must not pay very well."

"Any vans?" Chalky asked, becoming impatient.

"Nothing even resembling it. Not even a pickup."

"Fucking great!" Chalky walked around the room and stared out the window for a minute, then came back to his desk and toyed with the phone.

From behind him, Herb said, "So, call her already."

"I need to know how Joanne Pinkers is doing," Chalky said defensively.

"I'll buy it, sounds like a good reason to me." Herb smirked. "I'll even leave the room if you're embarrassed." Everything that Chalky considered to throw at him would have hurt, so he turned to his desk and dialed.

After the usual paging and fooling around it takes to get a doctor on the phone, she answered. He felt his insides warm when he heard her voice. She sounded tired.

"Sorry to bother you," Chalky said, then asked about Joanne Pinkers. He avoided any mention of last night, afraid she'd bring up what he had been there to ask. He was unsure of how to handle it.

"She's withdrawn, won't talk to anyone. Gone into a shell. Fortsam's working with her. I don't know what the prognosis is right now."

"Poor woman," Chalky muttered. He passed on the issue of questioning Joanne, then he told her about the two dogs. She was even more appalled than he had been. He said he'd get the photographer's pictures for her, that maybe she could see some similarity between the stitching or something. The fact that it would give him another reason to see her made him feel good. A reason with no guilt attached to it.

Peggy hesitated, then said, "I think there was someone in my condo last night." She told him about finding the mud and water after he left.

"I glanced out the window, but I don't see how I could have gotten mud on the sill. Maybe some water, I was pretty wet." He thought for a moment. "It makes me feel stupid that I was that careless." He hesitated, then asked, "Do you have a gun? You're pretty isolated out there."

"No."

"You want one?"

"No, but I have to admit, I'm pretty jumpy and getting worse

all the time. My girlfriend has been trying to talk me into buy-
ing one."

"Why don't I let you use one of mine until you can buy one?"
he asked.

"Let me think about it, okay? Besides, I don't know how to
use one."

"Point, pull the trigger. Guys with pretty low IQs have
worked it out. I could show you how in a half hour," he said enthusiastically, brightening at another chance to see her. She said
she wanted to think about it anyway. Chalky backed off. Pushing a gun on someone was bad news.

She mentioned that she was going to have a burglar alarm installed. He suggested that she have someone stay with her, at
least until it was activated, and that would give her time to think
about the gun.

"A burglar alarm is great if you've got neighbors who can
come to your rescue," he told her. "Problem is, even if the police are called, it could be twenty or thirty minutes before they
arrived. Plenty of time for really bad things to happen and for
the bad guy to get away."

They sat in comfortable silence for a moment, then Peggy
asked, "You said you'd call me today about the question you
were going to ask last night?" Her voice sounded tentative, as
though she felt nervous about bringing it up. "Joanne Pinkers, is
that what you wanted to know about?"

"Yeah, I guess," he said without conviction. They talked a
minute or two longer, then he hung up reluctantly and banged
his forehead with the heel of his hand. "I guess! Stupid!" He got
up and walked into the coffee room for a cup of coffee. If he
was out of the room, he could avoid Herb's questions. He paced
around the floor, then came back into the office and sat. Herb
was mercifully quiet. Finally, Chalky told him about Joanne
Pinkers and the pictures. So, it was back to Gomez.

They called the hospital and found out that tonight was
Gomez's day off. He was scheduled to work the following
night. No, the lady had no idea where he was. Yes, she would
call if they heard from him. Yes, she would keep quiet about
Chalky calling.

Chalky went in and explained to the captain that they had a

positive ID on a suspect in the case. Chalky wanted a twenty-four-hour stakeout on the rooming house. After Chalky related the circumstances, the captain refused on the basis that it was a weak connection, then gave him the usual story about the budget, etc. Chalky expected to lose, but nothing ventured, nothing gained.

"Where to now, Goyem leader?" Herb asked when he returned.

"Gomez put his mother down as the closest relative. You want to take a shot he's there?"

"She lives in San Diego?" Herb was incredulous.

"So, we could drive in shifts." Chalky smiled.

"Funny," Herb said as he straightened his desk. "My brother Bernie's coming in from Chicago tonight. Beth will cut me off if I work on Sunday. You going to have the uniforms follow up on Gomez?"

"Probably."

"Probably hell, you can't go there alone," Herb said.

"Sure, if I go I'll take help. Don't let the face fool you, I just look stupid." Herb left, and Chalky sat for a long time and stared at the clock on the wall. He'd been doing a lot of that lately.

Saturday night. He was getting horny as hell, but the thought of romancing some twit for a couple of hours of slap and tickle was really losing its attraction. He went through the list of possibilities, then reflected on the gray-eyed doctor. Now there was a woman with some substance. Christ, he felt he could actually talk to her if they could ever get by this awkward period, but he'd already pushed his luck and was uncomfortable about calling her again tonight. Besides, a class act like that was probably already booked up.

Well, there was always Giselle. She'd slipped her number to him a couple of times, and he'd promised to call. He'd been tempted two or three weeks ago, lying in bed thinking about that flawless body of hers, and the way it wiggled in all the right places. But it would almost be like taking advantage of someone who was retarded. She had the body of an adult, but the mind of a child, a very spoiled child. And then, how the hell would he get rid of her when the party was over. No. I don't need that kind of grief, he thought. The phone rang.

It was Yoko. She had a set of the pictures of the dogs. She was leaving, so he asked her to leave them in a nine-by-twelve envelope outside the door to the lab when she left. He said he'd pick them up on the way home.

"One last question, about the dog, the one that's alive?" he asked.

"I don't want to talk about that," she said. "I'm seriously thinking about quitting this place." Chalky was shocked. It seemed so out of character for her to express displeasure about anything.

"Anything I can do?"

"Yeah, you can get me a new boss. He's working tomorrow to catch up, and said he's going to put that little dog to sleep in the morning when he comes in if he hasn't heard from you. I tried to talk him out of it, but he ignored me. That's one of the reasons I called."

"Son of a bitch! He said he would wait two days."

"He claims its crying is upsetting his work. The poor little dog is just confused and in pain."

"You think he'd let me have it?"

"I already asked to take it, and he refused. I don't have a place for it, but I think I could find someone to give it a home." Her voice broke.

"You have an extra key to the lab?" Chalky asked.

"Yeah, why?"

"Don't ask. Just put it in the envelope with the pictures. I'll see that you get it back."

She hesitated for a long moment, then added in a weak voice: "I kind of like her. Could I come to your house and see her some time?"

"See who? I don't know what you're talking about," he said, chuckled, then hung up.

chapter//thirteen

Carlos had picked up the van and driven by Peggy's condo around six o'clock. Since there were no lights on, he assumed she was still out. He was confused about exactly what he was going to do, or how he would do it, but he had a constant compulsion to get even with her.

Cut her and leave her alive, or dissect her into smaller and smaller pieces, those were his options. Either one would be satisfying. The dogs were good practice, but they satisfied none of his needs, his cravings. His waking hours were spent thinking about cutting her and the unbelievably erotic pleasure of feeling her warm blood well up. Her voice now invaded his dreams too, like a stuck record player: *"Ragged, unprofessional, ragged. . . ."*

He pulled the van in back of the condo he'd parked behind the prior evening. It was overcast and getting dark and shadows were black in the trees. He thought about his job at the hospital. If he could get her, that chicken job was not important. Screw them. He could always get another one. Besides, after he did the doctor, they'd snoop around, ask questions, get closer, and sooner or later they'd knock on his door.

Yes, when he took care of her, he'd have to move on. His hands shook with excitement, and he could feel the sun on his back—hot, burning, and relentless; and he could taste the dry, orange dust in his mouth.

"Ragged, unprofessional, ragged, unprofessional . . . gotta get the *puta*, gonna get her . . ." he mumbled in a fevered tone. The vision was just on the edge of his consciousness . . . pushing, pushing, trying to get in . . . and . . .

His patience with waiting was almost gone.

• • •

The lab was still and black, and the lock to the outside door
snapped when it turned. Chalky imagined that it echoed down
the hall and they could hear it at the security desk in the front.
Shit! He was a damned good cop, but a questionable crook. Not
daring to turn on a light, he picked his way through the office. It
was dark. Illumination filtered in from the lights on the grounds
and reflected off the far wall, but it was still hard to see where
he stepped.

He banged his foot on the leg of a chair, cursed as softly as he
could, then continued toward the lab door. He listened. Quiet as
a mummy's tomb. Did the bastard kill her already? If Parker
did, he'd be at the orthodontist before tomorrow was gone.

It was even darker in the lab with only two windows filtering
in the weak, warm light. All the old movies came back to him.
He could visualize knocking a beaker of corrosive acid onto
himself, or tipping something that would explode and set the
whole lab on fire. Forever scarred, he'd have to wear a steel
mask, lurk in a bell tower somewhere, and just come out at
night.

"Ugh!" He slammed his thigh into a stool, and it tipped over
onto the floor with a crash. Try to explain this to the captain if
someone comes, idiot! he thought.

A weak woofing sound; a testing sound.

She was alive.

It came from under the table to his right. Then, a low whine.
He could imagine the little dog moving, then being hit with a
flash of pain. How frightening it must be to wake in this strange
place and have to endure what she'd gone through. He fumbled
under the table for the small cage, then lifted it up and carried it
to a desk in the dim light of a window.

He talked in soothing tones to the little dog as he searched
around for something to carry her in. He'd get nailed if he
walked out the front door with this cage. Finding a pile of laun-
dered cloths about eighteen inches square, he took a handful
and laid them on the desk. He gently lifted the puppy from the
cage, and wrapped her body in them.

"If we're going to pull this caper off, kid, you're going to have to cooperate by being really quiet." He tucked her inside his coat. The puppy was warm against his side as he locked up and moved quickly down the hall. She seemed content to have someone touch her, and remained calm as they passed the guards who stared at their television as he walked out. Maybe I'm not such a bad crook after all, he thought. What a disappointment for Parker when he comes for her with his needle in the morning. Wish I could be there.

The dog lay quietly on the seat next to him all the way home still wrapped in her towels. The rule was, no animals in his apartment, but what the hell. He'd deal with that problem when he came to it. What were they going to do, call a cop?

When he got home, his inclination was to feed her something, but her eyes kept drooping closed. He made a bed of blankets on the bathroom floor. She was asleep before he laid her down. He closed the door and went into the kitchen and opened a bottle of beer.

Trying to figure how this was all going to turn out was difficult, but right now he felt damned good about the whole thing. Damned good.

The doorbell rang.

He glanced at the clock and it was almost nine. His first instincts were that someone had come for the dog already. Ridiculous! He opened the door.

"Hi, cutie, you alone?" Not waiting for an answer, Giselle flounced in the door wearing high heels and a raincoat, her cloud of perfume trailing behind. Chalky was so shocked he just shut the door, then watched as she sidled over and sat in a chair by the fireplace. Her hands were jammed into the deep pockets and stretched the coat tightly around some of her best parts. She stared at him like a cat surveying a mouse. Her collar was open and he could see her ample cleavage with no evidence of any undergarments. He cleared his throat and could feel himself losing this one already.

"How'd you know where I lived," he asked weakly.

"Asked," she said seductively. Who she asked was of no importance. He could feel his temperature rising and his loins ache. God! What a crummy time to do this to me, he thought.

"You want a drink?" He was trying to put off decision time a while longer. If she wanted to talk, he had no idea where to start. At thirty-six, he thought hard rock was something you sat on.

"Nope."

Inane thoughts bounced around, like: But I'm so much older than you. Does your mother know where you are? Are you sure you should be doing this? Pretty tame stuff to fight what his hormones were doing to him right now.

"Well, Giselle, what can I do for you?" he asked lightly, trying to regain some control of the situation.

She stood, licked her lips and stared at him, then tossed her high heels off. He watched as though hypnotized. She struggled out of her raincoat and stood in front of him.

She was naked.

"Jesus," he said involuntarily.

She smiled. Her breasts were high and perfectly formed, her stomach flat, legs long and supple. God! She had the body of a lean gymnast. Pinch an inch? No way. He had the feeling that he was watching a grade Z porno flick in three-D.

Giselle turned and walked into the darkness of the hall, toward his bedroom, not bothering to look back. Her skin was flawless and her muscles rippled invitingly as she glided— moving with the grace and confidence of a lioness sure of her prey. He could feel his stomach twinge with desire.

"Coming?" she asked over her shoulder.

"Damned near," he said softly.

He got up and turned off the light.

"Just stay for tonight," Peggy said as she dropped her purse on the counter and turned on the lights. Carrie followed her in the door and put a couple bottles of Chablis in the refrigerator to chill. "The man from the alarm company is coming to explain it to me at eight-thirty, in forty-five minutes. I'm not going to be able to sleep until the thing's installed. They said they might be able to do it tomorrow."

Peggy hung their coats in the hall closet. She instinctively went into the den, checked the lock on the window, then came back into the kitchen.

"Bull!" Carrie said. "An alarm, no matter how great, is only a feel-good. What you need is something to make very large holes in the piece of garbage who's creeping around here scaring the shit out of you."

Carrie patted her purse. She'd brought her gun. "The hell with the laws," she had said when Peggy told her it was against the law to conceal it in her purse. "Who'll know," she added emphatically. "I'll have the damned thing in my hand if I have to shoot the bastard, and he's sure not going to be in a position to tell anybody."

Carrie was pretty much the opposite of Peggy—aggressive, outspoken, and used colorful language casually. Peggy was a long way from demure, but tried to take a softer approach to get what she wanted. Carrie felt the primary cause of trouble in the world could be laid at the feet of the male of the species. With Peggy, the jury was still out, even though she'd had to fight the male-dominated system through medical school. "No point in struggling, it's simply the way it is," she'd said to Carrie's anger.

"Look, if your alarm isn't working by tomorrow night, I'll hang around. Odds are they won't be able to do it until next week, tomorrow being Sunday. Hell, what am I doing any different than I'd be doing at home?" Carrie asked. Too impatient to wait for the wine to chill, she went to the refrigerator, took out a bottle, and opened it. She poured it into two glasses filled with ice cubes. They both settled in the living room, sipped their wine, and listened to the wind caress the trees.

"Chalky, the detective, says I should have a gun too," Peggy said. "He's a nice guy. Said he'd show me how to use it." Peggy could count, one-two-three, before the invective came back. Saying anything positive about a man always set Carrie off.

"Nice guy? Pegs, the guy's a cop. Nice cop is an oxymoron. It's like saying, military intelligence. And why are you calling the cretin by his first name, for Christ's sake?" Peggy smiled. She was used to Carrie and ignored the man-bashing most of the time.

"He was really nice to me even though we got off to a bad start. Besides, in case you haven't noticed, he's tall, blond, well built, and extremely good-looking in a rough sort of way."

"Yeah, and he probably makes a fifth of what you do and sleeps with whores off the street?"

"God, that's ridiculous. You're really being a snob. I get the feeling the man's very good at what he does, and as far as women are concerned, I think he has more class than that. He has excellent taste in women . . . he seems to like me," Peggy said. She smiled, then flushed. It was the first time she'd acknowledged that she was flattered by his bumbling attention. Besides, she'd had enough of smooth men, Brad being a prime example.

"Class! Give me a break. Where'd you get that idea?"

"Just a feeling, I guess."

"Your mother would have a blanking heart attack if you brought something like that home to dinner," Carrie persisted, talking about him as though he were an inanimate object.

"Well, my mother didn't have to sleep with a lethargic, flatulent cat every night when she was my age either." Peggy was defensive. It was getting darker in the room as the last of the light filtered from the sky.

Carrie prepared to release a new barrage when the doorbell rang. She jumped up and went over to her purse, opened it, put her hand in, then whispered, "Get the door, Pegs, I'm ready."

"Relax," Peggy said, then chuckled as she went to open it. "It has to be the man for the security alarm, put that away." She peeked through a side window that had a view of the front porch area and added, "It's him." Carrie relaxed and closed her purse. The bell rang again.

The man from the alarm company was a grandfatherly type who beamed and patiently batted Carrie's objections down one after the other with the ease of long practice. No, he promised only security, simply the best system for the money, not perfection. After promising it could be installed on Sunday, he checked his schedule and said it would take approximately a week to install it. Peggy asked if he would do it on Sunday if she paid extra for the installation. He initially refused, but after Peggy offered him a hundred fifty dollars extra for installation, he changed his mind. She was too nervous to wait. He agreed to be there around noon tomorrow and have it active by evening.

Peggy gave him a spare key to install it in case she decided to go away during the day. He said he'd stop by at six P.M. tomorrow evening to pick up a check and explain how it operated.

That was what she wanted to hear, so he was out the door by 9:30 with a signed contract.

Carrie was annoyed that Peggy accepted the first price without bargaining. Three thousand and some miscellaneous numbers seemed fair to Peggy. Hell, people normally paid for their gall bladder or appendix operations without haggling. Besides, she had the old-fashioned concept that you had to let a merchant make a fair profit if you wanted the job done well. And having something that could save her life installed correctly seemed pretty important right now.

After he left, they drank Chablis and talked about men for a half an hour. Peggy dropped the subject of Chalky and mentioned the confrontation she'd had with Fortsam in her office and that set Carrie off on another diatribe about exploitation by men. In her characteristic rapid-fire dialogue, she punctuated every other sentence with "fucking men."

She insisted that Peggy file a formal harassment complaint at the hospital, but Peggy refused. Peggy felt that she could control him herself. Peggy left unsaid the fact that she also knew that she'd be in for some rough weather with the other doctors if she did. The male doctors would publicly defend her right to complain, but in the back rooms, they'd quietly label her a troublemaker and a bitch. Carrie was a GP, finishing her residency, and planned to set up a private practice with the help of her family, so she was partially insulated. A young surgeon like Peggy who needed referrals to get started had to avoid that type of reputation, deserved or not. No. Peggy had to handle Fortsam herself the next time he became aggressive.

It had been a long, tiring day for both of them. Peggy was first to yawn. It was after ten and the gaps in the conversation got longer and longer.

"You ready to call it a night?" Peggy asked.

"Yeah, I guess so. I've always fought going to sleep since I was a kid, always thought I was going to miss something." Carrie laughed, then stood. Outside the wind blew leaves against the windows. It was getting colder and was threatening snow in some of the higher elevations, especially in the Snoqualmie Pass to the east of them.

Carrie had intentionally left the television off because she was tired of listening to the newsmen constantly harping on the mutilation atrocity of Joanne Pinkers. They were down to interviewing neighbors since Joanne's mother had effectively shut them out, and no other family members lived in the area. Then there were the so-called experts giving their opinion of the type of person who was capable of the crime. The news had gradually escalated in frequency, and the unanswered question at the end of every program was—who's next? God forbid that he didn't do it again and they'd have to develop another story, Peggy thought.

As they carried their glasses into the kitchen, something fell with a crash in the garage. They both froze and looked at each other. Peggy could feel her heart skip a beat, then instantly speed up. Adrenaline doing its job, she noted.

"Your garage door closed?" Carrie whispered. She walked over to the counter and stood in front of her purse, head cocked, listening. The kitchen door led to the garage.

"I know I closed it, but it was open last night when Chalky came by . . . and I'm sure I closed it then. Maybe something's wrong with the opener." Carrie glanced at her and Peggy realized that she had avoided telling Carrie about Chalky's visit to avoid criticism.

Carrie pulled her gun from her purse. It was a small chromeplated automatic. Peggy stared at the gun as though it were a snake. The wind gusted and another clanking sound came from the other side of the wall.

"Sounds like the wind blew something down," Carrie said. She cocked the automatic with her other hand. Peggy cringed at the action. That's what you do when you shoot somebody, she thought.

"You're not going out there, are you?"

"You going to be able to sleep if somebody doesn't?" Carrie asked. The tacit answer was no. Peggy'd spend the night staring at the ceiling, nerves tingling, waiting for the next sound.

"We should call the police," Peggy finally said.

"Great. What are you going to tell them? That you heard a couple of sounds?"

Peggy could hear the police chuckling at her on the phone.

Go close your garage door, lady. If you see a prowler, then call us.

Another gust; another clunk.

"That's it, it has to be open," Carrie said. "I'll go out and close it." She headed toward the door. Peggy considered getting a knife from a drawer and following, then realized how ridiculous she'd look to Carrie. The garage door was open, and Carrie was going to close it, that's all. She hated the fact that her imagination was out of control.

Carrie stepped through the door with the gun lowered and a blast of wind hit her. She blinked her eyes as dust and particles of dirt peppered her face. Carrie snapped on the light and searched for the garage door switch with her free hand and found it. Peggy leaned apprehensively into the garage and watched.

Carrie pushed the button. The door hummed, the chain jerked, and the door closed, effectively cutting off the sound of the wind. It touched the garage floor, reversed, then went up.

"Damn!" said Carrie. She jabbed the button again and the door repeated the cycle. The lone sixty-watt bulb in the wall socket made long black shadows behind the car. The wind swirled and rattled dust against the back wall again, then settled between gusts.

"What now?" Peggy asked. "Should we leave it open?" The frigid air raised goose bumps on her arms. Peggy kept glancing into the blackness in the driveway. The yawning opening made her nervous.

"Hell no, we'll do it manually," Carrie said. Peggy had no idea what she was talking about and watched. Carrie walked to the door of the garage, laid the gun on the roof of the car, then reached up and grabbed a rope hanging from the opener chain. She jerked hard and it popped from the relieved pressure when it disconnected. Carrie climbed down and pulled on the rope. The door rolled easily and stayed in place when it touched the floor.

"Who needs a man," Carrie said and smiled. She slid a manual bolt into the side of the track, locking it. "Now, whatever you do, don't touch that button. Okay?" Peggy nodded. Carrie continued, "In the morning when we go for breakfast, we'll have to get the car out, lock the garage door from the inside, and leave through your front door. Monday, you'll have to call the builder to come and adjust this." Carrie indicated the opener, then picked up the gun. Peggy was really glad she was there. Peggy snapped off the light and quickly shut the door on the black garage.

Back in the condo, Peggy was still nervous. She wanted to ask Carrie to search the garage, but was afraid she'd laugh at her. They should have looked around on the dark side of the car, and in and under the car. She'd lock the deadbolt between the kitchen and the garage, and that would make her feel safe. For now.

Peggy went to all the windows on the ground floor and checked the locks as Carrie rinsed the glasses and cleaned the sink and counter. In the den, she double-checked the window, then stared into the blackness of the yard. The thin saplings in the distance whipped back and forth in the gusts, giving the illusion of dark forms dancing in the yard. Peggy shivered. The window was freezing to her touch and the frigid wind pummeling it leaked in around the sash. Goose bumps again. She hugged her arms, shuddered, and turned off the light.

"You think I'm a coward?" Peggy asked in the kitchen.

"Don't be ridiculous, Pegs. I'd be nervous living out here in the boonies by myself too. I can't believe you don't move back into the city like a civilized person."

"Good. Then you won't make fun if I ask you to do one more John Wayne thing for me?" Carrie laughed as Peggy gave the front door one final check, then walked to the bottom of the stairs, hesitated, and asked, "Would you think I was being paranoid if I asked you to take your gun and check the bedrooms upstairs before we go to bed? I'm sorry. I know I'm really being a pain."

"Yes, I think you're being paranoid, and no, you're not a pain. I was going to do it anyway." Carrie retrieved the gun from her purse and went up the stairs. Peggy hovered at the bottom and waited, feeling stupid, much as she had when Chalky had performed the ritual the night before.

She could hear Carrie's cautious footsteps in the first bedroom. Doors slammed. Peggy could see her in her mind, holding out the gun, opening doors, looking under the beds and behind furniture. Jesus, what a coward you are, she thought, then shivered. The fire popped and hissed. Have to close the doors to bank that fire before I go to bed.

Upstairs, the sound of Carrie walking in the master bedroom—

Then—stumbling steps and a scream—

A shot! Loud, concussive—

The sound of a body falling!

Peggy shrieked and waited a tick of the clock.

She shouted, "Carrie!"

Another thudding sound and a groan. Panic rose in Peggy's chest as she ran toward the door and snatched her keys as she passed the counter, then banged into the dark garage. He's inside and he's killed her, her frantic mind shrilled. She threw open the car door, got in and slammed it, then fumbled through her keys. As she was searching for the right one, the door leading to the condo banged shut on its automatic hinges—

Inky black!

"My God!" she shouted. Her circuits failed to compute—she just kept sorting the keys. "Think!" She reached up, explored the roof of the car, found the interior light, and switched it to on. Finding the car key took another second, then she jammed it into the ignition. The inside of the car was lit in a soft, warm glow, but beyond the windows, it was black. She locked the doors and started the car in almost the same motion.

The garage door behind me—it's still closed! Her fist banged the opener button. Above, in the blackness, the mechanism made a popping sound, hummed, then stopped. Peggy glanced into the rearview mirror. It's still closed! She jerked on the headlight switch, and the bright flash of lights on the walls shocked her.

"Jesus! The door is locked . . . it's locked closed!" Should I risk getting out and try to open it by hand where I could get trapped—or should I put the car in reverse and smash through the plywood door?

Her mind wrestled with what to do when the door to the condo opened and the wall light snapped on—

"Pegs! What the hell are you doing?" Carrie shouted from the open door.

Peggy stared at Carrie through the windshield and was suddenly aware that she was racing the car engine and her own face was constricted in panic.

Carrie limped to the car window. She no longer had the gun.

Peggy hit the button, and the window slowly whirred open.

Carrie said as she grimaced, "I tripped over that damned cat of yours and the gun went off. Damned near fractured my pelvis when I fell into the wall and then to the floor."

"There wasn't anybody?" Peggy choked out.

Carrie's face convulsed in laughter and she leaned back against the wall helplessly.

Peggy watched her, and gradually a smile broke at the corners of her own mouth.

"Shit," Peggy said, then reached down, shut off the engine, and climbed out.

Carrie still giggled and was having trouble getting her breath.

"You hurt my cat?" Peggy asked.

Carrie shook her head no, then exploded into another gale of laughter. She bent and choked from the convulsions. Finally, she controlled it, straightened, and wiped her eyes.

"No, the cat's fine," Carrie answered through a chuckle and swallowed. "But you've got new roof ventilation." Peggy walked in the door and Carrie followed. "My hero," Carrie taunted under her breath.

"Give me a break. I never said I was brave or anything." Peggy walked into the living room and closed the glass doors on the fireplace to bank the fire. God, Monday is going to be hell at the hospital, thought Peggy. The story would be all over. She knew it was too good for Carrie to keep to herself. Her face flushed when she thought of the smiles she'd get from the staff.

The two women turned off the lights downstairs and went up to their separate bedrooms. Peggy came in to say good night while Carrie brushed her teeth in the hall bathroom.

"You wouldn't consider not mentioning this to anyone?" Peggy asked, looking sheepish.

"Not a chance," Carrie said through the foam in her mouth.

"I'll have to pay to get the hole in your ceiling plugged up, so I have to get something out of this."

"I'll have it fixed—how about then?"

Carrie rinsed her mouth, straightened, pretending to think deeply, then said, "Naw—I like it better the other way."

In a light vein, Peggy said, "Good night, bitch," then walked into her bedroom accompanied by another round of Carrie's laughter. She wondered how funny it would have been if someone had been standing in front of the gun.

After the lights were off and the sheets started to warm, Peggy's cat thumped up on the covers and stretched out alongside of her. She roughed the fur on his back. He stretched and purred softly.

"Sidney, I'm going to have to get you a bell," she whispered. The cat rattled louder. She remembered her statement to Carrie about sleeping with her flatulent cat. She turned over, hugged her pillow, and stared through the window at the outline of the moving trees on the horizon—swaying and dancing rhythmically like ghostly figures keeping time to the moaning wind beyond the glass. She squeezed the pillow harder, thought of Chalky, then smiled.

"Why didn't you ask me?" she whispered in a sleep-clouded voice.

He smiled down, ready to kiss her, then held her gently in his arms as she fell asleep.

chapter//fourteen

It was after one A.M. when Carlos walked away from the driveway of the burned-out house. The van was in the garage, the satchel hidden, and he'd have to walk to work and finish his shift. *Damn!*

"Bitches!" He lashed out into the wind and darkness. "I'll cut you both!" He sliced the air with his hands making long, slashing strokes.

He had waited impatiently for the man with the truck to leave the doctor's condo. Waited and waited. Finally the bastard came out and drove away. Then more waiting, to make sure the man was gone, all the time his fever rising, the excitement burning his stomach and groin.

Finally, Carlos had climbed out of the van into the penetrating wind, pulled his bag from the side door, then withdrew a prybar to force open the same window he'd entered with no trouble last night. The doctor'd probably have it locked this time. When he snuck around to the rear and checked the window, it was locked, but she had the door to the room closed again. Closed. Impossible to hear him break in if he was careful. *Stupid.*

He listened, then carefully worked the bar under the edge of the aluminum flashing. *I'll just bend the lock up*, he thought. *I'll tie them both up first, then do them one at a time, the lady doctor last. Yeah, she had to be last. Stretch it out as long as possible. Listening from the other room, she'd scream and beg, and that would make it even better, even better.*

The saliva dripped from the corner of his mouth as he jogged along. He started to get hard again thinking about it.

135

"Bitches!" he screamed into the night. A couple of dogs barked in the distance, and he shook his fist in return.

Just as he had been ready to pull down on the bar and pop the window lock, the crazy *puta* had fired the gun at him from the window above.

Shot at him! The fucking *puta*!

Must have seen me or heard the noise or something. But how the hell could she know I was out there? I was being quiet. How could she have heard me?

Carlos lived under four miles from the hospital, and he could see the lights from the complex in the distance. Now he was running through a mixed area of businesses and old, tired homes. A twangy country western song drifted by on the wind from a bar a block away, tires squealed, a horn honked, a random shout. All nonsense sounds as he focused straight ahead.

The urge to cut, to feel the flesh parting, was almost more than he could bear. He'd fantasized about it so long, for so many years, then he had finally done it. The sensation was three or four times more exciting than he had thought it would be. Cocaine, crack—he'd tried them—they were great, but not even close. With the second slice into the Pinkers woman's arm, he'd ejaculated all over the bed, over and over again, almost uncontrollably.

Now, the terrible tension inside him was almost bursting, ready to explode again. He'd been so close tonight, then the damn gunshot—

He took the stone steps to the hospital two at a time, made his way around to the side and the employees' entrance. He stopped breathlessly at the time clock. His card was gone. How could that be? He'd received a tongue-lashing last night from his supervisor, Miss Jackson. She told him to shape up or ship out and to show more responsibility, and on and on. *But they can't fire me, I'm too valuable,* he thought.

"Hi, man," Cooper said from a door as he walked by. "Jackson's havin' a shit fit. You seen her?" He grinned. Carlos glared and kept walking. *Bastard loves it.* "She said for you to come down to her office in the basement if'n I seed you, man!" Cooper finished.

"Seed this, motherhumper!" Carlos shouted and held up his

middle finger over his shoulder. He could hear Cooper slam the door behind him as he continued toward the elevators. The hospital was active for late at night, and two people stepped off the elevator when he got on.

One young girl was crying, whining about another person being too young to die, or some shit like that. Carlos ignored them.

In the basement, a couple of people were in the hall when he smashed Miss Jackson's door open without knocking. He glowered down at her where she sat behind her desk.

"Where the hell's my time card!" he snapped, still boiling from the frustration from earlier in the evening. As he stood over her, his hands opened and closed with barely controlled rage. He had taken all he was going to take. He'd reached the breaking point with the people who controlled his life.

Miss Jackson raised her two-hundred-pound-plus girth from the chair as though bouncing off a spring and spat: "You smart-mouth son of a bitch, how dare you talk to me that way!" Her black face was now reddish-black. "Get your locker cleaned out, you're fired!"

Suddenly Carlos turned quiet and cold as he glared at her malevolently, his fists clenching and unclenching. He wanted to kill her, to rip her apart with his bare hands, to cut her. As his flat eyes bored into her, she glanced down. Her mouth worked as she smoothed her flowered skirt and lowered herself into her chair, obviously trying to regain her composure because she recognized his threat.

"Ahem," she cleared her throat. "You've been a problem for too long, Carlos. You've been given three written reprimands. I told you last night—"

"Shut up," he hissed without moving his riveting eyes. "Shut up or I kill you." His voice was even, as though discussing the weather.

Miss Jackson's eyes widened. She coughed again, then looked around. There was no way out of the room except by him. The fear in her eyes showed that she believed he might try. He could see her measuring him, trying to decide what to do. *Come on, bitch!* She took her handkerchief from the pocket of her sweater and wiped her neck.

"I'd like to ask you to leave now, your check will be—"

"Fuck you, bitch." His gaze was fixed. The heat rose up his legs, through his stomach, and into his chest. His whole being was filled with the need to crush her.

"Wait a minute, you can't—" she said, then stopped. His skin flushed and the moisture pushed its way to the surface of his face. In the distance the round orange sun started to grow . . . burn . . . move . . .

She stared at him and her mouth dropped open. Breathing faster now, her eyes darted back and forth trying to find a way out. She stood—then, marshaling the courage, charged around her desk intending to shove by him, obviously expecting him to step aside. Instead, he moved into her path, coiled his arm, and hit her in the middle of the forehead with all his strength.

She fell back, both arms windmilling, and her head hit the bare tile floor with a loud cracking sound.

He was on her instantly like a rabid wolf. Clawing, biting, scrabbling over her huge form, looking for a way to kill her quickly. His fingers sunk into the fat folds around her neck. Semiconscious, she made gargling sounds as he gripped and regripped his hands to find the right hold to cut off her air.

Gouging, pressing, driving his fingers into her throat, he held her long after her sounds stopped. He groaned heavily from the effort. Finally, he released her neck, stood, and wiped his moist hands on his pants. He spit down onto her blank face. Her bulging eyes continued to stare up at the ceiling. Sweat poured off his skin and his breath came in quick explosive thrusts, not only from the effort but from the unchained savagery.

"You shouldn't a made me mad, lady. You shouldn't a done it," he whispered. Damn. He needed time. Time to get away, time to think about what to do.

Carlos banged out into the hall. It was quiet except for a voice coming from a door thirty or forty feet away. As he trotted toward the elevators, his steps echoed. He realized what he had to do.

Opening the storage door, he pulled a surplus gurney away from the wall and wheeled it down the hall. Stopping at the laundry-room door, he hesitated. Inside, Maria worked near the door, and three women labored at the dryers and folding tables, their backs to the door.

Carlos darted into the room and grabbed a couple of sheets, hoping to get away without Maria noticing him. She caught his movement out of the corner of her eye, glanced up, and smiled. She followed him through the door.

"Where you been?" she asked. "Miss Jackson is looking for you." Her large eyes studied him, then took in the gurney. She wore tight jeans and a T-shirt that clung to her taut, small body. Her long black hair hung loose and glistened with highlights.

"Go back to work, I got it worked out," he snapped and threw the sheets on the gurney.

"You talked to her?"

"Yeah."

"Oh, by the way, I got that doctor's address for you. What did you want it for?" Maria asked.

"I gotta do something, you gonna be here for a while?"

"Sure." She smiled at his question.

"I'll be back in a half hour or so. You wait here." She nodded, and went back to work. He pushed the gurney to Miss Jackson's office. She lay where he had left her. No one had come in while he was gone. Carlos sweated as he wrestled her dead weight up onto the gurney, then covered her with the sheets.

Breathing hard, Carlos pushed the gurney down the hall, around a turn, then toward maintenance. The small, secluded room with the cabinets, his hideaway, was unlocked as usual. When he got the gurney into the room, he pulled it to the wall, then pushed Miss Jackson off and let the body thump heavily onto the concrete floor. He dragged her lifeless form to the shelving in the rear. It took him fifteen minutes of straining to force her large bulk into the small space behind it. When he finally had her wedged in, he covered her with extra sheets.

The hall was clear when Carlos left. He pushed the gurney back to where he picked it up. He got a mop and cleaned up the urine from the floor in Miss Jackson's office, then he went into the bathroom and washed his face. He tried to not look at himself in the mirror.

Carlos's hair was still damp and stuck together in clumps. The vision that had been threatening to come had receded into the distance and was now only a low ringing in his ears. One more thing to do.

Maria smiled again when he peeked around the door and he motioned for her to come. The other women continued working without noticing. She walked into the hall, beaming.

Carlos walked down the hall a couple of steps, then turned and said, "You gotta leave with me."

"Leave?" Her brow furrowed. "Why?"

"'Cause you have to—" He put his hand on her arm and his stomach turned over with the desire to cut into her skin.

She studied him for a moment, then said, "Jackson might fire me if I just leave."

"Jackson won't know." Carlos grinned. Maria cocked her head questioningly. "She left on an emergency, won't return tonight." She glanced at the door and back, as though trying to decide. "Important," he added. Maria's eyes softened at his voice. She got her coat, then followed him down the hall, up the stairs, and into the cold windy morning.

As they disappeared into the darkness, disturbed by their passing, a dog howled into the night.

chapter//fifteen

Sunday morning was depressing as hell for Chalky. He woke with a bad taste in his mouth. When he went into the bathroom, he jumped when he saw the little dog lying there looking up at him inquisitively. How quickly we forget. That made him smile.

The night before with Giselle had been a disaster performance-wise. At least from her point of view. Somewhere around two o'clock she grabbed her raincoat and left as quickly as she had come, with a couple of mumbled "I have to's." He knew it was bullshit, but he was just glad she was going. As expected, conversation the night before had been almost non-existent and was confined to words like "faster" and "harder" and geographical directions to her on-buttons.

She had showed up solely for several hours of uninhibited sex play, and he'd fallen short by at least a couple hours. When he was ready for a nap, she was getting revved up. She needed a sixteen-year-old with the libido of a rutting stag, then again, maybe that's any sixteen-year-old. He tried to remember. Goodbye, Giselle, he thought.

"No vets open today, kid, so it's just gonna be you and me," Chalky said to the dog. He knew he had to take her to a vet for a general checkup, and to make sure her surgery remained uninfected. The puppy seemed to be in good shape, as much as Chalky knew about dogs. He'd had only one as a child. Sparky had been a dachshund with energy that lasted all day. His arm would get tired of throwing a ball before Sparky gave up.

Chalky washed the dog in the sink, then dried her fur with his hair dryer. Not having rear legs on a dog posed some sanitary problems that he had not considered. Somehow, he'd have to

141

come up with a solution to that. He smiled when he remembered how Giselle had freaked out the first time she went into the bathroom to do whatever it is that women do after sex. A little squeal, and she was back in bed. She lost her enthusiasm for all of fifteen seconds maybe. She had no curiosity about what the dog was doing there, she just disappeared under the covers again to try to resurrect his flagging interest.

Chalky carried the dog into the kitchen and laid her on the floor on a folded towel. The puppy watched him with growing interest as he fried a couple of hamburgers for her breakfast. When he finished and drained them, he crumbled them into little pieces. She ate with gusto. Nothing wrong with her appetite. Like a doting mother, he sat in a chair beside her and watched her eat.

The doorbell rang. He looked from the dog to the door, trying to decide whether he should hide the puppy or not. Landlady, dog catcher, or Parker-the-prick standing there with his needle saying, "Let me in, Fuchs, I need to kill that dog." The animal was quiet during the night, so no one in the building could know she was here. He opened the door. It was Herb.

"Surprise. What happened to your brother from Chicago?" Chalky asked as Herb walked in. Herb was dressed casually in an open shirt and coat sweater.

"They missed the flight. Coming in tonight."

"How about Beth. She going to be pissed, you being out on Sunday?" Chalky asked.

"Probably, but I can deal with it." Herb noticed the dog and laughed. "You've got to be kidding me," he said as he knelt down. The dog's tail wagged as Herb scratched behind her ears. Herb looked up. "Parker's going to have a cow, dude!"

"I can only hope." Chalky picked up the dog, holding the towel under her, and carried her into the bathroom. He spread papers on the floor at one end hoping she'd be a little more selective the next time since she was able to scoot around on her stumps. A clean blanket on the floor for her comfort and a bowl of water, and she was set for the morning. Her head was tucked down, and her eyes closed before he shut the door.

Without talking, Chalky slipped on his coat and the men walked to Herb's car. It was a miracle—the sun was out. That buoyed Chalky's spirits slightly. They talked about other things, but they tacitly knew they were going to try to pick up Gomez. After Giselle left last night, Chalky had stared at the dark ceiling and reflected on Joanne Pinkers and the poor little dog in his bathroom. The more he thought, the angrier he had gotten. He had to force himself to not dwell on it so he could go to sleep.

"How'd you get the dog?" Herb asked.

"Long story. Basically I stole her." Herb nodded and dropped it. He was sharp enough not to say anything. They drove along in silence for a couple more minutes. The sun had gone back behind the clouds. The miracle was over for the day.

"How do you know when you're over the hill?" Chalky asked. He decided not to tell him about Giselle using and discarding him last night, mostly because it was his style to keep his mouth shut about his adventures with women, and partly because—all things considered—it was a very ugly story egowise.

"By my guess, you're over the hill when you ask someone: 'Am I over the hill?' " Chalky punched his arm and they both laughed.

"What makes you ask a question like that?"

"Charge it up to brain damage. So, we going to pick up this Gomez, or what?" Chalky asked.

"That's what I'm here for, *compadre*," Herb said. Chalky smiled and settled in the seat. The fact that Herb was out on Sunday without being asked cemented their relationship as far as Chalky was concerned. His last partner, Slade, was the kind of guy who went by the rules. And the rules said you were supposed to take Sunday off. Chalky sort of went by the rules too, but he knew that sometimes there were more important things. Coming in on Sunday was a minor inconvenience. Picking up this piece of human garbage was right up there in importance. God, just think if we left him on the street a day longer, and he mutilated some kid. All because of some stupid rule. A wound like that would never heal.

"Fat Phil's for breakfast?" Herb asked.

"Let's change our luck and eat at Denny's this morning." Herb shrugged his shoulders. It had been a while since Chalky'd eaten at Phil's on Sunday, and he was unsure whether the sex machine was there this morning. Right now, his pride could stand a break from her.

Denny's was buzzing with activity. Chalky ordered a Southern Slam. It was a gut-buster with gravy on a biscuit, eggs scrambled, bacon and sausage. Herb had toast and coffee. The two men talked mostly about the little dog. Chalky was still silent on how he'd picked up the animal last night. No point in letting Yoko's fanny flap in the breeze after she'd done him a favor. The less Herb knew, the better. Most of the conversation centered around how Chalky was going to deal with the animal's handicap. Stealing the dog was something he did out of gut instinct. Not a lot of planning there. The one thing that he knew for sure was that he'd never deep-six the little tyke.

The drive back to Gomez's neighborhood went a lot quicker this time because they knew where he lived. They argued about whether to evacuate the surrounding apartments, then decided that this would be a cakewalk and it should go down with no hassle.

Besides, the guy had no felonies, as far as they knew. Right now, he was only a suspect. A suspect who had been ID'd by a couple of eighty-year-old eyes from a distance. He knew they'd need a hell of a lot more evidence than that to nail him to the wall. Any first-year attorney could shoot him down if that's all he had. An eye chart tacked to the wall in the courtroom and the case would be history.

The halls in Gomez's apartment building were still permeated with the oppressive smell of mildew when they entered. They passed a couple of residents in the halls as they made their way to the second floor, but the neighbors stared straight ahead to avoid eye contact. Friendly place.

"Think either of us should be outside in case Señor Gomez gets spooked and makes for a window?" Herb asked.

"Second floor? Not likely."

They knocked on the door of apartment 2C. Inside, they could hear the sound of something drop, then footsteps. The steps stopped at the door and a voice asked, "Who's there?" with a degree of apprehension. Apparently, dropping in on each other for morning coffee in this building was not the norm.

"Police!" Chalky shouted with authority. "Open up!"

It was silent inside for a long moment, then Gomez asked again, "What do you want?" Chalky and Herb looked at each other. That response was definitely a bad omen.

"Open the door, Mr. Gomez—police!"

More silence.

Chalky got nervous. Maybe he should have listened to Herb.

"Tell me what you want first," Gomez said.

"Think we've got a live one," Chalky whispered to Herb. He pointed to the stairs. Herb drew his gun and headed down, tiptoeing the first few feet.

"Open the door, or I'll have to force the door!" Chalky said a bit louder after he waited about a minute to give Herb as much time as possible to reach the exterior window.

The footsteps inside retreated away from the door, as though Gomez was trying to sneak off. Chalky heard a muffled banging inside, then realized that Gomez was trying to break loose a reluctant, probably painted-closed window.

"Crap!" Chalky hated to be physical this early with that damned Southern Slam still lying there like a lump. He took a deep breath, pulled out his 9mm automatic, cocked it, and stood back.

The old, solid-paneled door sprung open with the first kick. Chalky entered with his gun extended. No one in the small living room. Just as he went through the bedroom door, a flash of red shirt disappeared out the bedroom window. Chalky ran to the sill and leaned out. A high bank was within jumping distance. Gomez was running along the driveway that led to the rear parking area. Herb dashed up with his gun drawn.

"You see him?" Chalky yelled from the window as Herb flashed past.

"He's mine," Herb shouted confidently, not breaking stride. Chalky was impressed with the way his arms and legs pumped. Chalky hung by his hands, then dropped to the grassy ground and rolled. His ankle pained him when he stood, but he followed as best he could. He had no way of knowing whether Gomez was armed or not, but they had to assume he was. If he was guilty as suspected, he sure had a hell of a motive to lay down some heavy fire. "Should have called for backup! Stupid!" Chalky grumbled as he hobbled along.

They ran through the parking lot, being cheered on by two or three people from windows, and entered a thick stand of cedar trees. Limping, Chalky fell farther behind. He could hear Herb yelling all the necessary threats in the distance, but it was plain that Gomez was ignoring it. The harder Gomez ran, the more it appeared that they had their man.

The good news is, we found the guy, the bad news is, he could run faster than we could, he could hear himself telling the captain.

They broke out onto a parallel street again. The red shirt was quite a way in the lead, with Herb about thirty yards behind. They turned a corner onto a side street called Millstone. Herb stopped, looked at Chalky, then waited for him. Breathing fast, Chalky limped up. Herb was gasping too and his face was flushed.

"See him?" Chalky asked. They stared down a long block of decrepit, time-worn storefront buildings.

"Had to go into one of these buildings. No alleyways, and he wasn't far enough ahead to have made the next corner."

"You take that side, I'll take this," Chalky said. They split up and walked down either side of the street, looking into doorways, glancing into windows, and trying doors as they went along. Most of the buildings on the street were abandoned or were struggling retail stores. On Sunday, all of them were closed. Political posters plastered the windows of the abandoned ones.

Coming from the distance, Chalky could hear the discordant strains of people singing, backed by an organ. Church music? he wondered. He passed a shuttered shoe shop, an oriental market of some kind, another vacant storefront with posters, then he was there.

The door to the storefront church was open. The entry went back between two display windows. Inside, a minister faced a group of some thirty to forty people sitting on plain folding metal chairs lined up with their backs to Chalky. The minister was droning about the sins of omission. Chalky thought he said emission at first, then flashed on his lack of performance last night. Yeah, that was almost a sin . . . well, maybe as far as Giselle was concerned.

Chalky holstered his gun before he entered the door, but the minister obviously caught the motion. Chalky smiled up at him. The minister glared at Chalky as though he expected him to steal a metal chair.

Heads bobbed up as Chalky edged by. Most of the people were older with years of living etched on their faces.

"Have a seat, you're welcome," the minister said. Now all heads turned Chalky's way. Chalky nodded and continued to the front. On the far right, in the first row, a Spanish-looking man tried to hide behind a mountain of a black man. The Spanish man's red shirt was unbuttoned and he was breathing hard. Gomez. How sweet it is, Chalky thought.

Chalky walked over and took a seat next to Gomez and smiled. He kept one hand on the butt of his gun inside his coat just in case. Gomez's eyes were like those of a frightened rabbit. He definitely had something to hide. The minister intoned his admonitions again and all heads turned back to the lectern. Chalky continued to stare at Gomez and smile.

"You want to do this easy or hard," Chalky whispered. Gomez leaned away from him as though his breath were bad.

"You can't 'rest me, I'm in a church," Gomez said in a surprisingly firm voice.

"That isn't true. We were in hot pursuit. That changes the rules a little. Why don't you come with us, we don't want any of these old people to get hurt, do we?"

The minister had slowed and all but stopped his sermon. He glared down at the men who were interrupting him. Herb walked up behind Gomez and sat. He smiled when Gomez looked over his shoulder.

Gomez leapt to his feet and screamed, "These men are trying to kidnap me and I want sanctuary!"

"Sanctuary?" Herb and Chalky asked in unison. Charles Laughton playing the Hunchback of Notre Dame flashed in Chalky's mind. The people sitting around them leapt up in a confusion of scraping chairs and crowded for the exit.

"Sanctuary!" Gomez repeated.

"You have it, my son," the minister said in a pompous voice. He stepped forward and stood in front of the three men. The black man jumped up and lumbered out. The crowd thinned magically and only a couple of stalwarts lingered by the door to see the outcome.

"Minister, we're policemen, and this man is simply wanted for questioning," Chalky said, holding up his badge. He took Gomez by the arm and Gomez jerked away.

"All the more reason to give this man sanctuary," the minister said. His voice was vibrant now, apparently excited about the possibility of having a cause. Sticking it to the police was a hobby with a lot of people in the Seattle area. Chalky glanced around and the last two stragglers elected to leave hurriedly.

"Look, Reverend—"

"Look, nothing. This man is a guest of the Church of Delphi," the minister said.

"Herb, why don't you take the minister here into his office and call the station. Have the captain explain what our rights are in this situation. I'll wait right here and keep an eye on our friend." Herb looked at Chalky questioningly, then stood and walked toward an inside office door. The minister seemed undecided for a moment, then followed, glowering suspiciously all the time. They closed the door after them. Chalky smiled.

"You made me hurt my ankle," Chalky said as he leaned into Gomez. "That really pisses me off."

"Ask me if I give a shit." Gomez's dark features had the same hatred of authority that Chalky had seen countless times in the streets.

"You like dogs?" Chalky asked him casually.

"I hate dogs almost as much as I hate cops." Gomez glanced around nervously at the empty church.

"Wrong answer," Chalky said.

Carlos stared up at the burned boards above him. A small room under the basement stairs of his aunt's house had remained intact and he'd brought his clothes and blankets here after he left Maria last night. His time was running out. They'd come for him when they found Jackson. Time. That's all he needed. Time to get the doctor. *That bitch!* After he got her, he'd leave. Go somewhere else. He'd use a different name and get a job in another hospital in another state. Some place warm this time, like California or Florida or someplace like that. *I'll sleep a couple hours, then go by her condo again. So tired.*

As he drifted off to sleep, he could hear the sounds of the children in the hot, dusty field playing kickball, and he could feel the burning orange sun on his bare skin. This time, it felt comforting. He smiled and ran to join them. To play for a while before his mother called again.

"How'd you get him out of there without making any noise?" Herb asked. Gomez glared at them from the rear seat of the car. His hands were handcuffed behind his back.

"It was an intellectual decision on his part," Chalky said. "Had something to do with pain thresholds and stuff like that."

"Anyway, the captain talked to the minister," Herb said. "Appealed to his civic responsibility and told him we had the right to remove him."

"And the minister said?"

"Quoted Scripture, lots of numbers and so forth. All amounted to the fact that he wasn't going to cooperate."

"How'd he react when he came out and we were gone?" Chalky smiled.

"Off the wall. He's going to file a formal complaint. Says he's going to call the television stations and picket our headquarters."

"Great," Chalky said. The captain was going to go off like Vesuvius—probably bury them in the ashes.

It took about a half hour to get to the station. They took Gomez in an interrogation room and read him his rights. He opted to clam up. Doggedly they asked him a series of questions that included: Where were you on the morning of the Joanne Pinkers crime? Gomez was tight-lipped and finally demanded to call his attorney after another half hour of nonproductive, one-sided questioning.

Chalky went into the captain's office, requested and got a search warrant listing the items they were looking for: any kind of cutting tools, pharmaceuticals, clothing or articles with blood on them. They stopped by the courthouse and found Judge Beauchamp, who happened to be in on a fluke. He signed it, and they were on their way to Gomez's apartment.

Before they had taken Gomez in, they had dropped back by his apartment and secured the door with a padlock they found on the counter. Getting back in required bolt cutters because they needed the key that was in Gomez's pocket.

"Not looking good," Chalky said as he leaned on the counter in the kitchen. They'd searched both the living room and kitchen. Just the bedroom to go.

"I haven't found anything even close to surgical tools," Herb said, glancing up from the cabinet he'd been searching. "I don't think the guy even cooks anything. Can't even find a paring knife."

They both walked into the bedroom. It seemed unpromising at best. The dark room had a single bed and a chair with clothes hanging over the back of it, a *Playboy* magazine lying on the floor, and a closet. Tin foil was taped on most of the single window that was still open. Nothing on or under the bed or the chair. They checked the carpeting around the edges of the room to see if it had been lifted up anywhere. It was tacked solid.

"If there's nothing in the closet, we're finished," Chalky said. "According to the records, this guy doesn't have a car either." They opened the door. The interior of the closet was stacked high with boxes that contained the names of drug companies.

Chalky looked at Herb and smiled. "Jesus, Gomez has enough drugs here to start a pharmacy."

"I thought they kept this stuff locked up," Herb said as he took the top box and opened it.

"Has to be stolen over a long period of time. They'd miss this much, even in a hospital that large."

"Must be working with someone who has access to drugs in the hospital. Figure Gomez sells the stuff, and they split the profit," Herb said.

Chalky nodded. It sounded logical. Chalky brought his clipboard out of the kitchen and they itemized the drugs. After forty-five minutes, they finally reached the bottom of the stack. The final box was large, unmarked, and clinked when they slid it.

Chalky opened the lid and looked inside. It was filled with surgical tools, stethoscopes, and assorted laboratory glassware.

"Now we're getting somewhere," Chalky said softly. He

gently picked up each tool by the end, studied it, then returned it to the box. He frowned. They all appeared to be new. Chalky closed the lid.

"Those look spanking new," Herb said, echoing what Chalky was thinking. Chalky nodded with a defeated expression.

Chalky picked up the large box and said, "Let's get this finished. I want to take them to forensics to check for blood residue. The drugs will go to the station as evidence." After they loaded all of the boxes into the car, they came back and checked all of his clothes and shoes for traces of blood. None showed evidence of stains, old or new. Chalky was aware that the bag that the old lady said she saw the man carrying was still on the missing list.

"You think we've got our man?" Herb asked.

"Wouldn't it be great," Chalky said, "but the evidence so far doesn't add up."

chapter//sixteen

Peggy slipped out of bed early Sunday morning, dressed, and walked into the hall softly. She closed the door to Carrie's room to keep from waking her, then speed-walked a three-mile loop through a tract of homes to the south of her condo. When she came back, breathing hard and refreshed, she took a brisk shower in cold water. By the time she'd finished, Carrie was up and clinking around, making coffee in the kitchen. Peggy slipped on a pair of slacks, a tank top, socks and tennies, then walked into the kitchen and said good morning. Carrie sat down heavily and frowned at her.

"How the hell can you be so damned cheerful this early?" Carrie asked.

"Because I'm perky and sweet."

"Jesus, spare me." Carrie rubbed her head. "How long does that coffee take anyway?"

"Look, if you're going to moan and groan until you've had your coffee, I'm going to walk down and check my mail slot. I only think to do it once or twice a week."

Carrie nodded and glared impatiently at the coffeepot.

Residual wind from the storm the prior night still whirred through the trees as Peggy walked quickly to the entrance of the complex to keep from getting chilled. The mailbox area was a structure with a shingled roof over it. Mail was delivered into boxes that the owners mounted on a horizontal board at chest level. Below them were numbered, open slots for oversize packages. Peggy noticed that there were four mailboxes mounted now. That meant another family was moving in shortly. She smiled. Four down, fourteen to go.

She opened her mailbox and withdrew a pile of bills and several advertising flyers. It took her a few seconds to sort them and realize that they were mostly junk mail. As she turned to leave, she glanced at the parcel boxes. The one that was tagged with her number contained a package covered with black plastic. She bent and pulled it out. The name "Dr. Chandler" was crudely written on a card taped to the box. The box was wrapped in plastic, like a trash bag had been cut to fit, then taped closed. She tilted it back and forth and studied it carefully. No postage and light in weight, she noted. It had to be hand-delivered. She felt a chill, then hurried to her condo, looking around as she walked.

Peggy slammed and locked the door of the condo. She was surprised that she was breathing hard because there was no one around to threaten her. She laid the mail on the counter and dropped the plastic-covered package on the table next to the coffee that Carrie had poured for her.

"What is it?" Carrie asked, glancing up from the cup cradled in both hands.

"I don't know." Peggy sat. She took a sip of her coffee, then leaned back in her chair.

"So, open it already." Carrie's eyes were more animated as her coffee did its job. "Don't you want to know?"

"I'm afraid to." Peggy's bare arms were freckled with goose bumps. She rubbed them and stared down at the package.

"Jeez, Pegs, you're really a basket case. What are you afraid of, a bomb?" Peggy stared at the package, trying to decide whether to open it or not. "You want me to do it?" Carrie asked. Peggy nodded, then stood apprehensively as though not wanting to be near it when she did. Carrie shook her head and smiled.

Carrie went to the counter and refilled her coffee cup. Reaching into a drawer, she withdrew a small pair of shears, then returned to the table. Peggy stood at the end of the table and rubbed her hands together nervously. Carrie chuckled as she energetically snipped through the plastic, slid the box out of the wrapping, and let the plastic drop to the floor.

The box had a shallow lid taped carelessly at the four corners.

She ripped off each piece of tape, then gripped the lid on either side. She glanced up at Peggy, smiled, then lifted it. . . .

Her eyes widened as she stared down.

Trying to understand . . .

What she was looking at.

Then Carrie screamed.

And dropped the box!

Peggy leapt back—

As the bloody contents spilled to the floor!

Chalky and Herb dropped off the tools from Gomez's apartment at the forensics lab. Parker worked alone and was preoccupied when they came in. He told Chalky that running tests on the tools was out because it was Sunday, and that they had to be submitted through the personnel in the front office anyway.

Finally, after he'd made the point that he was in charge, he became a bit more reasonable and indicated he'd try to work on them tomorrow. Chalky waited for the explosion about the dog being missing, but Parker chattered on about other things. When Parker looked away, Chalky checked under the desk for the cage that he'd kept the animal in. It was still there.

Driving back to the station, Herb asked, "You suppose Parker doesn't even know the dog's gone?"

"Possible. He really gets his head into his work. Parker's nickname is well deserved in a lot of ways, but he does a damned good job when he gets down to it," Chalky answered.

A call came over the radio for Chalky to report to Captain Stone's office as soon as they got into the station.

Chalky said, "You see how this program works? You come in on your own nickel, then they start to tell you where to go."

"What the hell could it be?" Herb asked. "I didn't think Stone was on duty today." Chalky shrugged and pressed the accelerator harder. Whatever it was, it was probably important. People usually took Sunday off and filed complaints on Monday.

The weather had cleared and the wind had calmed as they pulled into the lot at the station. Herb sat down and started to work on their report while Chalky went directly to Captain Stone's office. When he rapped on the door, a muffled sound came from the interior that he assumed meant "come in."

Stone's office was small and functional with the odor of pipe tobacco in the air. Chalky tried to remember when he'd ever seen Stone without his pipe. Today was no exception. A blond woman sat facing Stone. She turned when Chalky walked in.

"Dr. Chandler," Chalky said and smiled instantly. She returned his smile weakly. She wore slacks and a sweater and sat with both legs together, huddled over a small box on her lap. She held it with both hands as though it were something valuable. Her eyes were puffy, apparently from crying.

"She's got something in that box that might have some bearing on your Pinkers case," Stone said as he pointed at the box with his pipe.

Chalky considered the possibilities, then gave up. Still smiling, he sat in a hard leather chair next to her. "The suspense is killing me."

"I found this box in my mail slot this morning at home," Peggy said, "with this attached to it." She held out the piece of paper with her name crudely written on it. Chalky picked the paper up by the edge, looked at it, and laid it gently on the desk.

Noticing how carefully he handled it, Peggy asked, "I shouldn't have touched it, should I?" Chalky just smiled indulgently. Mishandling evidence was normal for anyone without training. She set the box on the desk, as though anxious to get rid of it. He stood, bent down, and removed the lid.

"Damn!" he said huskily with emotion.

Four furry legs.

Jammed tightly into the box, the bottom red with blood.

Two of the legs had black and white fur.

Chalky thought of the little dog at his apartment in the bathroom. He put the lid on the box, sat heavily in the chair, and whistled like a deflating tire. The excitement at seeing the doctor had disappeared.

He rubbed his chin, then said, "You're going to have to reconstruct the last few days for me. I want to know everyone you've seen or talked to."

"My life is the hospital. It would almost have to be someone who works there, wouldn't it?"

"We have a suspect in custody right now. When's the last time you picked up your mail before today?"

"Two, maybe three days ago." He shook his head.

"If he did it, that would have given him plenty of time to drop the box off."

"Captain, I have pictures of some suspects at my desk, I'd like to show her—see if she can pick the man out as someone she's had contact with." Stone nodded and stood, obviously anxious to get back to reading the morning paper.

The captain shook hands with her, said he was glad to meet her, gave her a manufactured smile, then turned to his desk. Chalky picked up the box, and she followed him to his desk. He offered her a seat. Chalky took the box and put it on a shelf in the adjacent room since he knew that it upset her.

Chalky quickly straightened his desk, then reached into a side drawer for his file of suspects. Herb walked in and Peggy nodded in recognition. Chalky explained quickly what had happened and asked Herb if he'd take the box to forensics for dusting and storage. "Use your own car and go home from there if you want to," Chalky suggested. Herb chuckled. After he left, Chalky opened the file. He took the same ten pictures from the file that he'd shown the old lady and handed them to her.

"One of these men is the man we have in custody. Go through them and study each face carefully. I want to know if you've had any contact with or talked to any of them within, let's say, the last week."

She studied each picture, then gradually laid them onto a growing pile. Chalky's frown grew deeper as she rejected each picture. When she laid Gomez's picture on the discards, he looked up at her for any flicker of recognition. Nothing. That disturbing feeling that nagged him earlier when he took the cutting tools to forensics got stronger.

"I haven't talked to any of them at any time," she said with conviction, then rubbed her forehead in frustration. "You told me about those two dogs, then I read in the newspaper this morning about them being found with their back legs amputated—this has to be them, right?"

"It's in the paper?" Chalky asked incredulously. She nodded. Somebody had a direct pipeline into the department, and he knew who it probably was.

"The only one of those men I recognize at all is that Carlos fellow," she said, gesturing to the pictures.

"Which one is he?" She picked his picture off the pile and handed it to Chalky.

"How do you know him?"

"I've never talked to him, but I got the impression that he was listening to a conversation I had with one of the nurses."

"That's all? What was the conversation about?"

"Joanne Pinkers. We were discussing the removal of her arms. She asked if it was done by a doctor, and I told her I didn't think so, that the work was too ragged and unprofessional."

"How did you know he was listening?"

"Well, I don't, for sure. It's just that he dropped some things from a cart he was pushing at that moment, then looked very self-conscious while picking them up. The timing was almost as though it was a response to what I said."

"The stitches? If you saw another surgical procedure performed by this same man, would there be anything about the way it was done that you might recognize?"

"Maybe," she said. "I know that whoever did it is right-handed, from the angle of the stitches. The way the flaps were cut are unique too. Distinctive in that they were overextended and uneven. That's why it didn't appear professional."

Chalky banged his forehead with the heel of his hand. It was something that he had not thought to ask anyone, and yet it was so obvious now that he knew. He remembered Gomez lighting a cigarette with his left hand while he was being questioned.

"What's wrong?"

"My stupidity," he said and smiled at her. "Nothing wrong with you." He looked at the picture, then the file. Carlos Martinez. He just moved to the top of the pile for questioning. His gut instinct and the thin evidence against Gomez so far were telling him that he was probably not the man they were searching for. There was plenty of cause to convict him of robbery, but nothing else.

"Would you have a few minutes to drive to my apartment with me?" Chalky asked.

Peggy stared at him. "I have a very upset friend who went to her apartment to get some more clothes for a longer stay with me. She's going to hang around until this thing is resolved. Can I call her first?" He nodded. "This *is* strictly business, isn't it?" she asked with a smile.

"Of course," Chalky said. "Trust me, this is nothing but business. Might have everything to do with the case."

"It is getting late in the day," she said, "but okay, if it's important."

"It'll be clear as black and white when we get there."

It was 3:30 in the afternoon as Carlos left the burned-out house and drove the van directly to Peggy's condo. He knew it was dangerous, but he felt he had to check it in the daylight. Everything was closing in on him now. Soon they'd be finding Jackson's body, then there was Maria. Pushy Maria.

Going back to his apartment was out of the question because they'd be searching for him soon, but he had to take care of the doctor before he left town. Last night had been one long, fitful vision that tortured him. When he awoke sweating and thrashing around, he was afraid to go back to sleep. The bad vision—the one about his mother—kept coming back and back. He was so exhausted his insides quivered with tension.

As he drove down the doctor's short street, beyond her condo at the end of the cul-de-sac, he noticed flags and signs for an open house. Next to it was a large moving van, parked and unloading. A new family was moving in. He idled by the doctor's condo and was confused about what was going on. A smaller truck was parked in front. The sign on the side had a shield and the name of an alarm company.

"Bitch didn't waste no time," he mumbled. All the doors of her condo were open, including the garage door, entrance door, and all the windows. He saw a man working inside the garage. Doing something on the window that looked out at the condo next door. Her Cherokee was gone.

A surge of excitement passed through him. This was his chance to learn more about her and where her weaknesses were so he could get to her. He went to the end of the street, passed the signs and moving van, and drove toward her condo. He

pulled past her condo and stopped in front of the empty home
next to it, away from the open garage where the man was working. He climbed from the van and gently shut his door. Out of
his sight, he could hear the man still tapping in the garage.

Gotta hurry, just have minutes. He made his way across the
lawn, hesitated at the front door, and listened. Hearing no interior sounds, he made his way into the entry, moved lightly up
the stairs, and disappeared into the master bedroom.

"You took the dog without permission?" Peggy asked as
Chalky finished telling her how the dog came to be at his apartment.

"Yeah, I suppose I could get chewed out about it, but sometimes you have to do what you have to do," he said as he braked
in front of his apartment building. He was almost sorry they
were there. Being close to her in the car felt intimate, and her
subtle perfume was feminine and stimulating.

"I know what you mean," Peggy said, thinking about how
she was going to have to put Fortsam in his place. He ran
around and opened the car door for her. She smiled and appeared pleased that he was so anxious to be gallant.

Now, if I can just keep from acting like a geek, he thought.
Chalky walked to the door and hesitated for a second. No barking from inside. Good dog. As he opened the door, he realized
that the dog had no name yet. Good Dog would have to do for
now. The name the Verig woman had given her, Princess, was
definitely out.

Chalky glanced around the apartment and realized that it
looked pretty good for a bachelor pad. He was thankful that
he'd gotten the bug to clean the place up, otherwise he would
have been embarrassed to bring the doctor here.

She sat in the living room and waited while he went down the
hall to the bathroom. When he opened the door, the dog barked
sharply and energetically wagged her tail. With satisfaction, he
noticed a wet spot on the newspaper. He picked her up, and she
licked his hand. He took a towel and gently wrapped her and
carried her in to Peggy.

"Aww," she said involuntarily and reached out to take her.
The dog's tail registered pleasure.

"Check her carefully and see if you see any similarity in the stitching," Chalky said. He went into the kitchen and put on some coffee as she talked in calming tones to the little dog in the living room. As Chalky slid the pot into the machine, he wondered if this would be the right time to ask her for a date, then remembered her puffy eyes.

"Who could do this?" she asked when he walked in. The dog was lying on her back on Peggy's lap. She smiled at the puppy, but her eyes glistened. Chalky cleared his throat and bit the inside of his lip.

"What do you think—about the stitches?"

"Similar in many ways. Definitely a righty too, but then so are eighty percent or more of the people."

"No way to be sure?"

"The only thing I can say is that the stitches appear to be taken with the same triple-O nylon as Joanne Pinkers."

"That's something." The dog wiggled to turn over, and Peggy laid her gently on the floor. She lowered her head onto her paws and closed her eyes. "Damn, I just realized. I forgot to get dog food."

She smiled warmly and said, "You're a special guy, Chalky. Not many people would take a dog with this problem."

"Want some coffee?" he asked. Embarrassed, he wanted to change the subject.

Peggy nodded yes, and said, "Black, please." He poured a couple of cups and brought them into the room. The dog was sleeping now. Chalky suddenly felt awkward. The business end of their visit was over, and he was faced with small talk.

"You like your new condo?" he asked absently. He wanted to say something else but lost his nerve.

"I did, but right now, it feels a little threatening."

"That offer of a gun still holds. I have a couple of spares." She shivered, then rubbed her arms. "Still not comfortable with the idea?" he asked.

She nodded yes.

They sat for a long moment. Peggy stared at the sleeping puppy while he stared at her.

"You're very beautiful," he said huskily.

She was startled, then said, "Thanks. If I weren't so upset, I'd appreciate the compliment more." He took that as a cue not to go any further. "I really should be getting home. When I talked to Carrie, I told her I'd return in about an hour. She'll be worried."

"You're right." Chalky picked up the sleeping dog and took her into the bathroom. The dog barely woke, then collapsed asleep onto the pile of towels. "Hang in there, kid, I'll be back with some chow in a couple of hours." He glanced up. Peggy was standing in the doorway. He straightened. Her eyes glistened, and she bit her knuckle.

"I'm so scared," Peggy whispered. She moved gently against him and put her head on his shoulder. Chalky was taken aback, but it seemed natural to put his arms around her. She was warm and fragrant and so vulnerable.

They stood for what seemed like minutes to Chalky as her body shook with small sobs. He rested his chin on her forehead, turned, and kissed her temple gently. That too seemed natural. Suddenly she stepped back and rubbed her eyes.

"Sorry. Guess that's been building up." She tried to smile. Looking a little embarrassed, she walked toward the front door. He had an empty feeling, as though something valuable had been taken away. He wanted to kiss her, but knew he should wait. And asking for a date would have been awkward after her release of emotion. If it was going to happen, there would be better opportunities.

They drove in comfortable silence to the station, both lost in their own thoughts. Chalky dropped Peggy at her car in the parking lot. She asked him to wait a minute, then went to the rear of the Cherokee and opened it. She sorted through a case and pulled out a small sample bottle of antibiotics, brought it back, and handed it to him through the window.

"Your dog is basically very healthy. Right now, you only have to worry about infection. Break these in two and give her one twice a day, okay?"

Chalky thanked her profusely, offered to pay, but she refused. Said they were samples and were free. He started his car, and she leaned into his open window. As Peggy self-consciously fiddled with her keys, she said, "By the way, I'd like it a lot if you'd call me Peggy, please."

"I'd like that too." He smiled as she walked away.

Whatever happened the rest of the day, that put it in the plus column.

chapter//seventeen

When Peggy pulled in her garage that evening, the alarm man was still working—punching buttons, listening to beeps, checking windows. Anything having to do with electronics was an absolute mystery to her. She went upstairs, lay on the bed, and waited for him to finish. Her closet slider was open, and she wondered idly why he had to open that door. The tension of the last couple of days had drained her energy.

Carrie arrived with two large suitcases. When Peggy got up and helped carry them into the spare bedroom, she was amused. Carrie had enough clothes for an extended trip to Europe. While Carrie unpacked, Peggy swore her to secrecy, then told her about the black and white dog at Chalky's apartment. Peggy was touched with the way Chalky had treated the animal. How people related to and viewed animals was always a criterion she used in evaluating their warmth. Anyone who was cruel to one was checked off her list immediately. In telling Carrie, she intentionally left out the part about Chalky holding her in his arms. It would have just set Carrie off into another anti-male tirade.

At 6:30, the security man called her down and went over the operation of the system. Peggy was concerned about protection while she was gone, but primarily worried about someone breaking in while she slept. When she went to bed at night, there was a different sequence of buttons she had to push to arm the system. If a window or a door were opened in the night, the siren would go off instantly. Peggy was unsure what she'd do if that happened, besides panic, but at least she'd know if someone had entered. She paid the man, and he left. She fingered the brochure he gave her to study. Remembering everything he'd told her about all the possible functions seemed overwhelming. The only thing she really felt good about was that she'd told him about the garage door. He turned a couple of screws on the back of the opener, and now the damned thing worked like a champ.

Peggy studied the brochure, then dismissed it from her mind. She felt comfortable with Carrie here. She decided to read the brochure tomorrow and figure out how it worked.

Maria Lopez was a sound sleeper, so when her mother called her apartment at six in the evening and she failed to answer, her mother was amused instead of concerned. She usually called Maria at that time to talk for a couple of minutes before she got ready for work.

When her mother called at 6:30 without getting an answer, her mother got worried and walked the block and a half to her apartment to find out what, if anything, was wrong.

"Carlos?" Cooper pounded on the door again and there was still no answer. "Come on, man, I come to pick you up, we're going to be late." He raised his voice a bit and it echoed down the quiet hall.

He felt guilty about abandoning Carlos after he promised he'd pick him up, so he decided to stop by to keep his word. Cooper had yet to talk to him, so had no way of knowing whether Carlos had gotten his note. Besides, the note was the wrong way to handle it. If he was going to renege, he'd have to do it in person, that was the only way—the way his mama had taught him.

The door across the hall squeaked open, and a voice said, "Keep it down, idiot," then closed.

"Keep this down," Cooper said softly. He reached up and turned the knob. Crazy mother doesn't ever lock it, nohow, he thought. It was dark inside when it creaked open.

He stepped into the living room and stopped for a moment, trying to let his eyes adjust to the dim light that filtered in the dirty window. It was deathly still and Cooper was afraid to turn on a light.

He glanced toward the bedroom door. It was open a crack and light flickered through the gap. Cooper remembered Carlos huddled naked in the room, with the candles burning, then silently admonished himself for being stupid enough to return. This spooky man made the hair stand up on the back of his neck.

"Carlos?" he asked tentatively. No mumbling came from the room like before, only silence. Get away from here, you moron—just git! He stood for a moment, arguing with himself, then moved toward the door. Although Carlos was strange and hostile, Cooper had a certain fascination about this crazy boy. His curiosity strained at the leash. A quick glance, then he was out of here.

The smell of candle wax was strong—as though it had been burning for hours. He pushed the door open and peeked in. The candles on both sides of the bed had burned down to the nub, and the wax lay in puddles around the bases.

The smell of raw feces hit his nose—

Cooper flinched away in revulsion. His mouth was suddenly dry. He knew his voice would scratch if he tried to speak.

A form lay on the bed, faceup, under the bedspread, unmoving. A small, frail figure. Draped on the pillow, the hair exposed above the bedspread was long and black. A woman's hair. Cooper froze, waiting for some movement, but there was none. In addition to the foul smell, the air in the room was heavy with strange odors. Medicine, metallic—sort of coppery, moisture, warmth, and smoke.

He thought, Man, check it out, then get the hell out of here! Where does it say, you got to check anything? Get moving now! You got no business here.

He scanned the room, then glanced quickly into the shadows in back of him, half expecting someone to be there. If someone had been, he knew his heart would have stopped. He was alone with whoever was in that bed.

Cooper inched to the foot of the bed. The candlelight flickered off the walls as they threatened to go out. His skin crawled. Whatever happened, he was staying away from this place. No—never coming back no matter what my mama says, he thought.

He walked to the side of the bed and reached for the top of the thin chenille bedspread. The candle sputtered, and he yanked his hand away from the cover. Damn!

Steeling himself, he grabbed the blanket, ripped it toward the bottom of the bed, and jumped back at the same time.

His throat closed on the sound that leapt to his throat—

"My God," he croaked. He knew she was dead without feeling her pulse.

Chalky surveyed the food he'd bought for his refrigerator. He'd cleaned all the plates of unidentifiable green things the other night and had removed everything down to the wilted lettuce and celery. To start fresh had cost him almost a hundred dollars. He picked up the block of cheese and laid it on the counter. The small dog was at his feet, lying on a towel. Her front legs pushed her body up, showing real interest for the first time.

"I know you're going to get spoiled as hell, but what the hey," he said as he cut off a piece of cheddar and gave it to her. He shook a pill from the small bottle of antibiotics, cut one in half, and wrapped it in the next piece. It disappeared just like the first one.

"Peggy to me—to you—with love." The dog watched him intently. Her eyes were brighter. "You're a good dog, you make me feel good." He picked her up and looked at the stumps of her legs, then shook his head. Getting used to what that crazy had done was going to take time. The stitches were pulled tight and were a normal pink color. No sign of infection. He set her down gently and opened a can of dog food. Putting half of it in a bowl, he then carried her and the bowl into the bathroom. She was eating enthusiastically when he closed the door. He went into the living room and checked his watch. Ten o'clock, and he was feeling sleepy. He thought of getting a beer, then rejected it. Picking up a novel by Dean Koontz, he opened it to his placemark. The lead character in the book was a lot like him— manipulated and running all over hell with no idea what was going on.

The phone rang. Damn! On Sunday it had to be bad news. He glanced at the clock again, sighed, and picked up the receiver.

"Yeah?" He listened for a full minute, pulled out a piece of paper and wrote down an address, then said, "I'm on my way."

Beth was annoyed when he called, saying Herb had worked all day on his day off, and that had to be enough. Chalky was silent. Beth knew he was just doing his job, but leaned on him anyway. She reluctantly gave the phone to Herb who sounded almost as upset. Chalky could hear the sounds of loud voices and laughter in the background. Apparently Bernie and his family had made it.

"You want to pass?" Chalky asked. "I can handle it."

"And listen to you piss and moan for days, forget it. Who is it this time?"

"We don't know who right now. More important is where."

"You're not going to tell me, right."

"That's your penalty for being bitchy with me. You have to wait 'til we get there."

"You're really hard to like," Herb said.

"You love me, admit it."

"Swing by. I'll be ready."

As Chalky got in the unmarked car he'd borrowed and started it, he was filled with a mixture of déjà vu and extreme irritation. It was going to be a long night. A murder scene could take hours. He wondered how it would be to have a job that had regular hours. Boring as hell, he decided.

Herb was waiting on the curb and jumped in the car as soon as it stopped. It took another fifteen minutes to reach the scene of the crime. They had the right address all right. Three black-and-whites sat in front with their lights flashing, plus the coroner's wagon and a couple of unmarked cars. What a crowd. They pulled into the driveway and parked, then went up the steps of the aging apartment building.

"God, these places all look the same after a while," Chalky said as he recognized the smell of mildewed carpeting when they walked into the hall.

"Okay," Herb said. "Enough with the games, already. Who lives here?"

"Carlos Martinez."

"You're shitting me. And the victim?"

"Stone-cold. Young woman. No name yet."

"Why'd they call us?" Herb asked.

"Arms," Chalky said, making a slicing motion near his shoulder. "Gone." Herb winced.

"Jesus. Dead? Sounds like our sicko has graduated to the big leagues."

A young detective met them in the hall and gave them the information he had. He'd called the coroner and crime-scene people before he was told Chalky and Herb were working on the no-arms-lady case. They thanked him for the work he'd done and he left, glad to be going home.

Chalky and Herb looked around at the gray, Spartan living room where a young black man sat nervously on the dirty couch talking to a patrolman. They shook their heads. The bedroom was lit brightly and the sound of male voices came from the doorway.

The patrolman glanced up, stopped writing, and sauntered over. The three of them walked to the other side of the room and talked in hushed tones.

They made introductions around, then the patrolman said, "His name's Cooper. Works at Crosier Community. Stopped by to pick up this Martinez guy. Nobody answers, so he walks in and finds the stiff in the other room." He motioned toward the bedroom.

"He know the girl?" Chalky asked.

"He just knows her as Maria. Doesn't have any idea what her last name is. She works with them at Crosier makin' beds and stuff like that." Chalky glanced at Herb. Martinez was the man they had been looking for. "According to this Cooper guy, she had the hots for this Martinez, but he can't see her for dirt."

"They weren't dating?" Chalky asked.

"Hell, according to him, Martinez wouldn't give her the time of day. Last time this Cooper saw her was last night about eight or nine o'clock. Didn't see her the rest of the evening then. He assumed she went home or something."

Chalky thanked the officer, then went and talked to Cooper, who could only add that he thought that "Carlos is one strange dude," in his words. They asked him to hang around for a few more minutes, then went to the door of the bedroom where the men were finishing up.

Chalky stood by the door and asked, "Ready for us?" Lyle Marshall from the coroner's office walked over to them and snapped off his pair of rubber gloves.

"Ready as we'll ever be. Going to take her out when you finish." He glanced around the depressingly dingy room and smiled wryly. "Slice of heaven, huh?"

Chalky and Herb edged up to the waxen nude figure on the bed. Her thin, well-formed body in life would have been seductive, but in death was chilling. Her skin was bluish-white in contrast to her shiny black hair, but their eyes were drawn to where her arms should have been and the neatly sutured stumps. The bed was covered with caked-over blood that had dried to a blackish-red.

Chalky noticed dried semen on the edge of the sheets and on the stomach of the body. The odor of excrement, blood, medicine, and candle smoke made their stomachs do the rumba.

Lyle watched from the door as they checked each stump carefully. Even with Chalky's limited expertise, he could recognize the right-handed stitching. It was something he'd prefer not to be an expert on. He had a sample of the work sleeping in his bathroom at home.

Lyle said, "Liver temperature's about fifty-eight degrees. Figure she bought it around nine to ten o'clock last night." Lyle smiled. Just another day at the office for him. Dead people were his business. The skin on his face was stretched tight, his cheeks were drawn, and his complexion was sallow. Reminded Chalky of the guy who always played the undertaker in the old black-and-white movies, circa 1950s, except Lyle had more hair.

"The arms?" Chalky asked.

Lyle shrugged his shoulders and said, "Gone."

"Gone?" Herb said. "Jesus, let me off at the next stop, this is getting weirder all the time." He rubbed his stomach and swallowed deeply.

"Raped?" Chalky asked.

"Won't know for sure until we do the tests, but my guess would be no," Lyle said.

"Bleed to death?"

"Check her neck closer," Lyle said. Chalky and Herb bent and studied her throat. Both of them tried to avoid looking into her filmed-over eyes. Yellow and blue marks lined her neck on both sides. Her tongue protruded slightly. When they forced themselves to check her eyes, they noticed the whites and the lids were blotched with broken veins.

"Strangled her?" Chalky asked.

"Not a lot of question about it," Lyle said. "Son of a bitch cut her arms off and sewed up the stubs neat as a Thanksgiving turkey. She survived that, I'd guess, barely, then he strangled her. We'll confirm it on the autopsy, of course, but right now I'm ninety percent."

"So, you think Gomez and Martinez are working together?" Herb asked Chalky.

"I think Gomez is a thief, nothing more," Chalky said. "People who do this sort of thing don't exactly make deep and long-lasting relationships."

"I guess so. Would be hard to find two people anywhere with this kind of a perversion. You thinking Martinez is a loner then?" Herb asked.

"Can't see much doubt about it, right now he's elected as far as I'm concerned," Chalky said. They stepped out of the room while two men bagged her body and removed it. Lyle smiled, nodded, and was gone.

Herb and Chalky searched the apartment for additional evidence, but found nothing that would give them a clue to Martinez's whereabouts. Martinez had obviously left in a big hurry. Clothes were scattered in the bedroom and lay on the floor of the closet. No evidence of the satchel either.

They went into the living room and stood for a couple minutes watching the activity wind down around them.

"I think we need to get to the hospital," Chalky said.

"You think he's going to be just hanging around?"

"Possible. We're not dealing with a Phi Beta Kappa here, you know. He probably figures it'll take days to find her, that he's got some slack."

After talking to Cooper for a few minutes more, they took him with them. They wanted the vehicles and people out of there as soon as possible with a couple of uniforms left on stakeout inside the apartment in case Martinez came back in the middle of the night. It was 9:45 as they raced through the dark streets. Cooper was quiet in the rear seat while twisting his hands in his lap.

"You think he'll put up much of a fight?" Herb asked as he checked his 9mm automatic and clatched a round into firing position.

"I hope he does," Chalky said under his breath. "This guy needs to have his ticket canceled. If they put him in the cashew ward, he might escape and start again." On the way, Chalky slammed into a parking lot and pulled up in front of a pay phone. "I want to call Peggy," he said, and was out the door. Peggy's phone rang four times before she answered. If she had been sleeping, there was no way to tell.

"We've narrowed down the search for this crazy," he said after he asked her if everything was all right. He told her where he'd been and what they'd found. Maria was a stranger to her.

"But you said you had a suspect," she said.

"We found her in the apartment of the guy you picked out, that Carlos. We're pretty sure he's the man we want."

"God." Her voice quivered.

"Be sure you don't let anyone in tonight unless you absolutely know who it is. Your alarm working?"

"Yes, but I don't know how to set it," she said in a frustrated tone of voice.

"Take the time to figure it out. I have to go. I'll drive by your place later to make sure you're okay if we don't pick up Carlos."

"Thanks, you're thoughtful." Her voice was softer.

"It's the least I can do for someone I'm crazy about," he said, then hung up before she could answer. He had shocked himself and stared at the phone for a moment. It had just popped out.

When Chalky got into the car and swung onto the street, he was smiling from ear to ear.

Carlos stretched out. He was lying in the white van parked in the trees. His mind was in a fevered state. He'd started toward Peggy's condo, then had to retreat to the truck when his ears began ringing and the multicolored visions marched in front of his eyes. He had stumbled back and dragged himself inside the van before he lost consciousness. Now, he twitched and sweated, re-

living the hell of the dark death room over and over in his mind.
Outside, the rising wind masked the sound of his groaning.

Peggy settled into bed and fell asleep hugging her pillow. *It's
the least I can do for someone I'm crazy about*, kept going
through her mind. The games were finished—he'd said the
words. She thought about getting up and figuring how to set the
alarm, but she was too tired. Besides, Carrie had her gun and
Chalky was coming by later to check on her. She felt safe and
sleepy.

Crosier Community was lit up and glowed a welcome as they
drove around to the side of the building at Cooper's direction.

"This is where you go in?" Chalky asked of Cooper as he
nodded to a side door. Cooper said yes and continued rubbing
his hands. Chalky idled into the middle of the lot. He parked in
a spot he hoped would be inconspicuous.

"All right if I don't walk through the door with you guys?"
Cooper asked. Chalky smiled and said okay. He could understand why a black man would be reluctant to appear to be too
friendly with the police.

"Good idea," Chalky said. "Wait about ten minutes before
you go in. I'm hoping if he's there, we can take him without a
big fuss, but you never know." Cooper smiled. He liked that
idea. "Time cards are right inside the door?" Chalky asked.
Cooper nodded.

"Who's your supervisor?"

"Miss Jackson, 'cept she disappeared last night too."

"Disappeared? Why wasn't it reported?"

"No big deal, I guess. They's people coming and going all the
time in housekeeping." Cooper was getting more nervous.

"When was she gone?"

"About the same time as Maria, last night. Lordy. You figure
he did her too?"

"Probably coincidence," Chalky said. "She's probably in
there working right now. Wait ten minutes at least, you hear."
Cooper nodded. His smile was gone. Chalky had the feeling
he'd wait a lot longer than ten minutes before he came in, if he

came in at all. Chalky and Herb walked across the lot and in the side door.

It was warm inside. They went up to the time clock and shuffled through the cards. When halfway finished, a guard looked out a hallway window wearing a frown and a questioning expression. Herb smiled and held up his badge. The guard nodded, watched them for a moment, then disappeared back into the room.

"Not only isn't he punched in, there isn't even a card for him here," Chalky said as he ruffled the cards in annoyance with his fingers. The third person they asked directed them to where the housekeeping supervisor could be found and they went to the stairwell leading to the basement. They clanked down the steel stairs, not wanting to wait for an elevator, then walked in the direction they thought the office to be.

The heat and humidity were stifling as they passed the laundry. The women working inside bent over the machines and tables, and their arms and faces shone with sweat. Chalky poked Herb on the arm and said, "See, you don't have it so bad."

"I'll trade with them, they don't have to work with you." Chalky chuckled. "You think this Martinez will shoot it out?" Herb asked.

"If he has a gun. This guy is capable of anything—anything at all."

Carlos jerked when a limb from a tree broke off in the wind and banged the side of the van. He was lying on his back staring at the ceiling of the van. Carlos rubbed the sleep from his eyes, sat up, and looked around. He shivered like a dog shaking water from its fur, then reached down and rubbed his pants. They were wet and cold to the touch, and his mouth felt dry. He'd been sweating and tossing around. His body ached and he felt drained of energy. This had been one of the worst visions so far. He shook again.

What if I don't come back the next time, he thought. Death carried no fear, no threat, but living and reliving that same vision, over and over again for eternity would be many times worse.

He wavered and stared through unfocused eyes, then the

whirring of the gentle wind and the night sounds finally returned him to the present.

"Bitch!" he spat. One last thing he had to do before he could drive out of town. He had almost four hundred dollars and enough clothes to get by on. It was a big country, and when he finished with her, he'd just start driving and let the road lead him to a new life.

Carlos crawled painfully on his hands and knees to the side door of the van and slid it open. The cold night air was like a blow to his wet body. He shivered and pulled on a sweater. Grabbing his bag, he jumped to the ground and slid the door closed.

It was time.

chapter//eighteen

The small office had a hand-printed sign saying simply, "Miss Jackson—Supervisor." Chalky and Herb opened the door. A short black woman looked up from the desk. They introduced themselves and asked if she was Miss Jackson. The girl smiled, said no, and gave her name as Jean. She appeared nervous and worried. Said she'd called Miss Jackson's home after she failed to check in this evening and nobody answered. Miss Jackson lives alone, she said.

"When was she last seen?" Chalky asked.

"About eight or eight-thirty last night," the woman said. "Just disappeared after she was supposed to talk to that Martinez boy. You think she's okay?"

Chalky and Herb glanced at each other.

"I assumed she went home sick when she didn't show up for lunch. We was supposed to eat lunch together," she added.

"This Martinez, you seen him tonight?" Chalky asked.

She shook her head no.

"That boy is plum crazy," Jean said. "Lots of us stayed as far away from him as possible. Miss Jackson say she going to have to fire him for sure, 'cause he don't show up regularlike."

"Where was Miss Jackson last seen?"

"She gone talk to Martinez right here, in this office." She shook her head and tears shimmered in her eyes. "I know something done happened. That Martinez, he so crazy. She always be havin' to dig him from a corner somewhere."

"Digging him out?" Chalky asked.

"Yeah. She mentioned he had a room where he hid down here

somewhere. Everytime he be missing, she find him in there lying down, actin' strange and crazy."

"Where's this room she was talking about," Herb asked.

"This floor, down that a way somewheres, toward maintenance." She pointed in the direction. "I never knew for sure, and I didn't really care. I just wanted to stay away from him."

Chalky and Herb thanked her and walked back into the humid hallway. The lights were dim down the long, dank corridor. Chalky reached over unconsciously and patted the gun in his holster.

"You really think he could be there?" Herb asked.

"Doubtful, but worth checking." Chalky led the way. As they walked along, Chalky looked in the doors on the left; Herb the ones on the right. In a couple of the unmarked doors, people glanced up from worktables. They smiled, and he nodded and closed the door. One room was filled to the ceiling with solvents and cleaning equipment. As they continued on, their footsteps sounded hollow and otherworldly.

Another room was jammed with discarded equipment, gurneys, and garden equipment. The throbbing of heavy machinery became louder as they approached the turn in the hallway. They followed the bend to the right. Chalky opened the first door on the left. A foul odor assaulted Chalky's nose and he grimaced. No sign or marking on the door.

"Hello there," Chalky whispered. He recognized that smell, no question. The interior was inky black. Chalky fumbled along the wall for a switch and found it. A single bulb snapped to life, illuminating a small, jumbled room with cabinets across the rear wall.

"Herb! Over here," he called to Herb in the hall. Chalky pulled his gun and moved cautiously into the room. Carlos was probably gone, but until he was caught, care was the order of the day. With his gun out, Herb followed him through the door.

"Jesus," he heard Herb whisper and knew the stench had hit him too. "What's that?" Herb asked.

"It sure isn't rat shit," Chalky said, then held his hand up to his lips as he worked his way around the room, looking under and in back of the cartons and debris.

Chalky finally reached the back of the room and walked to

the end of the cabinets and peered into the narrow space behind
them. The stench was stronger here. He winced and had to force
himself to keep from retreating. In the reflected light from the
weak bulb, Chalky could make out a huge mound under white
sheets.

Herb came up behind him and watched him for a clue to what
he could see in the thin opening.

"I'm afraid we've found Miss Jackson," Chalky said, talking
in a normal tone now. He holstered his gun.

"That what that smell is?" Herb asked.

"Body gases combined with excrement," Chalky said.
"Smell it in a confined space once and you don't forget it."

"Can you get in there," Herb asked. Even as he asked,
Chalky crawled on his hands and knees into the opening.

"I'm going to have to burn my clothes," Chalky said when he
was almost there. He was calm. Whoever it was had to be dead
and no threat. Chalky pulled the sheet away. A wave of odor
came stronger. He tried to breathe through his mouth as he felt
for a pulse on the woman's swollen wrist. Seemed stupid, but it
was part of the job.

Finally, he stood and quickly worked his way back to where
Herb waited.

"Let's get the hell out of here," Chalky said and burst into the
hallway. He bent over and took in huge gulps of untainted air.

"Call the coroner and Detective Latcka. I want him to beat it
down here and handle this for us so we can take off." Herb went
to Miss Jackson's office and called the station because his portable unit failed deep in the building.

"Miss Jackson, she dead?" Jean asked Chalky while he was
waiting.

Chalky nodded and said he was sorry, but she ignored him
because she was sobbing so hard. While they tried to calm her,
Chalky thought of Peggy. It was beyond question this Martinez
was out of control now. The fact he had Peggy selected as a victim made his blood run cold. The image of her in her condo and
Martinez wandering around free filled him with a feeling of un-
ease, but he had to wait. Time dragged before Latcka finally
showed up. Chalky was thankful he'd gotten there before the
crime-scene people—saved the long explanations.

They filled him in on what had happened, then Chalky turned and ran down the hall with Herb following. He took the steps two at a time, ran to the door, and into the night. He could hear Herb's shoes pounding the hall floor behind him.

They were in the car and racing for the exit when Herb asked, "You want to call her first?" He withdrew the mike from its holder.

"We can be there in fifteen minutes. I'll drive flat out. When we get there, if he hasn't shown, I'll spend the night in her living room, you can go home." Chalky could feel his stomach churning. He wondered, She *is* safe, isn't she? She had an alarm system and her girlfriend is there with a gun. Relax. You're just tearing yourself up over nothing.

Chalky had his lights flashing and siren going as they raced up the on-ramp to the I-90 and he kept the car at a constant eighty miles an hour. The traffic was light and they barreled along until they reached the off-ramp at Issaquah. A mile from the ramp, Chalky called dispatch and told them to call Issaquah police and let them know he was investigating in the area. He only hoped they could get through this without any backup help. Working with these small-town police departments could get real sticky.

When he got within a mile of her condo, he turned off his rotating light and siren and slowed to fifty miles an hour. His heart thudded in his chest as he pulled off the main drag and made the turn onto her dark street.

Little after eleven. He slowed and idled past her condo. It was dark. He rolled down the window. No strange sounds or screams. He breathed deeply. Feeling a little foolish, he drove to the end of the cul-de-sac, turned around, and considered driving back to the station.

"You know, these backyards would be a great place for someone to park and wait," Chalky said as he slowed again. He switched on his spotlight and directed it into the trees alongside of each of the condos as he passed. He slammed on his brakes and came to a stop.

"What?" Herb asked. "You see something?"

"Not sure," Chalky said, then backed up slowly. He stopped again. He shined the light off into the trees behind a vacant unit.

A flash of white. "Come on." He pulled the emergency and grabbed his flashlight, then climbed out and ran alongside the condo into the rear yard. Chalky had to step carefully because scrap lumber was strewn around on the ground. As he got closer, he could definitely see something white in the trees. He focused his light on the last small stand of trees, then slowed. It was a vehicle. A white van.

Chalky drew his gun and approached the van from the rear. The only thing he could hear was his heart beating, the sound of the wind in the trees, and in the background the sound of his cruiser idling.

When he moved along the side of the van, he looked up. A bunch of flowers drawn in airbrush right behind the rear window. The name of the flower shop had been crudely painted out in an off-color white. Whoever did it must have liked the flowers, but wanted to get rid of the name.

He jerked open the door and said, "Police!"

Empty.

He ran to the other side and slid the side door open. Inside, there was nothing but a few tools and a blanket lying on the flat floor. Chalky reached over and pulled the blanket to him. He unrolled it and jumped when its contents tumbled to the floor.

Two bloody arms.

Cut off just below the shoulders.

A woman's arms. Small. Maria's.

Herb came up in back of him and said, "Jesus, no," when he saw the white arms.

"Come on," Chalky said. "He's in there now!"

Chalky hesitated for a second, then aimed at the rear tires and fired two shots. The tires exploded and went flat instantly. The sound echoed among the deserted buildings. The two men ran to the idling cruiser. Chalky grabbed the key from the ignition, then raced up two doors to Peggy's condo. At the front door, Chalky hunched down and called dispatch and told them what he'd found and about the shots he fired into the van. He told them to call Issaquah for backup, but it was questionable if he could wait. Wait for backup, they told him. He switched off and slipped the transmitter into his inside pocket.

"I can't wait, partner. I know he's in there now. We can't afford the time," Chalky whispered.

"I'm with you," Herb said. "You want me to go around back?"

"Go!" Chalky yelled and slammed into the door. It held and he backed up and kicked it again. No time for niceties like knocking. This time the door exploded away from the frame and he was in the dark living room.

No alarm. Dammit, Peggy. Why didn't you set it? he wondered.

"Peggy!" he yelled up the stairs. He fired a shot into the ceiling. If Carlos was up there, he wanted him to know for sure he was here so Carlos'd stop whatever he was doing.

A muffled sound came from the darkness, then a scuffling. He approached the foot of the stairs cautiously. A dead man was no help to anyone. "Peggy! Police!" he shouted again.

A gunshot roared; a muzzle flash lit the interior—

The bullet slammed into the wall next to him and sprayed his face with plaster fragments.

"Jesus!" he yelled and fell to the floor.

Another gunshot and the tinkle of glass as another bullet hit the front window.

"Get out of here or I'll shoot again!" A woman's voice with a waver in it. God, that's Peggy's friend.

"Police! Don't shoot. Police! Let me turn on the light." It was quiet from the top of the stairs. Chalky stood and flipped the switch. The light made spots dance in front of his eyes for a second.

"Who are you? What the hell are you doing? What were those gunshots outside?" The woman was standing at the wood railing with the gun pointed into the living room.

"Police, Sergeant Fuchs." As he climbed the stairs, she lowered her gun. "Is there an intruder in here?" She just shook her head, confused. Her eyes were heavy with sleep. He ran to the landing.

The door to the master bedroom was closed. He opened it. The light from the hall shone on the bed where Peggy lay, tied at the wrists and ankles, naked, a piece of tape across her mouth. She was struggling, trying to get loose. Two candles were on either side of the bed. They were unlit and one nightstand held a display of medical instruments. A leather bag was on the floor. He glanced up. The window was open and the miniblinds fluttered in the breeze. He scanned the room quickly, then ran to the window and looked out. In the distance, he could hear the sound of yelling and footsteps.

"Herb! You okay?" he yelled as he leaned through the window. Herb was too far away to hear. Two shots exploded from the trees. He grabbed his transmitter and yelled that shots were fired and an officer needed help. After finishing, he checked the distance to the ground and decided his injured ankle was too sore to take another second-story jump, then dashed out the door and down the stairs.

As he ran around into the dark backyard, the sound of more gunshots came from the trees. He estimated the distance to be forty to fifty yards. Trying to run in the direction of the sound of the shots, he slowed to let his eyes adjust to the darkness. He stopped and listened.

His breath came in deep gasps. He tried to breathe shallowly so he could hear, but the only thing that came back was the wind through the trees, frogs croaking, and the rumbling traffic from the main drag about a hundred yards away.

How in the hell could they have disappeared so quickly? Suddenly he felt helpless and stupid. Standing in the dark, not knowing exactly which way they went, and being torn between continuing on or running to the house to see if Peggy was all right. At least her arms are still attached. While I'm out here stumbling around, the bastard could double back. But how about Herb? I can't return until I know if he's all right, he thought.

Chalky jogged in the general direction of the last sounds, trying to move as silently as possible. The forest floor was almost totally black and crunched loudly where he stepped. He whipped his flashlight back and forth, trying to get a glimpse of color, anything. He ran faster to make up for the time he knew he'd lost.

In the blackness, he tripped.

Reaching desperately for something to grab hold of, he rolled down an embankment and his head smashed into something hard. Flashing lights and pain ricocheted through his brain. He was out for a few seconds, then he moved.

The first thing he heard was the soft trickle of water. He was lying in a few inches of moving water. He sat up and felt his head.

His forehead was warm. Blood. Damn! He felt around where he lay and was relieved to find his gun in the dirt by the water. His flashlight was smashed so he left it. He stood and water rained from his shoulders and back. Scrambling up to the top of the bank, he stopped and listened. Nothing.

"Herb! Where are you?" he yelled. Silence again. He cupped his hands and tried shouting in each direction, and got no results. It had been a long time since he had felt the anxiety that overcame him when he turned and headed through the woods toward the condo.

He broke into the clear and could see the roof line in the distance. In back of him, he could hear the sound of sirens coming closer.

Thank God, he thought.

As he walked out of the last of the trees into her yard, two police cars skidded up to the front of the house. Chalky could see people standing on their lawns a couple of doors down pointing toward Peggy's house. He knew the policemen would be tense and have their guns drawn because they were responding to a shots fired report. Chalky called, "Police," as he rounded the front of the condo at the same time they approached the door. He held his hands up so they wouldn't feel threatened.

"Who are you?" a short cop asked, leveling his automatic. Chalky stopped on the sidewalk. The policemen were about ten feet away.

"Seattle police. Reaching for my badge, relax." He held it up as they came forward. "Inside—woman injured," he said, after he was sure they saw it. He was first into the door. "The bad guy's gone," he shouted over his shoulder as he ran up the staircase. He stopped at the door to the bedroom. Inside, Peggy was untied and wrapped in a thin housecoat, sitting on the edge of the bed. She snuffled softly. Carrie stood by her and looked up at him accusingly.

"Peggy, you all right?" Chalky was out of breath. She rose

and met him as he came forward. Peggy leaned close to his
chest, crying, whimpering, and talking, trying to explain what
had happened through her fear.

"I woke up . . . and he was on the bed with me, he had a gun
and . . . oh, God . . . I was so . . . I couldn't get away . . . when I
tried to scream, he . . ."

"Shhh," he said softly. He kissed her cheek gently and could
taste her salty tears. "You're okay now."

"Mind telling me what's going on here?" A deep voice from
behind him. Chalky had almost forgotten about the police. And
Herb? What had happened to him? he wondered.

"Just a second." Chalky held Peggy away and studied her
eyes. "You okay?"

She nodded. "Your head?" she said and reached up. Chalky
took her hand and kissed it gently.

"It's nothing. You sit here until I return." Chalky guided her
to the edge of the bed and lowered her gently.

"But your head . . ." Peggy said weakly.

"Relax. I'll be back in a second." He glanced at Carrie who
stood glaring at him as he talked to Peggy, then went out and
shut the door.

"Thank God you guys are here," Chalky said as he ran down
the stairs. "My partner chased this guy into the woods. They're
still out there somewhere."

He explained who they were looking for and gave them a description. He explained that Carlos was wanted for murder now
in addition to the maiming of the woman and the dogs. The pa-
trolmen were young and their adrenaline was high. This was
probably the first thing of this kind they'd had in Issaquah, a
normally quiet bedroom community. Chalky led them through
the backyard.

Herb being silent for minutes unsettled Chalky, but dwelling
on it right now would interfere with doing his job.

"Jerry! You take one of the cars and go down the street and
patrol to the south. He's liable to be looking for a ride," one of
the policemen shouted. Jerry ran toward the car. He turned to
Chalky and said, "Show us which way he went."

They all took off at a lope following the path Herb had taken.
When they got to the deep ditch, Chalky stopped and yelled to

Herb again. Still no sound from the woods, just the wind and the sound of frogs croaking in the blackness. The forest floor was thick with growth, and it was impossible to see any tracks in the dark even with their flashlights. They crossed the ditch and climbed to the other side and continued for another twenty or thirty yards. All the time, Chalky could feel his fear building.

He thought, If Herb is here, and all right, he'd be able to see or hear us, unless . . . Chalky tried not to think about the unless.

The men came upon a patch of blackberry bushes that was impossible to get through. They skirted them on the right. Another half hour of searching and they broke onto the main road. They stood and watched the traffic go by in frustration, wondering what to do.

"You have a K-9 unit available?" Chalky asked.

"Yeah, we can scare one up." He pulled his portable unit from his belt and called dispatch and told them what he wanted. He clicked it onto his belt. "Twenty minutes to a half hour before he's here. Meantime . . . let's head back the way we came. Spread out a little," he called to the three other men. They slowly worked their way back in the direction they'd come and found nothing.

When they got to the condo, Chalky took the men over to the van. They slid the door open. It was empty inside except for the arms, the blanket, and an old coat. Shocked epithets came from the policemen who came up behind and shone their lights through the door. Chalky wrapped the arms in the blanket to protect them. No one had returned to the van. Carlos was still in the woods somewhere.

They went to the condo. When they got there, Peggy was dressed and sat at the dining-room table, drinking a fresh cup of coffee. Carrie was opposite her, still glowering.

"I didn't hear a damned thing," Carrie said defensively, "or I'd have shot the bastard."

"Nobody's blaming you," Chalky said. "We were lucky we got here when we did, that's all that matters." He looked at Peggy and she shivered. She had been a pinprick and a few cuts away from being an ex-surgeon. Peggy's lip quivered. Chalky wanted to take her in his arms and comfort her, but the condo was filled with people.

"Back window in the den was popped open," said an officer coming into the room. "That's how he got in."

"Stupid," said Peggy. "All I had to do was figure out how to set the alarm, and I'd have known when he broke in. Being lazy almost cost me everything."

Chalky reached up and rubbed his forehead and checked his blood-covered hand. "Damn," he said. "You have any Band-Aids?" Peggy grabbed him by the arm and steered him into the downstairs bathroom. She took a hand towel and soaked it in warm water, then cleaned the cut on his forehead.

"You're a mess." She noticed his wet, dirty clothing. He smiled weakly. Peggy's eyes filled with tears again, and she choked out, "You saved my life. If you hadn't fired that gun when you did—" He put his fingers up to her soft lips.

"Don't think about it. He won't get another chance." She pressed the towel hard against the wound to stop the bleeding. The heat from her warm body radiated against him through her thin clothing. She looked into his eyes and he could feel his body melt.

"I'm crazy about you, you know that?" he said softly. She started to say something, then swayed up against him and her free arm slid around his other shoulder. Their lips met gently. Hers were soft, yet vibrant and searching. She came alive in his arms and hungrily pushed closer. Their tongues met lightly and electricity surged through his body.

"Ahem," the officer cleared his throat behind them. "Sorry. Thought you'd want to know—the K-9 unit just arrived." Chalky could hear him walk away from the door. Chalky drew back, then kissed each of her eyes gently. Her breath was hot, urgent, her eyes heavy-lidded.

"I have to go," he said huskily.

"You're still bleeding." She dabbed his forehead with the soggy towel.

"Doesn't matter." He pulled her close, gripping her upper arms, and kissed her hard this time, then walked out of the bathroom. When he left, she leaned against the sink.

"Let's move it," the officer said impatiently to the men outside.

"We've got a possible officer down in the woods and he needs our help—NOW!"

chapter//nineteen

Carlos breathed hard as he flailed through the thick brush. He had worked his way about thirty yards back from the other side of the highway. The woods were thick. He could hear the traffic rumbling off to his right, but he had to stay away from the road even though, in these woods, he was moving slowly. When the policeman shot at him in the dark, he had turned and aimed his silenced gun into the blackness. It spit lead into the bushes several times. He had no way of knowing whether he'd hit him or not, but the thrashing in the underbrush behind him had stopped.

"Cop probably hid. Yeah," he gasped. "Because he realized I was armed. Cops are cowards anyway. They only beat on people who are defenseless. Yeah, that was it." He tried to run faster, but his lungs burned from the cold air. Up ahead, he could see the halo of lights.

Bitch! It was easy. Actually easier than I figured. Getting that window open with my crowbar was simple. Then sneaking up and actually surprising her sleeping in bed. Pathetic! Stupid cunt! If it wasn't for those gunshots . . . he thought.

Carlos broke out of the woods into a neighborhood of homes with manicured lawns. He jogged through a yard and onto the sidewalk, stopped, and checked around. Newer houses. *Late now, don't know what time.*

He moved along the quiet street looking for a car or truck he could steal. His mind was in a panic for the first time.

I'll never, never go to jail. I have to escape. I'll die before I'd let them catch me. Gotta get away from this area.

189

Another half hour and the police'd have the whole city blocked off and it'd be crawling with cops.

Can't hide in the woods. They'll come for me at first light. With dogs and stuff like that. Have to get away. They have the van by now . . . and Maria's arms . . . they know for sure it was me.

He checked a brown Toyota pickup sitting in a driveway. A dog barked from the yard. It was dark in the house. *Damned door's locked, no keys*, he thought. He jiggled the handle, then felt his pockets. Nothing to hotwire or break the ignition switch off with. He had to have a car with keys. He looked at the house. If someone was home . . . he could force them at gunpoint to give him the keys . . . but he had no way of knowing how many people were there . . . or whether they had a gun. Too risky.

Have to find a car quickly, or I'll have to go to the main street and force someone to stop.

Ahead, in a dark area between streetlights, a yellow Ford Mustang. He worked his way up behind it. He studied the windows from a distance. They were tinted, so seeing in was impossible. Then he heard a low moaning sound. Someone inside. He smiled. His adrenaline kicked in again, and he moved closer. The sounds were louder as he crossed in back of the car and went up to the driver's door. Standing right next to the car, the windows were still obscure. The small car moved almost imperceptibly in a quick, violent rhythm. He knew instantly what was going on and grabbed the door handle. . . .

Carlos yanked open the door and the light flooded the interior.

"Jesus Christ!" A boy's shocked voice and a high-pitched squeal came from the interior at the same time. The front seats were pushed way forward. He leaned in just as two wide-eyed faces popped up from behind the front seat.

A young girl and a boy. Sixteen, seventeen maybe. Carlos smiled again, scooted in quickly, then leveled the gun at them. He slammed the door so the light would go out. The windows were steamed from their fevered lovemaking.

"Don't move," he said softly. The only sound was the heavy breathing from all three of them.

Carlos reached over, flipped on the interior light with his left hand, and noticed the keys dangling from the ignition.

"What the hell you doing? Get out of here," the boy said in an abnormally high voice. "You some kind of perverted sicko?" The boy looked foolish lying between the girl's arched legs with his pants down. The girl barely breathed, afraid to move. The smell of their lovemaking was pungent in the musky enclosure.

"You shouldna said that," Carlos said. "You shouldna said that at all. . . ."

Carlos smiled wider and carefully aimed above the boy's wide eyes, slightly below his tousled, moist hair.

The dog's handler had Chalky bring him Herb's coat from the car. Even though the men were eager to pick up the chase of Carlos, they knew Herb had to be located first.

"Herb is probably injured, lying out there somewhere," Chalky said. "Time's important. We have to find him now!"

"Relax, Sergeant," Sharp said to Chalky. "I know you're up-tight, but let us handle this our way." He yelled at one of the men to go and get the coat from the van so they could scent the dog for Carlos after they found Herb.

The dog snuffled around Herb's coat, then his handler took him into the rear yard where he barked and was off at a gallop into the black woods. The officer holding on to the chain could barely keep up with the excited dog. Chalky ran behind with the other men, crashing through the underbrush. Chalky hated this. He was used to being in charge, but in their jurisdiction, he was allowed to come along only as a courtesy.

On the other side of the ditch, they turned to the right and followed the scent for about twenty yards, then headed for the road again at an angle.

Ahead, the dog barked frantically and stopped. The group of men in the lead slowed, and Chalky could see the random lights flickering in the dark. Chalky broke from the trees and found the men in a circle, around a fallen figure. The officer restrained his dog off to the side. He tried to calm him by patting his neck while saying, "Good dog, good dog."

Officer Sharp bent over Herb, his hand on Herb's throat feeling for a pulse. He looked up at Chalky. It was an eerie scene with the four flashlights lighting Herb's face and shoulders where he lay on the ground. His eyes were closed and the front of his shirt was covered with blood.

"Oh, shit," Chalky choked.

"He's dead," Sharp said.

"Bullshit! He can't be dead," Chalky yelled and hunched down on his knees. "Herb! Get up, damn you! You've got to help me!"

"Listen to me . . . he's dead!" Sharp insisted, putting his hand on Chalky's shoulder to restrain him.

"Jesus, no—he can't be," Chalky said and touched Herb's neck to feel for a pulse. Herb's neck was cold and there was no pulse. "Damn it to hell!"

Officer Sharp stood and called his headquarters on his handset. Chalky could hear him talking in the background, but everything had disappeared from his mind except the figure of Herb lying on the ground. He thought of going to get Peggy to see if she could help him, but knew too much time had passed. There was no way to resuscitate him now. He was beaten and Herb was gone, forever.

The men strung yellow tape around the bushes in the area to protect the crime scene. Chalky walked in a daze slowly back to the condo. In the distance he could hear the dog barking again. They had scented the animal for Carlos and were following his trail now. Somehow, the life had drained from Chalky, and the need to catch Carlos had disappeared. Right now he wanted to see Peggy again, to protect her, to reassure himself she was all right.

When Chalky reached the condo, the homicide detectives had arrived. He sat at the table for a long time and talked to them. Peggy sat with him and watched his face. She was hurting for him as well as herself. Her voice shook when she answered their questions. After another hour and a half, the medics removed Herb's body from the field and carried him to the coroner's wagon. It was impossible for Chalky to watch. It was too painful.

Chalky rode into the police station and sat for another couple of hours answering the same questions time after time. He was beginning to feel like a suspect. After he was there forty-five minutes, Captain Stone showed up and sat in on the questioning. He was quiet, just offering a comment now and then.

It was getting into the early morning hours when Chalky drove to Peggy's condo. She and Carrie were still up and an officer cruised up and down the street occasionally. The officers had long since given up the search in the field and were on the streets looking for Carlos.

For some reason, Chalky was sure Carlos would escape tonight. He had disappeared like vapor. Weakness washed over him. Exhausted, physically and emotionally, he knew his thinking was faulty.

Peggy answered the door and let him in. Peggy and Carrie sat at the table staring up at him.

"I'm so sorry," Peggy said. She stood and rested her hand on his arm. He nodded. Outside, another patrol car idled by.

"Sit down," Peggy said. "Let me get you something to drink." Chalky shook his head no.

"A week. About a week. That's how long Herb and I worked together," he said. "Has a wife and a new baby." He walked over and pulled out a chair, sat heavily, and stared at the tabletop. "What a waste."

"I'm sorry," Carrie said. "How awful."

"What are you going to do?" Peggy asked. He shook his head as though trying to clear it.

"I'll have that drink now," he said. Peggy got up and poured him a shot of bourbon. She set it in front of him and rubbed his shoulder with the other hand. He drank the whole glass without putting it down, then said, "My first instinct is to get drunk, but I have things to do." Peggy looked at him questioningly.

"First, I have to get you girls out of here," Chalky continued. Carrie started to say something, then stopped when Peggy glanced at her. "He's going to come back, you know." He rubbed his forehead and winced. "I won't try to pretend I understand what makes him tick, but he has some kind of an obsession about you. I don't think he's going to stop until you're dead or maimed—or he's dead or in prison." Peggy hugged herself, shivered, and sat down.

"Go where? I could go to my mother's, but I don't want to put her in any danger," Peggy said.

"It's settled," Carrie said. "You're coming to my house. I'll do the whole place in land mines if I have to."

"No," Peggy said simply. "Absolutely not. The only thing that kept you alive tonight was the lucky fact you sleep soundly. If you had gotten in the way, he'd have killed you."

"I'm not afraid," Carrie said.

"Yeah, I know you're not, and I love you for it, but Chalky's partner wasn't either. He was brave as hell and see what happened to him." Chalky wore a pained expression when she glanced up. Peggy said, "Sorry," and he looked back at his glass. He got up and poured another shot of bourbon and downed it at the counter.

"You're staying with me," Chalky said.

"Great. And what a great job you did of protecting her the last time," Carrie said with hostility.

"Carrie—shut up!" Peggy shouted. "If it wasn't for him and Herb, I'd be dead right now, or worse than dead. Just shut up." Carrie got up and stomped up the stairs.

"Put something together," Chalky said. "Take your time and make sure you've got what you need for several days." She nodded and went upstairs. Going to make peace with Carrie first, he knew. They were both under a lot of pressure. He knew they'd work it out in a day at the latest.

While Peggy was upstairs, Chalky poured another shot of bourbon, then pushed it away. He had to keep his wits. He already felt the calming effect of the first two in his bloodstream. I need to be calm, controlled. Until I catch this crazy man, he thought.

He knew Captain Stone would be going by Herb's house right away, probably as he stood there, to tell Beth the terrible news. He wanted to go, do it himself, but it was against regulations. He'd call her about nine or ten in the morning. Maybe he could soften it a bit by telling her how courageous Herb was, about how he'd helped save Peggy at the last minute. It might not seem like a lot to her right now, but as time passed, she'd have the comfort of knowing he gave his life for a reason.

When Carrie came down with her suitcases, Chalky helped

carry them to her car. She apologized to him for what she had said. Chalky told her to forget it. Peggy came down, gave her a peck on the cheek, and Carrie drove off into the night. Back in the house, he went upstairs, picked up Peggy's packed suitcase, and carried it down to his car.

Chalky went into the garage, searched around, and finally found a hammer and nails. He then went into the den and nailed the window shut right through the aluminum sash. It was unimportant, he thought. It will have to be replaced anyway. She left her Cherokee in the garage, with the garage door still locked in place.

They drove away from her condo at 3:30 in the morning. Chalky was going to call the Issaquah police before he left, but changed his mind. If they caught Carlos, fine; if he escaped, fine. Nothing he could do about it either way. They'd call him if they found him. He was exhausted and had to conserve what little energy he had left. Peggy leaned back in the seat and closed her eyes. The emotional impact of what had happened had enervated her too.

Chalky could feel the tears fill the corners of his eyes as he started the engine and pulled out into the street. He was glad it was dark. Peggy was breathing deeply, obviously drifting off or already asleep. He reached over and smoothed her hair to reassure himself she was okay.

"I'm coming for you, crazy man," he said under his breath. "Just pray I'm not the one to find you, you bastard!"

chapter//twenty

Chalky sat staring at the fire he had built in his fireplace. It was almost five in the morning, the quietest part of the night, the time before people woke up and began another day, the time he should have been sleeping the soundest.

When he and Peggy had gotten to his apartment, he took her bags into his bedroom, changed the sheets on his bed, and kissed her gently. She was pliant, like a rag doll, drained of energy. He had reluctantly closed the door.

Under the circumstances, sex was of no importance, but he wanted to stay and comfort her for a while. Knowing she needed the healing sleep, he forced himself to leave.

Chalky crept to his car and drove to the station. He took Carlos's picture and description and had them put out an APB. Waiting for feedback from the Issaquah police seemed a waste of time. He knew Carlos had already gotten away.

When he drove back and tiptoed into his apartment, it was refreshingly silent. Even the dog was quiet. Peggy was physically and emotionally exhausted, so he was sure it had been only minutes before she was undressed and in bed. It was toasty warm from the fire. The urge to get drunk, cry, or do anything had disappeared. His body and mind were floating free, eerily devoid of normal emotions.

All Chalky could think about was Beth, wondering what she was doing right now. He knew there would be no rest for her at all in the next few days.

Words were meaningless at a time like this. Chalky thought about what he would have liked to say to Herb. About how much he liked him, and how happy he was Herb was his partner.

Damn! Men are so damned constipated about discussing their
feelings. Expressions of approval would have meant a lot to
Herb, he was trying so hard. Men never say those words to each
other until it's too damned late. It was the same remorse he'd
felt when his father died two years ago. Chalky was always going to say he loved him for what he'd done for him as a boy . . .
someday. But someday never came—then suddenly it was too
late.

Damn. Women never seem to have those regrets. They use
the dumptruck theory in off-loading their emotions, so they're
never more than a couple days behind, most of them. Just back
up to your door, and whump! A yardful.

Chalky heard a small mewling sound from the hall. Instantly
alerted, he sat up straight. He touched the end table where he
had put his gun. Could it be Peggy crying? The sound came
again. He relaxed and smiled.

He got up and went into the bathroom and picked up the furry
puppy and brought her into the living room. He laid his gun on
the floor next to the couch and lay down next to the dog. She eagerly settled in next to him. It was soothing for him to rub her
soft, warm coat and let his mind concentrate on stroking her.

The room was cozy and comforting as they both closed their
eyes.

At 8:30, a horn sounded outside, and Chalky woke with a
start. His mouth tasted like the bottom of a canary cage. He carried the dog out onto the small lawn, and she was able to clum-
sily relieve herself. Good dog. He looked around. The landlady
was still in bed. Back inside, he opened some dog food, fed the
puppy, and closed the bathroom door.

Chalky went in the bedroom, got some fresh clothes, show-
ered, and changed in the bathroom as quietly as he could. Peggy
was still motionless under the covers. He walked over to her
and checked. Lying on her side, her rib cage rose and fell rhythmically. God, she's beautiful, he thought. He tiptoed out and
shut the door gently.

At the dinette table, Chalky wrote her a note, leaving all the
telephone numbers where he could be reached. He said he'd be

home early, around three or four, and they could go get her car from the condo. Meantime, relax and have a good rest. He filled the page in with X's and O's. He chuckled. The last time he did that was in high school.

Before he left, he called the sheriff's station at Issaquah. The morning honcho indicated they had searched the entire area last night and Carlos's trail led to a housing development and disappeared. They assumed he had stolen a car, but none were missing from the neighborhood when they door-knocked. He said they were still working on it, and that he should call back later. Chalky shook his head, thanked him, and hung up. It was precisely what he had expected. Evaporated into thin air. He shook off the feeling Carlos was more than human. Stupid. Carlos was just lucky. Chalky considered calling Beth, then thought better of it. It was fortunate she had family there at this time.

On the street, the sky was overcast, mirroring his mood. KIRO News predicted, "Snow in all the higher elevations," as they put it. That could mean anything. The morning temperature had been in the high thirties.

"Just what we need," he groused. The drivers in Seattle were pole-axed whenever it snowed, drove like a bunch of tourists from Florida and abandoned cars helter-skelter as though trying to escape an atom blast. Snowed maybe once or twice a year, but it always seemed to take them by surprise. And then, there were the city bureaucrats. Their solution to everything was, if it's slick, pour sand on it. Sand. Christ, talk about high tech. They were probably doing that back at the turn of the last century.

Chalky stopped at Fat Phil's for a quick cup of coffee. He already had a caffeine headache along with his other problems. Sitting at the end of the counter, he kept a low profile. Fortunately, Giselle was off this morning, saving him a different kind of headache. The few stragglers would be ignorant about Herb, but it was safer to avoid all conversations. His stomach still felt quavery, so he passed on solid food.

It was about 10:30 when he walked into the squad room. Three or four heads popped up, then returned to their work. It was tacitly understood by the men that when someone was lost in the line of duty, any conversation with their partner about the incident should only be brought up by the partner. The men always gave the person a lot of space. Chalky appreciated that this morning.

"When you're up to it, Stone would like to talk to you," Detective O'Brien said, then looked down at the papers on his desk. Chalky nodded.

When you're up to it? Stone usually simply said: "Get your ass in here, now!"

"Sorry about what happened last night," Stone said. "Rosen had a lot of promise. A class guy. I liked him. How do you suppose he actually came to take the slug?" Stone leaned back and packed his pipe with his perfumed tobacco as usual. Chalky knew he had been at the station last night and had heard it all, but he wanted Chalky to say it again, just for the record.

"Shit! Had to be a one-in-a-thousand blind shot. I figure Carlos fired at sound or flashes. You couldn't see your hand in front of your face. Not even a moon." Chalky pulled out a chair and sat down.

"I'm not leaning on you right now, Chalky. But the shooting team is going to ask you some pretty tough questions about what happened. They're going to want to know why you didn't wait for that backup car."

"Screw procedure. I was trying to save someone's life. Had minutes, maybe seconds to do it. Given the same set of circumstances, I'd handle it the same way."

"Okay," Stone said in an uncharacteristically soft voice. He looked up and noticed the bandage on Chalky's forehead. "You had that checked?"

"Yeah. Had a doctor look at it," Chalky said, and flashed on Peggy at home in his bed. "It's nothing." He reached up, rubbed it, and tried not to grimace when the pain hit him. "You've seen Herb's wife?"

"Yeah. Early this morning."

"Tough?"

Captain Stone nodded his head and took a puff on his pipe as though reflecting on the scene. "Real tough," he said. "Herb's brother was there though. Guy named Bernie. Took charge of the situation. Stand-up guy."

"Think I ought to wait to call her?"

"I can't tell you. Use your own judgment on that. You want some time off? You've got vacation time coming. I can assign somebody to this."

"Bullshit! I want that bastard's head skewered on a spit! I don't have time to sit around and lick my wounds."

"Figured you'd feel that way. We're assigning you two men. We've got his picture and description distributed. With any luck, we'll have him in a couple of days, one way or another."

"I want a stakeout at Dr. Chandler's condo," Chalky said forcefully. "You think we can talk the Issaquah police into handling it?"

"Doubt it. They didn't seem too cooperative last night. Might get them to let us handle it though. The chief over there is an old friend of mine." He tamped his pipe, then leaned forward. "Let me ask you. This Martinez struck out there, Chalky, and had uniforms crawling through gullies looking for him. Why in the hell would he return?"

"Trust me. He's got a thing for that lady doctor. He's off the deep end. He'll be back, I know it. I feel it in my bones."

"She going to cooperate?"

"One hundred percent. She moved out and is staying with a friend." A damned good friend, he thought. "I want to sucker this Carlos with a female officer who could pass for the doctor. Set it up with her and an extra man, starting tonight." He was eager now, leaning forward in his chair.

"You have any ideas for the female officer?"

"Only one I know of who has the same build, except for the blond hair." Stone nodded and waited. "Jeanette who works vice on the night shift. The dark hair can be cured with a thirty-dollar wig."

"Have you talked to her?"

"No, but she'll do it. I know her."

"Set it up, I'll back you. Until we get you a permanent assignment, I want you to work with Merrick, okay? I'll talk to the chief in Issaquah right away. Under the circumstances, I think they'll let us set this up in their jurisdiction. Call me in an hour or two."

Chalky stood, said thanks, and walked to his desk. He got a cup of coffee.

Merrick, he thought. A fifteen-year, know-the-ropes detective. I could do worse.

At his desk, Chalky sipped his coffee and watched the activity around him for a few minutes. He knew he was putting off the call he had to make. When he finally got up the nerve, Beth's phone rang four times before Bernie answered. He told him what Chalky wanted to know. Beth had finally started to grieve and had cried herself to sleep after she saw Herb's body in the morgue. Herb was going to be cremated tomorrow and she planned to have a private service. It was what Herb wanted.

"He thought you were one helluva guy," Bernie said. "Talked about you all the time." That made Chalky feel even worse if possible. Any energy he had managed to work up sifted away when he hung up the phone.

Merrick came over and awkwardly expressed his regrets about Herb. They talked about him for a couple of minutes. Chalky mentioned the stakeout and that the captain supported it. Merrick grumbled, but agreed to take the first watch in the early part of the evening.

Chalky called his apartment. It was eleven o'clock and he assumed Peggy would be up by now. Four, five, six rings, then he hung up. Could she be sleeping that soundly? Had to be. No way that crazy could know where she was. Chalky decided to go home earlier if possible. Maybe around one or two.

He had work to do in the meantime. . . .

Had to start assembling his rat trap.

Olympia. The first time he'd ever been there. Carlos finished showering, walked into the bedroom of his motel room, and fell heavily onto the bed. He'd driven seventy miles to this town in the middle of the night, coming down Interstate 5, then up 101 to an off ramp called Black Lake. He had stopped at a small service center, parked, removed the license plates off an old Buick, and put them on the Mustang. He smiled as he looked up at the ceiling. Cops were so stupid. If you had the nerve, you could get away with anything.

Knowing he had to get rid of the bodies in the back seat, he drove south about six or seven miles, past a large lake he guessed was Black Lake, then into a thinly populated, forested area. Along that road, he'd stopped and dragged the two bodies from the back seat into the forest and covered them with brush. Searching them had been a bonanza for him. The boy had almost four hundred dollars, the girl eighty-five and some change. The boy also had several small packets in his pocket of what he presumed were amphetamines. Assuming that explained the money, he left them in the boy's pocket. Carlos removed all their ID to give himself more time if someone found them immediately.

After Carlos'd dumped the bodies, he drove for another half hour through dark, winding back roads and had found himself at this old hotel on the I-5 freeway, south of the city of Olympia. The Tyee Hotel. It had a large, well-populated parking lot to bury the car in. In the dim lights of the lot he had searched the car. The only thing of value to him were two hunting knives he found under the front seat.

After Carlos settled in the room, he sat on the bed and withdrew one of the knives from its sheath. It had a razor-sharp ten-inch blade. He studied it. Knives fascinated him. Crude, but deadly, it would be a formidable weapon and tool. His head was hot with fever. Carlos cradled the knife on his chest as his eyes slowly dilated. His body was sweating even though he was naked. The hot sun was coming again.

Maybe, maybe I can make it go away. He reached up and drew the tip of the blade across his chest. Blood welled up from the thin line. The sun retreated in size. He smiled and pulled the point across in the other direction making an X. The sun retreated farther into the recesses of his mind.

"*Ragged, unprofessional, ragged . . .*" The lady doctor's face floated across his mind and a surge of raging hate engulfed him. He could feel the heat in his body increase.

"I had her . . . I had her!" he screamed at the ceiling. "Fifteen minutes! That's all I needed!"

Bastards! Bastard cops! My tools, my precious tools. Because of her, they're gone, and I have to figure some way to replace them. Cut her, cut her up!

Until he left this town and got another job in a hospital, he'd have to make do with what he could buy in stores.

I'll slash—gouge—rip her—tear her insides out!

Carlos dropped the knife to the floor and rolled back and forth across the bed in frustration and blind rage. Minutes later, his flailing calmed. His thoughts ran together like watercolors blending into a cesspool of unfocused torment.

The blood was warm on his chest and his ears rang louder as he drifted off into a disturbed and fevered sleep.

Jeanette was a sweetheart and readily agreed to be Chalky's bait in the stakeout. Blond hair. No problem. She had a wig collection that included any color he wanted. Chalky thanked her profusely and hung up. He called the chief and was told they had permission for the stakeout, but nothing outside the unit. No chasing, no cowboy stuff. Chalky chuckled to himself when he hung up. He'd do whatever was necessary to nail Carlos. Period. If he had to do something outrageous, he would, then deal with the flack afterward. Screw the rules! After he finished that conversation, he tried his apartment again. Still no answer. He was getting concerned.

Peggy would have enough sense to stay away from the hospital, right? Even though she was one independent lady, she had to have more smarts than that. Chalky called the hospital and after the usual jockeying around, her voice came on the phone.

"What are you doing there?" he asked gruffly.

"I have patients," she said simply. "I can't ignore them just because I have problems."

"We're not talking problems here, we're talking one terminal problem. This guy is going to try to get you again, I know it. It could happen anywhere."

"I have things to do." Her voice was adamant. "I have another surgeon covering for me, but I have three post-op cases I have to follow up on."

"I'm simply worried about you," he said, more softly.

"I know, and I love you for it." Peggy had a smile in her voice. Chalky felt his face heat up even though the inflection was casual. "You might be interested that Joanne Pinkers came around. I just finished talking to her." She continued before he could ask, "She doesn't remember anything, nothing at all about what happened. Remembers a man who had his face covered with a ski mask. Had no idea who he was. I hope you're not mad that I asked."

"No, why should I be? Frankly, I haven't counted on anything positive from her since day one. Too much trauma involved. I've seen it before. When you're ready to leave there, I'll pick you up." He said it casually, not wanting to sound too possessive.

"You can't escort me around all the time, you're doing enough. I called the Jeep dealer, he's a friend of mine. They're going to let me use a demo Cherokee for a couple of weeks. Dropping it by in about an hour." She was silent for a couple of seconds, as though thinking. "I can't go back there for anything, to the condo, until you catch Carlos. I couldn't sleep or feel safe in that house for even five minutes."

"That'll work perfectly," Chalky said. He knew he needed the car in the garage for bait anyway. Have to leave the window uncovered so he can see it, he thought. Chalky told her what he intended to do with the stakeout. Peggy was excited about the idea. Anything, just so they caught him.

When they finished discussing the mechanics of how it was going to work, she was quiet again, then said in a gentle, happy voice, "I have a surprise for you."

"I've had all the surprises I can handle." Chalky felt his mind cloud when he thought about Herb and the insane night before.

"I know, but this is a good one . . . a great one in fact." Peggy's voice was lighter and teasing.

"Tell me."

"Don't be silly. How can it be a surprise if I tell you?" In spite of his mood, he could feel the corners of his mouth going up.

"When do I get to see it?" The image of Peggy in a teddy flashed into his mind and he rejected it. Having her this close to his life was tough enough without those kind of thoughts floating through his mind.

"Today. I promise it'll make you feel better."

"Great. Because the only thing that could make me feel worse is if something happened to you."

Chalky was still smiling when he hung up.

● ● ●

Carlos jerked up from the bed in the motel room. He moved around the room with a purpose. He pulled two small pieces of paper from his pocket and studied them closely. He took a road map he had bought at a gas station on the way to the motel and spread it on the bed. Turning on the light, he bent over it and traced a line with his finger.

"There! There it is." He folded the map down with that section on the outside. He had several things to buy on the way there. Candles, matches, smaller, sharper knives, and cartridges for his gun. He'd used the last two in the clip last night.

No, I won't get no cartridges. I'll only kill from now on with sharp tools and knives. Blades that cut and bring forth the warm blood, he raged inside. He smiled and got dressed slowly and purposefully.

"I'm coming to get you, bitch. I'll be waiting. This time no one will rescue you."

He made long slashing strokes in front of the mirror.

"You're dead, bitch! You're dead!"

chapter//twenty-one

Chalky went to Peggy's neighborhood, drove around, then when he finally assured himself no one was watching, he opened the front door and went in. Peggy had told him where she had hidden a key when he called. He pulled the nails from the den window. After working on the window with a bar and a pair of vise grips, he was able to get it to close and locked it.

Chalky then went into the garage to make sure there was nothing in front of the window in the garage. The Cherokee was in plain view. Checking each room, he satisfied himself the house was empty.

What if he doesn't come back for Peggy? He will—he has to, he thought. The real nightmare scenario would be if Carlos left the state and set up housekeeping somewhere else. He'd be caught eventually, no matter where he went. Guys like him can't stop, can't change. He'd be killed or end up in the looney bin, but it was important for Chalky's peace of mind and Peggy's safety that he get him.

Finally, satisfied everything was in readiness, Chalky locked up and took the key with him to make copies. He had to plant another key because Merrick and Jeanette had planned to meet at the condo at five o'clock, just before dark. Chalky'd be there for the second shift, midnight to dawn. He decided he'd have to fix the garage tonight so Jeanette could take the Cherokee when she went home. They'd have to forget the daytime. If he was coming back, it would be at night.

Right now, Chalky had to get to the apartment and try to get some sleep if he hoped to be alert late tonight. He reached over and patted the gun under his coat. Chalky thought of Herb. He then pictured Carlos standing in front of him, jerking from the impact of round after round he pumped into his body. No prison tennis or handball for Carlos. Simply cold, dark earth, someplace where Carlos could never hurt anyone again. Chalky remembered Herb again and gripped the steering wheel so hard his knuckles went white. Waiting was going to be tough.

"Peggy?" he called when he opened the door of his apartment. "You here yet?" Not a sound came back. He searched the apartment, room to room, then tapped on the closed bathroom door. No sound there either. He rapped harder, then opened it a crack and called to her again. Not even a whine from the dog. Chalky suddenly realized that maybe the dog was sick or dead and threw the door open. The towel and food were here, but no dog, no Peggy.

"Damn. She took her," he said to himself in frustration. Chalky immediately felt defensive. If someone from the lab had been there, maybe she had felt obligated to give the dog to them. "No, that's stupid, she wouldn't do that, she likes her." He walked through the apartment and checked all the windows to make sure they were locked. They were. He immediately discounted the possibility the dog might have gotten out. She could barely drag herself around. Call the hospital? He looked at the clock.

3:15. "Give her until four," he grumbled. She has to have the dog. Maybe she took her to a vet for treatment?

Chalky walked into the bedroom and lay on the bed. The room was dark from the blackout curtains on the windows. He had to have them because of the irregular hours he sometimes was forced to work. He could only sleep in the dark unlike most of the guys he worked with who could doze off anywhere.

Peggy had made the bed when she left, and he imagined he could still feel her lying next to him. He tried not to mess the covers up, so he kept his feet on the floor. Chalky cringed when he remembered the embarrassing evening with Giselle the other night right here in this bed. He shook his head in humiliation and his face unconsciously warmed at the image. It was going to take a while to forget that. Sex with her had been about as impersonal as a blow-up doll. At least a blow-up doll would have kept quiet about it afterward. She hadn't said anything, but he had a strong feeling it was coming in spades. Chalky wondered if she'd put it on the bulletin board in the restaurant. Chalky Fuchs is a lousy lay, he thought, then grimaced.

Peggy. He tried to imagine being with her and felt his stomach stir. Never again. Never again would he go to bed with someone he felt nothing for. He was wondering how his relationship with Peggy was going to end when he drifted off to sleep.

Peggy opened the door to the apartment after checking around carefully to make sure she was alone. She had doubled back a couple of times on the way home to make sure no one had followed her. Inside, she laid the little dog on the floor of the living room and watched her as she hesitantly pulled herself across the floor with her front legs. Peggy had seen people return from adversity, but this puppy could teach a lot of them a lesson.

"Want some water, sweety." The dog looked up at her and followed dutifully as Peggy walked down the hall toward the bathroom.

The door was open.

She froze.

Peggy tried to remember where Chalky parked his car when he was home. Last night he'd let her out in front of the door, disappeared around a corner, then came back and let her in.

Stop being a child, Peggy admonished herself. Carlos couldn't know you're here. She forced herself to move forward. Peeking around the doorway, she could see the bathroom was empty. She breathed deeply. "Coward," she whispered softly. She went through the partially closed bedroom door, then stopped.

Chalky. Sleeping. She smiled. He seemed years younger when his features were relaxed.

Peggy went to the edge of the bed and looked down on him. His unkempt blond hair fell softly over his forehead. His chest and shoulders moved slowly. He's exhausted, didn't even bother to take his shoes or coat off, she thought. She wanted to lie down next to him, put her head on his shoulder, and feel his strong warm body next to hers, but knew she'd have to work up the nerve to do it. How would he react?

Look, lady, I'm giving you a place to hide out, not marrying you, Peggy was afraid he'd say. She walked to the closet to get a blanket from the shelf to put over him. It had been a long time since she'd had warm feelings about a man. She unfolded the blanket, leaned down, and snugged it gently under his chin.

"Gotcha!" Chalky said as he smiled and reached up, grabbing her by the arms. She screamed in delight as he pulled her down next to him. "Caught you in the act of being a mother," he said playfully.

Peggy stretched out next to him smiling, her head braced on one hand, then said, "You want your surprise now?"

"If it includes you," he said, suddenly serious. Peggy leaned and kissed him lightly on the lips, then jumped up and stood by the edge of the bed.

"Close your eyes and I'll give it to you," she giggled. Peggy was having trouble containing her excitement. Chalky seemed puzzled, then said okay, and shut them, still smiling. "Give me your hand and stand up." He laughed deep in his chest, then sat up with his eyes closed.

"You're not going to hurt me, are you?"

"Only if you open your eyes before I tell you to." Peggy took him by the arm and led him slowly into the living room by the fireplace. "Turn around." She swiveled Chalky so he faced the room.

"Surprise!" Chalky opened his eyes. Across the room, the small dog followed, pulling herself along by her front legs, her body in a sling that had a small wheel on either side. The dog stopped in front of him, leaned back and peered up and wagged her tail, obviously proud of herself.

"You're kidding," Chalky yelled and bent down and looked at the contraption. "You did this?" The wheels moved smoothly and soundlessly as the small dog backed up a little.

"Thought you'd be pleased. I have a couple of good friends in orthopedics. Putting it together wasn't that hard." She could feel his excitement at their closeness. She wanted to reach out and touch him. "When she heals a little better, I think they can fit her with a couple of functional artificial legs. They won't work great, but she'll be able to—"

Peggy was interrupted by his strong hands closing on her arms. Chalky drew her hard against him and smothered her face with kisses, not touching her lips. She could feel his hips pressed firmly against hers as his body melted into hers. Her body felt weak as he softly caressed her neck, then worked up to her ears, then explored her earlobes gently. His breath came hot and urgent in her ear and he said loving words she was too excited to understand. She had an almost painful pang of desire. Suddenly she was hot between her thighs as moisture flooded her. It had been so long, so long.

Chalky stopped and held her face gently with both hands and stared into her eyes. Peggy knew he wanted her and was silently asking for permission.

"Okay," she said huskily. Chalky leaned and kissed her lightly on her hot, trembling lips. She felt any last reservations flow from her body as she leaned into him. Her legs were so weak she needed his support as they slowly walked as one down the hall and into the bedroom. Chalky closed the door, then moved to the other side of the bed and started to undress. Peggy hesitantly followed suit and they watched each other's movements as if in slow motion. His upper body, coming out of the shirt, was hairy, whip slender, and finely muscled. His stomach was flat, athletic. And he was hard. Rigid with excitement. Peggy drew in her breath, looked away, and took the rest of her clothes off. Even though it was dark in the room, he was lying across the bed watching her when she slipped off her bra and lay down next to him.

Chalky gently pulled her body close to him, then explored her lightly with the tips of his fingers. Peggy put her hands out and felt his chest, his shoulders and back, the tight muscles of his arms. Her fingers explored his thick mat of chest hair, tangling then releasing. It had been so long. He was going to take his time and she felt her body tingle with the pleasure of that. She wanted him so badly now, but he would not be hurried.

In a little while, his explorations continued with his tongue. His lips ignited her skin. His tongue probed her ears, then along the length of her long neck. As her hand stroked his face, he took each finger in turn and kissed it gently—then her hand—then her arm. Then he found her breasts. His gentle tonguing became a firmer suction, and he tugged at her throbbing nipples with his teeth, almost hurting her, but just short of it.

Peggy came alive and threw herself against him and kissed him hard, almost as though trying to get inside him herself. He felt strong and good and he trembled and she trembled too. They were both starving for each other. She rolled on her back, and he followed her as though attached to her. They both shuddered again as he entered her and she murmured softly. Chalky moved slowly at first, then she met him hard at each thrust. There was a melding, a communion to their lovemaking that went beyond the pure physical pleasure to something consuming, something deeper.

Peggy's skin pulsed with heat and electric tension as their movements became more frantic, more in perfect harmony, and she cried out, his face pressed close to her ear, his forehead buried in her fragrant hair, his breath on her throat, his body surging against and into and through her.

Peggy convulsed and Chalky groaned as they came together in pounding waves of pleasure. Finally, he was still but remained inside her, still kissing her neck gently, their perspiration blending; she could feel her body contract and contract into ever smaller orgasms. Finally, she breathed deeply and lay back.

Chalky got up to shower and she relaxed in bed for the first time in months. She'd never had anything shake her that much before and yet be so completely satisfying.

Chalky walked back in the room wearing a tattered bathrobe and looked at Peggy with a soft, almost embarrassed grin. He slowly clapped his hands together, then faster and louder, while he laughed with pure pleasure. She smiled and chuckled as he went toward the kitchen.

"Some wine?" Chalky called.

"Perfect," she said as she rose and went into the bathroom herself. "I'll be in the living room in a minute. Start a fire."

It was a special time for Peggy as they sat huddled together on the couch drinking their wine. The fire popped and flared and burned aggressively, giving out waves of heat that added to her feeling of well-being. The little dog came rolling from the bathroom and cocked her head as though trying to understand what they were doing.

"That was a special thing you did for my dog," Chalky said softly.

"My dog? Don't you think it's about time you gave her a name?"

"What do you suggest? Blackie? No, that's too pedestrian for a dog with character."

"She had us all laughing at the hospital. Her rolling around reminded me of playing on my scooter when I was a little girl."

"Scooter. Great name." He turned to the dog. "What do you think? Scooter okay?" The puppy wagged her tail. It was a done deal. Peggy sat up, set her wineglass down, and turned serious.

"I told them at the hospital I was taking a week off."

"I've got plenty of books if you get bored around here," he said, pointing to his bookshelves on the wall next to the fireplace.

"I might take a couple, but I'm not staying here."

"No? You're not thinking of going back to the condo, are you?"

"I'm leaving town. I called Mom and her cabin isn't being used at Snoqualmie Pass for three or four more weeks. It'll give me some time to catch up on my medical reading as well as time to think."

Chalky sat for a long minute, drank the last of his wine, then said, "Bad idea, kid. How can I protect you up there? What's wrong with just staying here?"

"I won't need protecting. For God's sake, this Carlos isn't psychic, you know. He can't possibly know anything about that cabin. As long as I'm sure nobody follows me, I'll be as safe as a bug in a rug. And staying here? I don't know right now. Maybe I need to be alone for a little while."

"I don't want you to go," Chalky said softly and put his hand on her lap.

"I know. I don't want to. It sounds trite, but I need some space. I need to think."

"Thinking can be harmful to your health."

"Not thinking can be a whole lot more dangerous," Peggy murmured.

"I can't break a man loose to go with you, but how about hiring a private security guard for a couple of weeks. I could arrange it."

"Don't be silly. I'll be completely isolated with no possibility that anyone could find me. The cabin has a phone and everything. Besides, I could take Scooter with me," she said. "You don't mind, do you?"

He shook his head no.

Chalky suddenly got up, went into the bedroom, and came out with a shoe box. He sat it on the coffee table ceremoniously. Opening it carefully, he withdrew a 9mm automatic.

"No arguments. You're going to learn about this gun, and you're going to take it with you."

She nodded. It was a small concession. It took him about a half hour to show her how to load and fire the gun. Peggy felt awkward and frightened when she held it, fully aware of how lethal it was. She had repaired a couple of holes in people made by guns.

"I'm going to leave in about an hour," Peggy said, looking at her watch. "It's five-thirty. I want to be up there before eight, and it takes about an hour in traffic."

"I can't change your mind?"

"That's one of the things you'll learn about me in time, I'm stubborn as hell." Peggy felt her heart lurch when Chalky stood and smiled. He would be easy to get used to. He held out his hand—an invitation.

"If we're going to say good-bye, we ought to get started," he said.

chapter//twenty-two

Snowflakes danced in his headlights as Chalky followed Peggy's car up Highway 90 to Snoqualmie. He blinked his lights for her to stop when they were on a long, straight stretch of road. She slowed and pulled off onto the shoulder with him right behind. Chalky climbed out and walked to her window, hunching into the wind-driven snow.

"Insane. Damn stuff came from nowhere," he mumbled. Cars passed by trailing a concussion of air, and the road was clear behind them in the distance. Nobody back there.

"Why'd you signal me to stop?" Peggy asked through her open window.

Chalky leaned against the roof of the car, hands in his pockets, and said above the wind, "Just being careful. Wanted to make sure we weren't being followed. I'm going to stay behind you all the way to the cabin. Check it out when I get there. I'd tuck you in if I had the time." He smiled. "You have plenty of gas?" She nodded. He bent farther in and gave her a peck on the cheek. "Crazy about you, Peggy." Her eyes glistened as she smiled. "You're sure that no one knows you're here?"

"Only one who knows is Carrie. I swore her to secrecy. Besides, who's she going to tell?"

Chalky shook his head, not liking the idea that *anyone* knew, but it was much too late to argue. "Drive carefully in the snow." He impulsively kissed her again, this time on the lips, then ran back to his car. They drove another eight miles and they approached the turnoff onto Amsterdam Road.

Chalky's radio came to life and called his car number. He answered, and they patched him through to Jeanette at the condo.

"You at the cabin yet?" she asked in a low voice difficult to hear.

"Just about. Why?" He could feel his hackles rise. She would only be calling if there was something wrong.

"Activity—out in back—someone sneaking along the tree line. It could be our man. Been there for ten minutes." Chalky could hear the tension in her voice. The line crackled with interference.

"Jesus—doesn't anything go according to plan?" he asked, not expecting an answer. Chalky slammed the heel of his hand on the steering wheel. "Hang on. Don't do anything radical. I'm on my way. I'll call you when I'm in the neighborhood." As he followed Peggy up onto the off-ramp, he flashed his lights again for her to pull over.

She stopped at a stop sign. Chalky drove up alongside of her, tires crunching in the wet snow, rolled down his window, and yelled, "Emergency, babe. I'll have to leave you here and go back. Call me at the condo when you get settled?"

Peggy nodded yes, smiled, then threw him a kiss. Chalky winked, rolled the window up, and gunned his car. It slewed sideways, then straightened out. He went across the freeway overpass and turned left onto the return ramp. Before he turned, he could see her pull onto the narrow road and head off between the towering trees in his rearview mirror. Even though he felt he was doing the right thing, his stomach churned at the idea of leaving her alone.

From where Peggy left the freeway, the cabin was six miles into the hills along the service road, then a mile up a private drive that led to two cabins, hers being the first. She drove slowly and carefully as her four-wheel drive rolled arrow-straight over the snow. Other homes populated the woods along this road. Even though several vehicles a day used it, the thought of being helpless in a ditch with Carlos on the loose froze her blood more than the cold.

Peggy looked into the back seat, then smiled. She'd wrapped Scooter in a blanket and had laid her on the rear seat and the dog's eyes were closed. She'd be good company at the cabin.

The snow-clad forest around her reflected the moonlight

shining through an opening in the snow clouds. As she reached down to turn up the heater another notch, a loose branch lying in the roadway banged the underside of the Cherokee. She jumped. Darn! What a baby, she thought.

Every five seconds or so, her eyes involuntarily glanced up to the rearview mirror. Peggy had put on a good act for Chalky, but alone in the woods, she suddenly felt vulnerable and exposed. Going back now would seem childish, so she just buried the fear.

"Nobody knows you're here, stupid." She could only be comfortable after she was locked in the cabin and had a roaring fire going. Peggy reached across the seat and touched the cold steel of the gun for assurance. No matter where she went, until Carlos was caught, it would be her constant companion. She made a vow to even take it with her to the bathroom.

Pull back the slide, raise it, lock my elbow, sight, and squeeze, she thought. Oh, yes—take off the safety, first—the damned safety—why can't I remember that? I mustn't forget to . . . God . . . will I be able to shoot at another human being . . . even to save my own life? All those years of study to preserve life. Can I take a life?

She remembered the terror she had felt when Carlos had tied her up. The answer was, yes, I could shoot, in his case, almost without thinking.

When the moment came, she'd know the answer for sure to that question. But, hiding here, she knew it would be unnecessary. Carlos can't know where the cabin is. No one knows except me, Carrie, and Chalky, she thought.

Peggy switched on KIRO News, hoping the sound of another voice in the car would settle her nerves. The chatter of two men instantly filled the air, talking about a new how-to book on investing. She missed the author's name. The conversation was babble to her, but company.

Peggy's eyes glanced up to the rearview mirror again. A pair of headlights in the distance, getting closer. She instinctively speeded up. The sound of the snow crunching under the tires rose an octave.

Another mile 'til the turnoff to the cabin, she thought. It's narrower there. When I go into the private drive, I'll switch off my lights and whoever is behind me will keep going on the main road if he's following the illumination . . . that's what I'll do.

Outside, the wind picked up, and the snow began to stick to the windshield. Peggy turned on the wipers, then cranked down the enthusiastic heater because it was already too hot in the car. Her hands ached, then she realized her grip on the wheel was twice as hard as it had to be.

"Relax, it's just a neighbor." She tried to avoid glancing in the mirror, but had to. The headlights were still there, but closer. Peggy pressed the accelerator, leaned forward, and stared out the windshield. She was near the turnoff, and it was difficult to see through the snow and churning wipers.

There! She hit the brakes, skidded, then straightened the car. When she stopped, two mailboxes were framed in her head-lights next to the narrow opening of the drive. Releasing an explosion of air, Peggy realized she'd been holding her breath.

Dropping the Cherokee into first gear, she bumped over the hump of the drainage ditch that fronted the entrance. She kept it in low and accelerated back between the trees. The road was almost impossible to see now that the snow covered the ground.

About fifty yards in she stopped and clicked off the lights. The sudden darkness shocked her. The only sounds were the hiss of the heater, the moan of the wind, the voices on the radio.

"If I have twenty-five percent of my investment capital in interest-bearing bonds, fifty percent in common stocks, what about the remaining twenty-five percent?" the interviewer asked.

"Well, Bob, that's where it starts to be fun." The author chuckled, obviously having a good time.

"Shut up!" Peggy snapped off the radio, then sat in the dark and squinted into the rearview mirror. Finally, she impatiently turned to watch out the rear window.

Off in the distance, the lights disappeared, then glimmered again as the other car moved between the trees. Finally, it slowed and stopped. Peggy's heart skipped a beat, then pounded faster. The lights began to back up.

Oh, God. He's stopping. Must be following my tire tracks in

the snow, she thought. A gust of wind rocked the Cherokee. She jumped. Her nerves were raw.

The lights from the vehicle brightened, then bounced up and down. He's in the drive! Oh, no! He has to be following me. She knew that her neighbors, the Carters, never came up to their cabin in the winter, and theirs was the only other house on this road. Beyond that were miles of tractless forest. This drive was the only way in and out.

Peggy turned, fumbled for the lights, hit the horn button, screamed, then found the switch. The headlights lit the drive. The ground was almost pure white now with black patches showing here and there.

Peggy's hands shook as she jammed it into low again, scraping the gears. The wheels shuddered, grabbed, then pulled her through the opening in the trees. The lights behind her were only thirty yards away and closing. She could feel panic overtaking her as she pressed the accelerator and fishtailed between the trees, bouncing as she went. A quarter mile to the cabin. What'll I do then? Can I make it inside before he gets there? she wondered.

"Don't panic! He can't possibly beat me to the cabin." Peggy knew once she got inside, she could barricade herself, then call the police or Chalky if she could reach him. With her gun for protection, she was safe.

"It's going to be all right, it's going to be all right." The words alone failed to do it. Peggy's heart trip-hammered, and her rapid breath steamed the windshield. When she turned the fan on to clear it, she jumped at the new sound.

"Damn!" She was irritated with her inability to control her reflexes. A loud thump echoed through the car as she tore off a fence post next to a tree. Peggy ignored it and concentrated on the ribbons of light that were her headlights. Angry snowflakes flew by at an almost horizontal angle—

I have to get to the cabin first, I have to! her mind shrilled.

Ahead, Peggy could see the dark outline of the hill and the three switchbacks. Behind, the other vehicle followed at a steady thirty yards. Its lights flickered as it disappeared, then reappeared from behind the trees. She slowed and took the first corner carefully, knowing it was dangerous.

In the three spots where the road made tight turns, huge guard timbers projected from the ground for safety. The first logs jumped up in her headlights and she made a sharp turn to her left, continued to climb, applying constant pressure on the gas pedal to avoid losing traction. Below, the vehicle slowed to enter the first bend, hesitated, then followed.

"Oh, no!" Peggy prayed it was someone other than Carlos—someone lost maybe—and when they came to the switchbacks, they'd turn back. The second group of timbers came into view. She made a sharp right and proceeded in the opposite direction. Because she had to slow down for the switchbacks, the lights behind her were closer.

Peggy negotiated the third and final one, headed to the top where it leveled out, then raced down the narrow road through the forest. In the distance, she could see the dark form of her cabin on a hill.

Behind, the lights flashed brighter as the vehicle rounded the last turn and pointed in her direction. As Peggy picked up speed, the Cherokee, still in first, screamed by the trees, the engine so loud it drowned out the click of the wipers.

Up ahead—the cabin. She focused on it and tightened her grip on the wheel.

"Beat you—you creep!" Peggy yelled as she slowed for the driveway. In back of her, the lights were nearer. The steep incline to the house turned in to the right and deep drainage ditches yawned on either side. The one on the left led down to a pipe that went under the drive. Peggy hit the bump at the entrance without stopping. The rear end slid sideways as she tried to barrel up the long drive to the cabin. She could feel her car sliding, then her lights were no longer on the carport at the top of the drive, but shone into the trees to the right. Her wheels lost traction—the engine roared even louder—the Cherokee tilted farther to the left, and it slowly drifted into the drainage ditch.

"No! No!" The Cherokee's wheels and frame thudded against the bottom, headlights pointed up at the cabin. It leaned precariously at a forty-five degree angle. The dog whined in the back seat as it thumped against the wall. The shuddering wheels echoed through the interior as the Cherokee clawed its way into the earth, struggling vainly to pull itself up. Peggy tried it in re-

verse, then first—back and forth—trying to rock it out, but she
could feel the wheels sink even deeper into the snow and mud.

She was stuck!

Outside, the heavy snow piled up on the windshield and rapidly obscured the now-slanted windows on the passenger's side.

The panic creeping up on Peggy filled her entire being. Her
hands shook almost uncontrollably as she continued to jam the
gearshift from drive to reverse and back.

She jerked around as the lights of the other vehicle came up
behind her. She'd lost any opportunity to make it to the cabin
before him.

Damn! If I'd jumped from the passenger's side as soon as I
came to a stop and ran in instead of trying to get loose . . .

Peggy stared at the car as though hypnotized. She could see
very little through the windows, just a dark outline behind the
snow-whipped lights of the other car. She reached down and
flipped off the idling engine so she could hear better.

"My gun! Dammit! Think!" Peggy felt the seat next to her.
Her heart jumped in her chest.

It's gone!

She glanced out the rear window. The headlights flickered as
a dark figure walked in front of one, then the other.

He's coming this way! Peggy felt in the dark for the electric
door locks, but just fumbled around. She snapped on the interior
light switch, then banged the electric lock button with her fist.

A comforting click!

A dark figure walked up the driveway, then disappeared as it
walked behind the snow-covered side windows.

The gun! The light still on, she looked at the seat, then the
floor. The velvety highlights of the gun gleamed on the passenger floor mat.

Peggy dove to grab it, but—

Something held her in place!

Struggling against her panic, she realized it was the seat belt
gripping her.

Peggy pushed the release, dove, and picked up the gun—

Tap, tap, tap! Knocking on the passenger door window. The
penetrating sounds were like electric shocks through her body.

Carlos was just the thickness of a window away from grabbing her.

Tap, tap, tap! Harder and more urgent.

Peggy's hand quivered as she put the gun in her left hand, her mind rehearsing what she had to do.

Grab the slide, pull it back. A cartridge flew out and hit her forearm. Already a shell in it!

As he rapped for the third time, a clear spot appeared in the snow on the window. A voice, but the confusing words just blended with the howling wind.

Rattle, rattle! The sound of him trying to open the door. Peggy pointed the shaking gun at the window, screamed, and squeezed the trigger at the same time.

Nothing!

The trigger was locked in position!

The safety, the safety!

The tapping sound on the window was louder and more insistent. It's going to break!

Peggy pulled the gun under the light—

Flipped the red dot on the safety catch up—

Brought it back toward the window—

It exploded!

The crashing sound in the enclosed car deafened her temporarily.

It was instantly dark—

Glass rained on her face and hands—

She was transfixed—too stunned to react—

Outside—

A high-pitched scream.

chapter // twenty-three

Peggy turned and was dumbfounded to see there was no hole in the window. Glancing up, she saw she'd blown out the interior light—

"That scream! That was a woman's voice!" Peggy leaned and looked out the clean spot on the window. The person was gone.

"That couldn't have been Carlos." Peggy climbed up and opened the passenger door with her left hand. The snow and wind slashed into the car, making her wince. With a struggle, she lifted the door all the way open, pulled herself through, and stood.

No one there!

The other vehicle still sat behind her, lights shining on the Cherokee. Peggy gripped the gun firmly for protection.

"Don't shoot, Pegs!" A woman's voice from the ditch on the other side of the drive.

Peggy inched over to the edge while brushing the snowflakes off her eyelashes. Then, as she held the automatic in front of her, she peeked into the deep ditch apprehensively. A dark-clad figure lay on its back, propped on one elbow.

"Why the hell did you shoot at me?" Carrie asked as she looked up. "Please put that gun away. I sprained my ankle and can't get up. How about a hand?"

"Oh, my God," Peggy said. "I could have killed you." Tears of fright blurred her vision as she slid down the bank and helped Carrie to her feet. They struggled to get out of the ditch, walked to the end, stepped on a drain pipe, then up onto the driveway. Carrie limped slightly. Peggy kept apologizing under her breath.

After they went inside, Carrie sat heavily at the dinette table. Peggy went quickly through the house, turned on all the lights, and checked the locks on all the doors and windows. Everything was secure. When she walked down the upstairs hall, she stopped for a moment, leaned against a wall in the dark, and rested her head on the cold surface. She felt guilty about leaving the dog in the car. She'd have to go and get her soon, it would get cold quickly. Her stomach was so tight from the protracted fear, she felt she might throw up. Peggy fought to control her feelings, hoping she could hide how upset she was from Carrie. After a couple of minutes, she breathed in deeply, then continued through the house.

The cabin was an A-frame design with an attached carport. In the rear and on one side, a sixteen-foot-deep wooden deck looked over a vista of cedar and hemlock trees. Although it was a black monolith at night, in the background was a towering hill of pines with just one small clear-cut area to destroy the symmetry. The entire back of the A-frame was glass, partitioned with rugged timbers. As Peggy pulled all the drapes closed, she noticed that the deck off the kitchen area and the steps down to the ground were covered with virgin snow. It was comforting to know no one would be able to move through it without betraying their presence.

"I'll put on some coffee for us, then I'll have to go and turn off the lights on the cars, get the dog out of the back seat, then pick up some wood for the heating stove," Peggy said as she opened a canister from the cupboard. "How in the world did you get up the hill so easily?"

"That's a Toyota four-wheeler I'm driving," Carrie said as she brushed her slacks.

"I wondered how you could follow me up the switchbacks. Where the hell did you get a four-wheel truck?"

"Pegs, you've hung around with that cretin cop so long, your language is sinking to his level."

"Let it sink. I'm tired of pretending to be Cinderella. He's my prince as far as I'm concerned."

Carrie pretended to stick her finger down her throat. Peggy laughed.

"Love may not be blind, but it sure as hell needs glasses in your case, babe." Carrie stood and stretched her arms. "Borrowed the truck. Belongs to Sherman down in the lab. He wants to get in my pants."

"Great—and you say I'm the one who needs a language check? What brought you up to the cabin? You said you weren't going to be able to come up." Peggy poured water into the container, slid it into the Mr. Coffee, and flipped the on switch. "You scared the hell out of me."

"No shit. Sorry about that. When you told me you planned to come up here for a few days, I considered it, and it sounded like a pretty good idea. I know it's kind of pushy, but I thought I'd come by and keep you company for a day or two. I need the rest. When I saw you turn in the drive, I recognized the lights of the Cherokee and tried to catch up. Bad idea, huh?"

"Understatement. You realize how close I came to killing you?"

"Not the brightest thing I've done, knowing how spooked you are. I figured you might have a damned gun, but I was scared for you when you slid in the ditch. I was worried you were hurt," Carrie said.

"Fortunately for both of us, I'm a poor shot."

"You weren't aiming for your interior light?" Carrie asked. "This is getting to be hilarious. We're both pretty pathetic when it comes to guns." They both laughed again, partly because it was funny, partly to relieve the tension.

"Want me to wrap that ankle?" Peggy asked.

"It's better already. Won't be necessary, but thanks anyway." Carrie stood, tested it, and smiled. "I'm going to the bathroom. When that gun went off, I almost wet my pants." She giggled.

"Yeah, well, you should have been inside my car. It sounded like a cannon. My ears are still ringing." Peggy patted the pocket of her coat where the gun hung heavily. "Coffee will be done in a second," she yelled at Carrie who'd disappeared down the hall. "I'm going out and take care of the cars and get the wood." She headed for the front door.

Carrie shouted from the hallway, "Pegs, when you get to mine, grab the paper bag on the front seat. I bought us some goodies, okay? Leave the luggage, I'll get it later." Peggy was silent, tired of shouting. When she opened the front door, the wind and snow laced her face and took her breath. She braced herself and walked carefully down the drive to her Cherokee, then struggled to open the passenger door. Snow fell off the roof and went down her collar as she climbed in.

"Great!" The coat was so bulky, she had trouble reaching the cold snow. Peggy picked up the unhurt dog in the blanket, petted and cooed to her.

She fumbled around in the dark, found the button, and turned off the lights. Before she got out and locked the door, she realized there was an inch of snow piled on the windows already. The ditch and the Cherokee would disappear under the snow by morning if it continued to fall this fast.

Carrie's truck still sat in the middle of the road, its lights pointed at the Cherokee. Peggy climbed up into the cab. The keys were in the ignition. She set the dog on the seat, cranked it over, and pulled the truck in front of the steep bank that stretched across the front yard. As she did, she could see the Carters' house, dark and foreboding, crouched back in the woods at the end of the street.

Peggy turned off the engine and the lights. Picking up the bag and the dog, she locked the door and climbed down. It was oppressively dark with the lights out. The wind whipped her hair, and the paper bag rustled. As she went around the end of the Toyota, she glanced into the black woods at the Carters' house, then froze in place.

A light.

Not bright, but there.

Peggy squinted. Her heart instantly accelerated. In an upstairs window, slits of yellow leaked between thin louvers. She walked to the front of the Toyota for a better view, then glanced at the snow on the narrow road.

Nothing. No tire tracks at all to the house. But there wouldn't be if whoever's there came here about an hour ago. There wasn't enough snow then to show tracks, she thought.

Peggy looked around into the black woods on all sides and shivered as a chill moved up her spine like a fluttering butterfly. She suddenly felt frightened, alone in the woods, even with Carrie in the cabin. She was comforted when she felt the heavy gun in her pocket against her leg.

"Stop being such an alarmist." Talking to herself was getting to be a habit. "That's probably just a night-light they left on. Or maybe, they left in the daytime and forgot it. That's it, they forgot it." A sense of dread grew as she hurried through the snow to her cabin. Peggy had a couple of bags of groceries in her car, but decided to get them in the morning. God knows, they'd be plenty cold enough there.

Peggy went in and set the bag on the counter. She put the dog down on the floor and took her from the blanket. Then she remembered the wood. She looked at the door apprehensively.

Do I want a fire bad enough to go out there? Peggy asked herself. If she were alone, there was no way she'd go back out into the dark. The wood was piled on one wall of the carport with a tarp cover. Three or four pieces to start it, that's all I need. A minute or so, that's all it will take, she thought.

Peggy went to the door and listened. Nothing but the sound of the wind. Do it and get it over with—you can't wait all night, she admonished herself. Opening the door, she leaned against the blast of wind and walked to the carport, around the corner, and into the garage. She surveyed the interior. Her neck was cold from the snow that had fallen into her collar, but she was barely conscious of it. What the hell am I doing up here at the cabin when I could be safe and secure at Chalky's apartment? she wondered. The idea of coming up here to hide had seemed so great when she was warm and comfortable, but now?

Grabbing an armload of wood, she ran to the door, slipped and stumbled, opened it, and went in. Once inside, she leaned against the door, tried to lock it, and the awkward pile of wood fell with a crash to the floor. Peggy swore, then bent to pick up the wood. Suddenly realizing her priorities, she reached out, latched the front door, and put the chain in place. She took a moment to try to regain her composure and wait for her heart to stop pounding and her rapid breathing to slow down.

"God, if I can get this scared over nothing, what would I do in a real emergency." She inhaled deeply, then knelt on one knee and picked up the cumbersome cold pieces of split wood.

"Sorry!" Peggy yelled into the dark hallway as she carried the wood to the stove. She chuckled to herself. The image of Carrie leaping off the commode in fright when the wood hit the floor was amusing. She could imagine what Carrie'd say when she came out. It was cold and clammy in the shut-up house. Within five minutes Peggy had a roaring fire burning. The heat felt good.

Peggy took Scooter into the front upstairs bedroom and settled her on a bed of blankets. She put down newspapers and gave her a dish of dry dog food and water. She took her out of her sling and wheels and checked her legs. They were healing nicely. The dog seemed to be spent from the excitement of the trip and lay down and closed her eyes again.

"This has been tough on you, kid. But it's going to get better soon, I promise. Have to remove those stitches in a few more days." Peggy left the door open a crack and went downstairs.

When Peggy walked into the kitchen, the coffee was finished and the fragrance was comforting. Coffee smelled like home to Peggy. Her mother had a pot brewing night and day in her home in Bellevue. As the stove warmed the house, Peggy's nose and fingers began to tingle with life.

Peggy took off her coat and brushed the snow from her collar, then draped the coat on one of the dinette chairs. The heavy gun in the coat pocket thumped against the wall. She thought of laying it on the counter for quicker access, then realized she was being much too paranoid.

Carrie's bag contained a pound of coffee, bread, butter, milk, doughnuts, breakfast rolls, and a box of brownies. All the basic food groups, she thought. Peggy put them away. At least Carrie had the presence of mind to bring something. I'll need some eggs. Forget them. I'll go down to the store in Snoqualmie in the morning for additional supplies.

"Oh, no!" She remembered her car slowly disappearing under the blanket of snow. "Have to call the Auto Club in the morning to pull it out." Dealing with it in the middle of the night seemed unreasonable. As isolated as this place was, if she called, the odds were they would respond only after this snowstorm was over.

Peggy hesitated, then listened. What the hell is taking Carrie so long? she wondered. Peggy poured a cup of fragrant black coffee, cupped it in her hands, sipped, then set it on the counter.

As she walked into the living room, she called, "Carrie! You fall in that damned thing?"

No answer. She moved into the dark hallway, listened, then tapped gently on the door. Light filtered out around the edges.

"Carrie? You okay?" She put her hand on the knob, and the door squeaked in a couple of inches.

No sound. Peggy's heart rapped against her breastbone again. She nudged the door full open.

The bathroom was empty, the light still on. Peggy stared, un-believing for a moment, then ran back to the kitchen table and pulled the gun from her coat pocket. This time she flipped off the safety before an emergency arose. She put her finger lightly on the trigger.

No more accidents, make sure of what you're shooting at, she thought.

Moving into the living room, Peggy shouted: "Carrie, where are you?" Her voice echoed through the house. Instinctively she knew she was alone. As small as the house was, Carrie should be able to hear her from any room. Downstairs, there was the living room, bath, kitchen, dinette, and a small den. Upstairs, two bedrooms and a bath. The living room and dinette ceiling went up two stories to a peaked roof. Stairs to the bedrooms were against the back wall of the living room.

"Carrie! Answer me, dammit. I'm scared—okay?" The reply, just the wind and the snow pattering against the windows that faced the woods.

Peggy breathed deeply, then walked into the hallway to the den and flipped on the hall lights as she went. She pushed open the door to the dark room, reached in, and clicked on the table lamp. It was empty except for the sparse furniture and a porta-ble television. A small window that overlooked the deck was still locked. God, what the hell's going on? She isn't downstairs—couldn't be, she thought.

Peggy came back into the living room. Her heart raced. She could hear it thump in her ears—130 beats a minute she esti-mated automatically.

Upstairs? Could she be? But why would Carrie go upstairs—for what reason. There was none. The bag with her clothes was still outside in the truck, wasn't it? I just brought in the groceries,

she reasoned. And after what happened outside, no way Carrie
would be playing with her knowing she was armed.

Looking up into the hallway leading to the two bedrooms,
Peggy could see there were no lights on. I have to go up and
check. I hate to do it, but I have to. As she slowly climbed
the stairs, a tree branch banged against the house. She jumped.
The tang of fear filled her mouth.

When Peggy flicked on the hall light, she noticed both the
bedroom doors were open including the one Scooter was sleeping in right at the top of the stairs. She went to the door of the
master bedroom first, hit the switch and glanced around.

Nothing.

Then the other one. Scooter lay still when she turned on the
light. Peggy kept the gun out in front of her at all times in a sim-
ulation of how she'd seen it done on cop shows. Both rooms
were empty; both windows locked.

"Oh, God! Where is she?" Peggy said under her breath as she
tried to control her panic. A shiver went through her body as she
hurried down to the kitchen. She stood in the dinette area, her
mind working overtime, her back to the wall, when she saw it—

The drape in front of the slider leading to the deck puffed out
as the wind whipped against the cabin.

The slider was open!

The gun in Peggy's hand quivered again, but she was too
scared to admonish herself this time. She reached inside for the
courage and inched toward the door. What's on the other side of
the window in the dark? she wondered. Can I open the drape?
No reason for Carrie to go out there the way she felt, not in this
storm! Not unless she had to—had to—had to— The phrase
echoed in her mind and chilled her more with each repeti-
tion. . . .

Peggy held her breath.

Like a moth drawn to a flame, she ripped the curtain aside—

The interior lights shone onto the deck. Heavy, wet flakes
hung on the screen as it flexed in and out from the pressure of
the wind. The clinging snow made it difficult to see through the
screen, but she could determine there was no one outside the
door. Peggy exhaled. Relieved, but still confused, she flipped

the porch light switch. No light. Must be burned out, she realized.

"Damn! Damn!" Peggy could feel tears of frustration well up, but tried to fight them off.

Carlos! Does this have something to do with him? Since this is the only window or door open, Carrie had to go out this door. I've got to know, I have to open it, see if her footprints are there . . . have to be sure . . . have to . . .

Peggy leaned against the glass door, peering back and forth to make sure no one was against the windows farther down on either side, then pushed the slider open followed by the screen. The cold air whipped into the room. She squinted into the distance . . . then glanced down. . . .

Tracks in the snow!

Peggy knelt.

The imprints of a man's shoe!

Heavy-laden.

The prints dragged, stepped, dragged, stepped, dragged through the surface of the snow leading to the stairs. Peggy edged out, unmindful of the raging wind, and looked into the ominous woods.

The tracks labored down the steps and vanished off into the blackness. In the distance, the light from her kitchen window shone on the snow, and she picked the tracks up again leading off between the trees. Then they disappeared in the direction of the other cabin—

"He's here—

"And he has Carrie," she whispered.

chapter//twenty-four

Chalky stopped at a 7-Eleven phone booth a block from the condo and dropped a quarter. Jeanette answered on the first ring.

"You sitting on the phone, Princess?"

"No—but it sounds interesting." Jeanette talked in a normal voice now.

"What's the status?"

"Little girl in the condo in the building couple of doors down snuck out and met her boyfriend in the trees behind this condo."

"You're kidding me? No other activity?"

"Not if you don't count the heavy breathing from behind the underbrush." Chalky could hear her smile.

"Be there in ten minutes," he said and hung up. Chalky was supposed to be there hours from now, but he was so keyed up, it was pointless to stay at the apartment. He'd give Merrick a chance to go home and readjust to the new schedule.

Chalky went in the store and looked at the magazines, then remembered he'd be sitting in the dark bedroom and bought a pack of gum instead. The man with the mustache groaned when he had to ring up the small sale. Chalky glared at him and bit his tongue.

When Chalky got into Peggy's neighborhood he cruised the whole area, then parked in a secluded spot on the access road near the entrance so his car would be unobtrusive. It took just a couple of minutes to walk to the condo. He made his way along the trees in back and snuck up to the den window and knocked. Merrick let him in.

"About time, Mr. Macho," Merrick said. "Nothing going on

here. No calls either. Quiet as a church." Chalky climbed
through the window and brushed himself off. It was easy to
convince Merrick he should leave.

Merrick went out the same window and disappeared into the
trees. He had driven his own car and it was parked up near the
entrance in front of an occupied condo so as not to draw attention. Chalky settled in the dark bedroom and checked his
weapon. He could hear Jeanette humming in the dinette area.

Chalky got nervous after a few minutes when Peggy failed to
call like she said she would. She has to be settled by now, he
thought.

In the kitchen, Jeanette played solitaire at the table, drinking
coffee. The stereo from the living room boomed classical music
that sounded familiar to him, but the title escaped him, as usual.
Finally, Chalky whispered to Jeanette from the door at a pause
in the music.

Jeanette came into the dark room, smiled, and said, "Change
of the guard, huh? Didn't hear you come in. What's the matter
. . . getting lonesome in here, Chalky-baby?"

"What time is it?"

"After nine—little bit."

"How about calling the good doctor for me, okay? I'm worried she hasn't checked in here yet."

"We wanted to keep this line open, remember."

"Jesus! Okay. But at nine-thirty, you have to call. I'm going
bug-house."

"Wanna fool around a little for old times' sake to take your
mind off the wait?" Jeanette asked, hands on her hips, smiling.
"Who'd know?"

"You wouldn't like it, Jan. I'm a lousy lay, I have it on good
authority. Besides, I'm spoken for."

"Rest-room wall at the station says you're great in bed."

"Don't believe it. I wrote that there months ago. Besides
that's my line. What're we men going to use if you broads steal
all our lines." He chuckled softly.

"God forbid you'd have to come up with some new ones." As
she walked away, she said, "Don't say I didn't give you a
chance." She bounced back to her chair and settled in. He knew

she was just kidding—he hoped. If she was serious, her marriage was in trouble.

The chair Jeanette sat in had a clear view to the street, and they made sure of that by leaving the drapes open. It was the "I'm home, come and get me" chair. They had little fear of Carlos shooting her through the window. His M. O. was to use knives on his female victims.

Finally, feeling guilty, she got up, came in, and leaned in the door. Chalky glanced up from where he sat.

"Don't worry, babe," she said. "Your cookie's probably taking a quickie nap or something. There ain't nothin' to bother her up there in the boonies, nothin' at all."

"My God, my God!" Peggy slammed the sliding door. "Oh, please, don't let him hurt her," she mumbled as she snapped the lock in place. She looked at the dinette table. In the center was a folded sheet of paper she had missed before, a flyer with a map from the Seattle area to the cabin on it. It was familiar. She picked it up.

The heading said: "Open house party." It was the flyer she'd had made five years ago when her mother and father bought the cabin. It had been sent out to all their friends. The only copy left was the copy in her—

"My God! He's been in the drawers of my writing desk in my bedroom. Carlos was in my condo!" The realization raced through her nervous system. "When?" She dropped the flyer to the floor in disgust as though it were infected by his touch. He'd intentionally laid it on the table so she'd know how he'd found her. She checked the door.

The footprints led away from the house. That means he had to be hiding in this house . . . waiting. Waiting while we came in the door and made coffee. Listened while we talked. Listened when I put my coat on and went back out into the cold. That's when he came out from where he hid . . . and sneaked up on Carrie in the bathroom. My God! With the memory of Joanne Pinkers still so vivid, the idea horrified Peggy.

Peggy ran to the phone, dropped the gun on the countertop next to it, breathed deeply, then dialed 911. She put the phone to her ear and mentally reviewed what she was going to say—

Peggy's gaze whipped around the room, then she suddenly realized the phone was silent.

No sound. No ringing. Not even a buzz.

She clicked the cradle up and down rapidly.

No clicking sound in her ear.

It was dead.

"Of course," she said softly to herself. "Why would you expect it to work? That's probably the first thing he did when he got here."

Peggy set the handle down gently, then glanced up at the clock.

Time. Time was her enemy. Time was Carrie's enemy.

Peggy remembered how important minutes, actually, seconds, were when Carlos had broken into her house.

If those gunshots had come five or six minutes later than they did—

Peggy shivered. Carrie! What's she thinking right now . . . how frightened is she?

Peggy studied the face of the clock as the second hand moved smoothly around the dial—each tick precious.

9:58 P.M. exactly.

Peggy's mind raced.

The truck? No. Even if I could get away, it wouldn't do Carrie any good. It would take at least forty minutes to get to a telephone . . . another half hour to forty-five minutes for someone to respond. Over an hour . . . God!

Peggy picked up the gun with her left hand and studied it as though seeing it for the first time. It seemed heavier, colder, and more lethal than before.

"I have to go," she said in a sober tone. "It's her only chance . . . at this moment he could be—" The image of him cutting into Carrie's arms was a blow to her midsection.

"Bastard! Bastard!" Tired of being intimidated, she grabbed her coat and slipped it on. Me! No one else. I have to do it— now! Peggy had the oppressive feeling she was walking to her death, but there was no alternative. Her conscience screamed at her to move—to try to protect Carrie.

That firm decision made, she felt her strength returning. She thought of the flashlight in the glove compartment of her Jeep, then discarded the idea. Walking around flashing a light in the dark would just make her a much better target.

When she pushed the slider open and stepped out, the wind lashed her hair and shook her conviction. The snowflakes were large and wet. Off in the distance, his tracks were quickly disappearing under the swirling snow as she reached the bottom of the stairs and headed for the other cabin.

It was pointless to look for footprints to follow, Peggy knew where she had to go. Only one place they could be. The only other refuge from this storm was two hundred feet away in the dark. As she moved, her head swiveled constantly—afraid she was the hunted—instead of the hunter.

Peggy wobbled in the deepening snow and slipped and fell to one knee. Her free hand came up wet and cold. She held it against her face to warm it as she continued into the wind and darkness.

The dark house loomed ominously. Much larger than hers, it was a full two stories with an enclosed garage, built for a family of eight. When she got closer, she glanced up at the windows. The only light on in the entire house still came from the second-floor window. The wind took her breath as she went along the garage.

Carlos's car must be in here, she thought. She placed her feet carefully to keep from falling again. No tire tracks in the driveway she could see. No window in the garage, but she knew his car waited patiently inside. She wondered idly what kind a crazy man drives.

He's watching me, I know it, she thought. As Peggy passed the dark windows in the rear, a wave of fear passed through her. Carlos could be waiting behind any one of them. She stepped away from each window as she passed, as though he had the supernatural ability to reach through the glass and grab her.

If Chalky were only here, he'd know what to do. I'll try the back door first, then the front if it's not open. Eight more bullets in my gun. That's all I have. I've already shot one . . . then . . . No, I only have seven, she remembered. One popped out in the car and is lying there somewhere. Seven, I'll have to hang on to that.

The yard was dark with the imposing house on one side, the

towering trees on the other. Peggy stepped up on the stoop in front of the door and tried to look through the glass. The screen door covering it was filled with snow, so there was no way she could see in.

Peggy'd been in the house before, and she knew the door led into a mud-room, then to an interior door that opened into a large country kitchen. She swung back the screen, then turned the knob on the door.

It was unlocked. Peggy had to concentrate on her concern for Carrie to beat off the instinct that cried: "Run, run!"

In the musty kitchen now. There were no cooking odors. Nothing had been prepared in here in weeks. Peggy stood silently, trying to listen. They had to be upstairs; it was the only place in the house that had showed any light. Dare I turn on more lights? she wondered. It had to be safer, right? She ran her hand across the wall, found a switch, and squinted with expectation when she flipped it.

No light again! He must have knocked out these circuit breakers. Or maybe this light is just broken. Dammit! Don't worry about that. I've got to get up there . . . to where Carrie is . . . to help her. Oh, God! I'm so scared. Can I do it?

Peggy's hand hit something hard . . . and it dinged.

Her heart raced as she searched the darkness with her gaze . . . then she realized what it was—

A telephone.

Could it be connected?

We leave ours connected because it's too much trouble to take it in and out in the spring . . . maybe . . . too much to hope for?

Peggy's hand touched the hard, cold plastic again and she felt for the receiver on the desk model phone.

She found it and inched it off the cradle.

The buzz in the silence of the room was audible before it reached her ear.

Thank God! Tears jumped to her eyes and she bit her lip.

Peggy clutched the gun in her right . . . the handle in her left . . . reluctant to put either down. Damn, she thought and gently laid the gun on the counter.

She put her hand on the buttons and tried to visualize them in the dark. Top left is one . . . bottom right, then . . . would have to be . . . nine. It was inky black in the room and she groaned inside when she thought about the flashlight sitting on the front seat of her car. No time . . . have to dial . . .

Peggy dialed by feel. 9–1–1.

The buzz changed to a busy signal.

"Damn!" she whispered.

Off in the darkness of the hallway . . . something clunked.

Peggy froze and listened. She set the buzzing handset down and picked up the gun and aimed it into the blackness.

Her skin was alive waiting for the next noise . . . but it was silent in the house except for the annoying busy signal and the wind moaning beyond the windows. She set the gun down again, clicked the line, then redialed 911.

Same busy signal.

Peggy's instinct was to scream in frustration, but she concentrated on counting the buttons with her finger. One, two, three—(next row)—four, five, six—(next row)—seven, eight, nine. Still have a row left, she wondered. Of course! The funny pound signs and the zero . . . in the middle . . . of course. I was hitting a funny thing for the nine!

She pushed nine and then the one—twice.

The phone rang. Relief washed over her.

Three—four—five—six—seven rings. Peggy whimpered softly. Twelve—thirteen—fourteen—

From the front of the house—something banged again. Peggy picked up the gun and listened with her other ear for more sound from the other room.

Twenty rings. Peggy clicked the handset down. No more time. She had to call her house and tell Chalky, then go save Carrie . . . NOW!

She carefully dialed her home number and was surprised when the telephone was answered on the first ring.

A woman's voice said, "Yes?"

Must be the woman detective, thought Peggy.

"Tell him he's here—" Peggy stuttered. Her voice was weak and sounded far off.

"Who's where?" the woman asked.

Click.

The line went dead.

Peggy choked and clicked it up and down.

The game was over. He'd cut this line too.

She set the receiver down and listened. Nothing moving. No sound.

No time, have to save Carrie, she thought. If Chalky comes . . . he comes. In either case, I have to go now. . . .

Peggy walked from the kitchen into the dark hall and held the gun up into the void. She could see the bottom of the stairs where dim light filtered down from upstairs. As she moved along, each doorway brought a new level of fear. Carlos could hang back in the shadows and leap at her at any moment. She'd never see him in time to be able to react and shoot.

A sound. Something clunked in the blackness. Where did it come from? It was impossible to tell. Peggy froze in place and the hairs on her neck tingled with anticipation. She willed the sound to come again. If she could know where he was, she'd feel better. Expecting him to attack from any direction was terrifying.

A snicker.

Low, yet out in the darkness somewhere. Carlos knew she was in the house and was enjoying her fear. Then another snicker. Soft, almost sibilant.

Bastard, crazy bastard! Peggy hated him for what he was doing to them. Please, please let Carrie be all right. She forced herself forward in spite of taut muscles that ached from the tension.

At the bottom of the stairs she turned and waved the gun into the blackness where she knew the living room to be. If he was in there, he could see her, but it was impossible to see him.

A shuffling from the living room. A mouse? Or Carlos? Peggy moved up the stairs toward the light emanating from the open doorway at the top. She took the first few steps quickly, knowing the farther up the stairs she was, the less vulnerable she'd be to physical attack from the dark living room. She noticed the light flickered as she approached the opening. Something burning? Candles? Must be candles or something—

A laugh from the blackness downstairs—she was able to isolate the sound this time about twenty feet away.

He's there!

A *crash!* Something broke on the living-room hardwood floor. Carlos is down there and is making noise intentionally. He seems to want me to know where he is, she thought. Her breathing and heart rate were so fast it was difficult to estimate what they were. A drop of sweat crawled down her neck and tickled her spine.

Why not attack me as I went by? No way I could be able to stop him. What does he want? It's almost as though . . . as though he wants me to know he's down there . . . but wants me to keep going . . . into the room . . . but why? she wondered.

Peggy sprang to life, ran the last four steps to the top, hesitated at the door, went through quickly, leaned back against the wall, and tried to take in the room in one sweep. Her gun followed her gaze. The light was from four tall candles, two burning on either side of a bed. He was gone . . . it was empty, except for . . .

Carrie lying faceup!

Her arms spread-eagled . . . her arms . . . still in place . . . thank God!

But she had a large pillow over her head—

Oh, God, Carrie! Did he suffocate you?

"Carrie?" Peggy said weakly. The figure was still. Peggy grabbed the knob and slammed the door to keep Carlos from sneaking up behind her when she approached the bed.

"Carrie!" Peggy shouted. Being quiet is stupid—he knows I'm here. Carrie lay motionless. "Carrie, are you all right?" Peggy's voice quivered when she tried to talk in a normal voice. Her body was so charged with adrenaline it would have been impossible to talk without shaking. Peggy looked at the closet. The door was closed tightly. Why worry about that . . . you heard him downstairs . . . help Carrie!

"Carrie, honey . . . I've been so worried . . ."

Peggy was at the bed—

"I've been so worried he would cut your arms off . . ."

She reached out and grabbed the pillow—

"God, I'm so glad to see that . . ."

She pulled the pillow away—

Screaming, Peggy leapt back and stumbled into the wall. The

gun clattered to the floor. She could feel her stomach involuntarily rejecting what it held, and she continued screaming through wet gasps as her diaphragm pumped her lunch and breakfast onto the carpet in front of her.

The ghastly image came in waves of horror—
The pillow moving—
The bed underneath—
Covered with blood—
Where Carrie's head should have been.

chapter//twenty-five

"Chalky! Move it!" Jeanette shouted through the doorway of the condo bedroom.

Chalky leapt up, already alert from the phone ringing throughout the condo.

"Was it her?" he asked.

"I don't know her voice ... but my guess would be yes," Jeanette said.

"What? What? What'd she say?" he yelled.

"Four words ... then it sounded like we were cut off—'Tell him he's here,' she said."

" 'Tell him he's here'?" he asked as he ran to the kitchen telephone.

"Yeah. Nothing more. Just that ... then whap ... the line went dead."

"Holy shit!" Chalky shouted and grabbed the telephone. He took out a slip of paper and dialed the number of the cabin. He banged the buttons on the wall phone like he was smashing bugs.

He said, "Damn!" when a busy signal came on the line.

Without hesitating, he called again.

Same thing.

Chalky hung up and tapped his fingers on the counter. "Maybe she's trying to get through here," he speculated. "What do you think?" he asked. "Should we wait?"

She shrugged. While they waited impatiently, she got up and went over and closed the blinds.

Chalky grabbed the receiver and tried again.

Same thing.

"Damn! Damn! Damn!" he shouted. He dialed the operator and identified himself and asked her to check Peggy's phone. She popped off the line. Chalky glanced up at the clock, shook his head, and rubbed his forehead. It took everything he had to keep from slamming out the door.

"That line's out of order, sir—I'll report it for—"

The receiver hit the cradle before she finished.

"He's there! The son of a bitch must have cut the line or something!" he yelled. Jeanette's response was to stand and pick up her purse. She took out her automatic and checked it.

Chalky called the station and talked to the desk sergeant. He explained he wanted him to call the sheriff's office at Snoqualmie and tell them to send a unit to Peggy's address immediately—that he'd go there himself as soon as he hung up. Chalky thanked him and banged the receiver back in place.

"I'll call Merrick as soon as you leave," Jeanette said. "If he can't come down, I'll take off."

"Bull! You can't stay here without a backup. Leave immediately. I've done enough stupid things lately. I don't want to worry about you too. If we're wrong about this thing at the cabin, you could be in deep shit here alone."

"I'm okay, big guy, honestly."

"No, I'm in charge of this stakeout. I say fold it—now. We're wasting time."

"What the hell, I wanted to do my nails tonight anyway." She sighed.

It took them five minutes to lock up and get the Cherokee out of the garage. Chalky climbed in, and she dropped him off at his car. He slammed the car door without saying good-bye and got in his car.

Driving moderately at first, he accelerated when he got to the main drag, reached through the window, put his magnetic emergency light on his roof, turned it on, and hit the I-90 on-ramp at over seventy miles an hour. He called in and had dispatch call the Snoqualmie Police to let them know he was going to be in their area and he was coming with his emergency lights on.

Something was wrong at the cabin—had to be. Could he get there in time? He looked at his dashboard clock.

10:18 P.M.
It would take at least thirty minutes to get there—a lifetime.

Peggy bent down quickly and picked up the gun she'd
dropped. Her body was cold from the frigid room and the fear.
She felt so weak, she was unsure whether she was capable of
any action at all. From downstairs, she could hear him snickering, louder than before. His voice sounded less and less human to her. Then, the sound of heavy, purposeful steps on the
wood floor.

Bang! A door slamming on the ground floor. Moving around
sounds.

Peggy leaned back against the wall, her entire system in
shock. She tried not to look toward the bed, at the horror on the
other side of the room. Peggy was hardened to dealing with ca-
davers in her training, but it was nothing like this.

Not when it was her best friend—not Carrie—

"Oh, Carrie, Carrie," she whispered. If I could have been a
little sooner . . . maybe I . . . The thought of the gore-covered
bedding made her nauseous again. She struggled to control her
gag reflex as she breathed deeply, her free hand up to her throat.

"Where's he going?" Peggy whispered in fear and frustration. "He knows where I am . . . why doesn't he come up the
stairs?" She tried to reason why he would let her pass by the hall
untouched. Now to simply go out the door? That's—if he did.
Carlos wanted me to come up here . . . to find Carrie . . . but
why didn't he follow . . . what's, what's he doing? Anything's
possible. His mind doesn't function normally. He could be
thinking anything—anything! If I'm going to survive, I have to
get a grip on myself. How can I delay him or get away?

She thought of Chalky. Any illusions about him coming and
saving her disappeared when she found Carrie's corpse. This
was reality—this was happening. If she was to survive, it would
have to be on her own—there was no one to save her. Even if
that woman understood what she was talking about and told
Chalky, it would be a long time before he got here. And . . .
what if I had a wrong number? she thought, then shuddered. I
don't know for sure who she was.

Outside, the wind howled louder and branches from a tree scraped against the window.

The dark staircase and hall? Impossible to face that again—there has to be an alternative! The image of opening the door and going down into that blackness was more terrifying than being up here with Carrie's mutilated body.

I could stay here, cover the door and window with the gun, shoot him if he came in. No! I have to get out! He might decide to burn the house down . . . blow it up . . . anything . . . he's not going to give up and go away . . . even as crazy as he is, he knows I have a gun . . . he had to see it when I was in the candle-light . . . he'll certainly be careful . . . not just walk in. . . .

"The truck," she whispered. But he's down there in the dark . . . and he's probably waiting for me to come through the door. If I could surprise him, sneak up on him for a change? If he's watching the door, I could . . .

Peggy forced her eyes to the bed, across to the window, then remembered the scratching sound. A tree? She held her breath and went to one side of the bed, concentrated on not looking at the body, snuffed the two candles, then walked around to the other side and did the same. The room seemed instantly colder. Her only chance of getting out unseen was to douse the light, so she and Carlos would be on an equal footing. She walked to the window, opened the shutters, felt for the lock, turned it, and pulled up on the sash. It stuck, then gave way. Cold gusts and snow whirled into the room.

Peggy squinted through the wind out at the slanting roof. The branches of two cedar trees extended over it, the needles of one scraping the house. She buried the gun in her pocket, felt for the truck keys, found them, patted the pocket, then ducked and stepped out the window. Her foot instantly slipped on the snow-slick roofing. It was so dark she could barely distinguish the outline of the trees.

Peggy strained to locate the truck in the distance, but the swaying branches obscured it. With her body outside and holding on to the windowsill, she lined herself up with the larger of the two trees and let go. She slid down the roof and collided hard with the trunk. She was vaguely conscious of the pain on her face and arms from where the branches had raked her as she slid. Reaching instinctively to save herself, she was able to hold on to a branch. She swung her legs back and forth, found a lower limb, and braced herself on it.

After Peggy cleared her head from the impact, she could taste the blood in her mouth. *This all seems so hopeless, so inept. How can I hope to get away if I'm so clumsy I keep hurting myself?* she wondered.

Feeling for each branch, she lowered herself from limb to limb until she was about five feet above the snow. The one she was standing on cracked, and she fell to the ground hard. When she landed on her back, the air slammed from her chest. She struggled for breath as the cold night air burned her throat and lungs. Peggy grimaced as she rubbed her jammed ankle. Her legs, arms, and face were on fire from raking the limbs on the way down. *Cut or abraded,* she knew. *The least of my worries.*

She sat up and looked out from under the tree. Nothing moved in the blackness. Off in the distance, she could see dim lights from her cabin. Pulling the cold automatic, she rose, bumped her head, and stepped from under the tree.

The truck was still hidden in the storm, but she knew where it was in relationship to the house. *In this dark, there's no point in being subtle. His vision will be just as limited as mine, so we're on equal footing.*

Peggy glanced back at the woods and considered running in that direction, but knew she'd be lost in just minutes. Chances of surviving overnight in this cold were practically zero. Her breathing had returned to normal, but her whole respiratory system was raw from the effort of sucking the icy air in and out. She limped through the snow in the general direction of the truck.

At the road, she could see the dark outline of the four-wheeler between the falling flakes. It was eerily still between the gusts of wind. No sign of Carlos. She walked faster as she got closer. In front of the truck, she turned and faced the blackness, scanning in all directions. Peggy held the gun out. It was heavy and her fingers could no longer feel the hard metal. She strained to hear, but there were no other sounds above the wind.

Working her way around to the driver's side, Peggy reached in her pocket and withdrew the ignition key with her free hand, then realized the door was unlocked. She jiggled the keys at the ready, because once inside, she had to start the truck and move quickly. The time she'd have might only be seconds. She peeked in the window. The interior was solid black—not even enough light to see the steering wheel.

"He could be in there," she whispered. I'll stand back after I open the door in case he is. When the light comes on—if he's there—I'll shoot him!

She grabbed the door handle, yanked it, and stepped back, all in the same motion. The interior light came on. . . .

Peggy stumbled backward and fell in the middle of the drive in the snow, then did a crab crawl several feet farther still staring at the interior of the truck. Her mouth was open, but nothing came out.

Eyes locked on the seat—
Where the stark overhead light shone down—
On Carrie's anguished face and shadowed eyes—
The mouth of the dismembered head hanging open—
As though trying to speak.

chapter//twenty-six

In the background above the wind, Peggy could heard a high-pitched screeching. Carlos's voice, insane with delight. She tore her eyes away from the truck to the blackness around her. He was somewhere in the woods behind her.

On her hands and knees now, she searched frantically through the wet snow and found her gun two feet away. The keys were still lost somewhere. No matter. With that horror on the seat, she had to get away from the truck anyway.

Peggy leapt to her feet and impulsively slammed the door on the truck to block out Carrie's haunted face and ran for the cabin—

She was able to scream at last. When she smashed against the front door, she jiggled the knob.

Locked? She struggled with it for a moment, then realized she had locked it earlier. Still screaming, she stumbled and slipped in the snow while running around the side of the house.

Charging through the open slider, she threw it closed and locked it. Her voice had settled into a keening sound emanating deep in her chest. Her breath came fast and ragged. She ran to the staircase, sat on the steps, and huddled against the wall. Shaking violently, she stared at the windows out of tear-filled eyes.

A fragile, terrified child again.

"How far down this road is the turnoff?" Deputy Arnold asked. The two men had left the Snoqualmie sheriff's office in their Bronco and were on their way to Peggy's cabin.

"About another two miles, I make it," Deputy James answered as he hunched his two-hundred-fifty-pound frame over the wheel.

"I can't believe we're responding in this kind of weather to a story as thin as that sergeant from Seattle gave you. Shit! This big city showboat says he *thinks* that doctor is in trouble?" Arnold said.

"Relax. Professional courtesy. We'll just mosey up there, check around, pick up our brownie points, then scoot on back. No biggie. Relax and I'll show you how this Bronco eats up the highway," James said.

"He mentioned the cutup killer from Seattle?"

"Yeah. Hollywood shit. Trying to impress me. Chances are when we get up there, she's not answerin' the phone 'cause she's screwin' some logger and can't be bothered."

"All the same—shouldn't we have called for a backup or something? I know I'm new, but ain't that procedure?"

"Give me a break. All that noise would break their rhythm."

"Doctors screw?" Arnold asked, smiling.

"Sure. Ain't you ever been screwed by some goddamned doctor? I have, lots of times." They both laughed hard and concentrated on the white road ahead.

Peggy snuffled quietly like an injured animal and could feel her reason return in small increments. Her instincts were to find a closet somewhere, roll into a ball, and go to sleep instead of facing up to this.

Crack! Crack! Something hard and metallic impacted sharply against the patio window. Peggy found herself standing and staring across the room at the point of the sound without realizing she had moved. The gun hung loosely in her hand—an appendage that seemed numb.

"Lady! Hey, lady!"

Carlos's voice. He shrieked loud and high-pitched to be heard above the windstorm.

"Hey, lady! Let me in!" The yell ended with a whoop and a laugh. Peggy could feel her fear slowly being replaced by anger. He'd just destroyed the life of her best friend as casually as she would swat a fly. She knew he had no control of his actions, but the urge to kill him was overpowering.

Crack! Crack! Hard against the window again. Peggy raised the gun instinctively and rapid-fired four times at the point she thought he was hitting. The glass of the sliding door exploded out into millions of tiny granules leaving only shards of glass around the edges.

Peggy was stunned. She expected it to make small bullet holes in the glass. The wind whipped into the living room and snapped the drapes back and forth. The huge hole sucked the warmth from the room almost instantly.

"Oh, lady! Now look what you done," he screamed and cackled again in an irritating laugh, his voice shrill and clear through the opening.

Four shots, her numbed mind computed. She glanced down at the gun. I have how many bullets left? Four from . . . from what? Seven! That's what I had . . . or eight? No—seven. That leaves only three. Less than half what I had originally.

"I can't shoot any more unless he's right in front of me," she whispered as if to impress it on her brain. "Right in front of me."

Bang! Bang! A loud thumping against the side of the house to the right. He's trying to terrorize me into using up my remaining bullets. Don't shoot unless you see him, she reminded herself. Three bullets between me and death or disfigurement for life. I mustn't shoot until I have him in my sights.

Crash! Tinkle! Upstairs. A breaking window. She started up the steps, then realized the gaping hole in the living room was an open walkway. He's trying to draw me up there so he can come through here. What can I do? That's stupid! If he's near the window—he can't be here too—even he can't be two places at one time, she thought.

Peggy ran up to the master bedroom and peeked in the door. The window had a foot-wide hole in it and glass sprinkled the floor. A heavy rock lay next to the wall. After surveying it, she turned immediately, went to the top of the stairs, and looked down on the gaping slider in the living room.

Peggy shivered as the cold air swirled around the room, then wondered if it was possible for him to have come in and hid somewhere in the twenty seconds she was out of sight of the opening. No—it was impossible—she would have heard him.

This elevated vantage point between the hall and the living room below was as good as she could ask for. She was confident she could hear him if he came through either opening and relaxed a little . . .

When the lights went out.

"The houses are dark," James said as they approached the cabins at the end of the drive.

"Which one is it?" Arnold asked.

"One on the right—the first one. That drive's a pisser," James said. "I'll park here on the flat. We can walk up. Don't want to chance the ditches like that other car there. Jesus—people can't drive worth a shit." He motioned to the mound of snow that was the Cherokee.

"I'll go up, you stay here. Shouldn't take more'n a couple of minutes, then we can be on our way. Can't believe we're wasting our goddamned time like this," Arnold mumbled as they stopped behind the Toyota almost obscured by the flying snow. James snapped off the lights, pulled out a small pocket-sized radio, and turned it on. A basketball game in progress filled the Bronco—a crowd roaring as the announcer described a fast break to the basket.

"Hey, partner. Isn't that against regulations?" Arnold asked.

"Don't be such a fucking Alice. Who'll know? You want to work up here, boy, you have to bend with the wind." He adjusted the volume slightly and put it in his breast pocket. "Hurry it up. I want to get back. Maybe we can stop and catch the end of this Sonics game."

"You could go in—and I could sit here and listen," Arnold said with irritation.

James chuckled, then said, "No. I like your first idea better. Take your time. Flash your light at me if you want me to come."

Arnold stepped into the snow, slammed the door, and made his way up the steep driveway and disappeared from James's sight in the swirling snow. When he got to the walk, he noticed there were partially filled-in tracks to the door. He directed the beam of his long-handled flashlight on the snow, and could see they continued around the side of the house. It was a small detail, but it alerted him to a new level of awareness. He considered blinking his light at James, grumbled, then decided to ring the bell instead. He was new, but he had his share of courage.

At the door, he found the small button and pressed it. With the wind whining through the trees it was impossible to hear if it had rung or not. He bent down and put his ear flat against the door and pushed the button again. No bell . . . electric must be off. Christ, maybe there's not even anybody here. That big-time Seattle asshole sent us on a wild goose chase!

He banged the door with the palm of his fist and yelled, "Police, open up! Police!"

Nothing. He looked at the door, then shook his head. Stepping away, he flashed the light on the walk again.

These tracks. They had to have been made about a half hour ago. The way they're only partly filled in, there has to be someone here. He followed them around the side of the house past the raised decking toward the steps. When he got to the stairs, he noticed the tracks were deeper. Fresh tracks. He went up the stairs and shone the bright light along the wall, then stopped it on the shattered slider window.

"Holy shit!" His body involuntarily tensed. He knew he should stop here and get James, but it was so far in the snow— and he wanted to take a quick peek inside the window—beyond the flapping curtains. He could call James through dispatch on his hand unit, but since they were supposed to both be investigating, it could be awkward if questions were asked. Damn!

He unsnapped his holster and withdrew his gun, then pushed the fabric aside and stepped forward onto the broken glass into the living room. Inside, out of the raging wind, it was deathly still. His heart pumped hard, his breath came fast. Should go back and get James, should go back . . . one quick look. . . .

"Hello?" he said into the blackness, his light working its way along the wall, and then . . .

The beam pinpointed a woman with wild eyes, pointing a gun directly at him—

He spoke to identify himself at the same time the gun flashed—

The impact as the bullets slammed into him—

Stumbling backward, he was falling, but felt nothing when he hit—

The blackness had cradled and warmed him before he landed.

Climbing up the pass, Chalky could see a pattern of red taillights ahead, with the sputtering of penetrating flares burning along the edges of both sides of the road.

"Damn! Another delay!" Earlier, even though he hated the extra time it took, he had to stop at the bottom of the hill and put chains on the rear wheels to get the traction his regular snow tires needed to climb the switchbacks to the cabin. He slowed and stopped.

An eighteen-wheeler had lost control and virtually disassembled in the roadway while he was stopped, putting on his chains. It had been coming down the hill on the other side of the highway, slid across the no-man's-land, turned over, then completely blocked his side of the road. Fortunately, it had missed other cars, but there was no way to get between the debris.

Traffic was already backing up behind him and he was rapidly becoming penned in. He felt his stomach knot when he thought of Peggy alone in the cabin. He looked around desperately for a way out.

The open area between the two roads was too deep to drive across; the berm to the right too piled with snow to get through. He called headquarters on his radio and asked them to connect him to the sergeant on the desk. The sergeant grumbled, "What do you want?"

"You reach them at Snoqualmie, and did they send a car up to the cabin like I asked? I'm buried in traffic on the hill here."

"Said they'd do it. Right away."

"Look, don't get ticked off, but will you call them and make sure they did. Peggy's life could be on the line here!"

"Jeez, don't get your ass in an uproar. Hang on, I'll call on the phone and be right back." The line snapped, and he was gone. Chalky could feel his tension building. What seemed like fifteen minutes was actually two and a half minutes.

"Chalky, if you can shake loose, you'd better do it. The office got a call in from a Deputy James saying he had heard shots fired from the interior of the cabin. He was calling for backup when his line went dead. They kept trying to call him and got nothing—no answer. They're thin as hell up there, but are sending four off-duty men. Talking to them now. They should be on their way in ten minutes."

"Thanks," Chalky said, and slammed the mike in its holder. He opened the door and leaned into the wind, then stood. He looked at the growing jam of vehicles in frustration. No emergency vehicles here yet. I can't wait, he thought.

Sliding down the bank, he slogged through the snow across the divider. Cars and trucks were parked on the other side of the road to rubber-neck at the accident in front of him.

He ran along the line of cars until he got to the end. The last truck was a shiny, four-wheel-drive Suburban with an older man in it. Chalky opened the door and leaned in.

"Police officer, emergency! I need your vehicle, step out please. You can wait in my vehicle there." As he spoke, he held out his badge, then pointed to his car pulled off the edge of the road in the distance. The man glanced at his badge, then at the car uncertainly.

"Ain't going nowhere with my car—it's new!" The man reached and tried to jerk the door closed without even waiting for him to get out of the way. Chalky grabbed him by the front of his coat and wrestled him from the seat, then stood him up and brushed him off.

"Sorry. I don't have the time to reason with you. Over there," Chalky said, smiling his "don't screw with me" smile, and pointed at his car again. "Door's open. I'll apologize later."

The man was saying something about he was going to have his job—he paid his taxes—Chalky worked for him—and on and on—

Chalky started the engine, backed up, and drove down the road the wrong way. Chalky heaved a sigh of relief that no lights of approaching cars were ahead of him.

Must be blocked on the other side of the hill, he figured.

He drove up the on-ramp to Amsterdam Road, then over the freeway and back into the woods—following the path Peggy had taken when he left her earlier.

Six miles to go. Peggy—be all right—be all right—

• • •

Peggy was terrified as she approached the figure lying on the floor and picked up the flashlight. She turned the beam on what she thought was Carlos's body, screamed, dropped it, and backed up to the wall. The light cracked when it hit and went out.

"My God my God my God! I've killed a policeman!" She looked around desperately. Her own gun was empty, and she dropped it as useless.

I have to get his gun . . . have to . . . only chance.

Carlos could be anywhere, and she knew she'd have seconds before he closed in on her.

It's on the floor somewhere . . . have to find it . . . I have to. . . . Peggy leaned down and felt around the floor. . . . He had something in his hand . . . a gun maybe . . . so it's here somewhere, if I can . . . the light . . . I have to crawl to the . . .

"Hello, lady."

Carlos's voice. Clear. Just a few feet away.

At the opening behind the drapes.

"You ain't got no more bullets, lady . . . I know . . . I heard your gun—it clicked." He chuckled.

Peggy heard the crunch of glass and could barely make out a dark outline stepping through the curtains. She froze in place, too frightened to move, still on her hands and knees. Her whole body turned cold.

"My mother . . . she could have lived too . . . if I could have helped her . . . you unnerstand, don't you, lady?" His voice was soft and appealing, almost reasonable. "Can't you see it . . . the sun . . . in the sky. . . ."

Peggy's mind churned. I have to move, I have to run . . . I have to make my muscles move . . . now . . . I have to stand . . . God, give me strength . . . I have to . . .

Carlos mumbled, "It's so hot . . . so hot . . . can you see the sun in the sky, lady . . . it means . . . I have to . . ."

Another crunch of glass galvanized her into action. He was only about ten feet away in the dark. Peggy leapt to her feet and ran toward the stairs, banged her leg into the rail, then ran up the steps as fast as she could.

She could feel his hands reaching, grabbing for her as in a

nightmare, but she kept moving until she knocked the master bedroom door open. She slammed it hard and leaned against it.

On the other side of the door, Peggy could hear Carlos laughing out of control as he approached. Casually, at an almost indifferent pace. Then his voice was near the other side of the door.

Carlos was in no hurry.

He knew the chase was almost over.

"Lady, don't keep running, you're going to hurt yourself! I got something here for you!" He broke into a chilling, hacking laugh that degenerated into a sound like rapid hiccups.

Peggy could feel his weight against the other side of the door—

Against her grip, the knob turned in her hands—the door was forced inward—

Screaming, she leaned her full weight on the handle, but it inched open anyway—

No way to keep the knob from turning—the door from moving!

Gradually she was pushed backward—her feet sliding on the hardwood—

As the door slowly opened.

chapter//twenty-seven

As Chalky got closer to the cabin, he constantly talked to himself, making deals, arguing, trying to convince the Almighty to give Peggy just one more chance. Chalky was neutral on religion, but even agreed to go to church every Sunday if He'd spare her. And Chalky meant it—at least right now.

"Maybe it's not him. Could be a hunter, or something could have scared her, or the gun could have gone off accidentally when she was loading it maybe." Even as he said it, he knew it was wrong. Hunter? In this kind of weather? Nonsense. The only thing left was an accidental or intentional firing. The most likely probability was she shot at Carlos to try to save her life—or God forbid—he had shot at her.

Then . . . maybe she shot the bastard! That would be almost too good to be true. He's been lucky up until now . . . not a dim bulb about covering his ass . . . but slipping away from reality more each day. Yeah, that's what happened. She shot him. Chalky had to believe that.

The image of her maimed for life was something he had to reject. It was unthinkable. Buried deep in his mind, it kept trying to creep into his consciousness, but he beat it back with positive thoughts. Not to Peggy. Not my Peggy. His eyes were hot and burned with unshed tears of fear and grief.

Chalky passed the entry drive, swore, then turned around and found the entrance on the second try. Recognizing the mailboxes in his headlights, he charged through the woods to the switchbacks. When he reached them, he stopped a second, considered how he'd attack them, breathed deeply, and took the first one with a running start. Even if I get stuck, I can make it

259

on foot from here. It's only a couple hundred yards down the road, he thought.

He made it. The Suburban struggled up over the last small hill, wheels spinning, engine roaring, and he headed for the cabin as fast as he could without losing it in a ditch.

Up ahead, rotating lights. A police car, and in front of it a truck of some kind. Chalky peered into the blackness hoping to see a collection of people talking in front, with Peggy smiling when she saw his car.

As he pulled up behind the police car, he realized there was no one in the yard, and the house was black and somber. Not a light on anywhere. His heart pounded in his chest, and his stomach was cold and achy. If Carlos was there, and they caught him, why would the lights still be off in the house, unless . . . unless . . .

Opening the car door, he jumped out into the wind and snow. In a conditioned reflex, his gun was in his hand without thinking about it. He jogged to the police car door window. It was coated with snow.

Chalky opened the door and leapt back when a man tumbled in slow motion to the ground. A big man. The sound of a basketball game came from his pocket adding another touch of insanity to the scene. Chalky bent over him. The light from the interior revealed a hunting knife buried to the hilt in the side of his neck. The mike still lay on the seat. Chalky grabbed the mike and keyed it and got someone at the Snoqualmie station. He told them about the dead body.

"There are going to be injuries inside as well as this officer. Send a couple of paramedic units too." The woman was hesitant at first, then agreed to. She told him to wait, that two cars should be there in minutes. "Sorry," Chalky said, "I have no choice, I have to go in." He hung the mike in its holder, then turned off the lights of the cruiser. Blackness reclaimed the yard and removed him as an inviting target from the house.

Chalky looked at the truck in front of the Bronco. Through the whipping snow, he could barely see the door was open a crack. He held his gun out and creeped up to the cab, then jerked the door open.

"Oh, no!" The air was forced from his chest. A head. So hideous, so bloody. He made himself stoop lower and studied it closely.

"Carrie?" he asked incredulously. "What?"

He had proof that Carlos was here, but Carrie? What was she doing here? His stomach sank. Was he too late for Peggy too?

Chalky slammed the door on the horror, turned, and ran toward the house. He tried the front door. Locked. Kick it down? No. Lose any possibility of surprise. Around back, see if something is open.

His lungs burned from the cold air as he hesitated, then climbed the steps of the decking. Something moving in the dark. He aimed his gun and moved closer. Drapes . . . but how? . . . it's open . . . broken window . . . by gunfire? Chalky moved the drapes aside with his left hand as he squinted into the dark interior, trying to make out something, anything. It was a black cave inside.

He stepped in. The glass crunched under his shoes. He jumped, then realized what it was. Upstairs, a dim light flickered from where he guessed the bedrooms to be. He stepped forward and . . .

His foot hit something soft, something big—

Stepping back, he focused on the floor.

A body—the other policeman.

He felt the man's face and neck with his left hand, feeling for life. Still warm. Strong pulse. Still alive, but in trouble. When he pulled away his hand, it was wet, sticky and warm with the coppery smell of blood. He wiped it on his coat and shivered.

"Hang on, buddy, help is coming," he whispered even though he knew the officer was unconscious. Outside the door, the wind howled up and down the scale. The curtains snapped.

The bedroom—the light—Carlos—

No noise came from the bedroom. Chalky strained to hear above the wind, but the only sound was the thumping of his pulse in his ears. The image of Peggy lying with her arms gone flashed. He shook his head.

Don't! he yelled in his mind. Don't!

If he thought about that it would make him too vulnerable . . . he'd stop thinking and end up like these two cops. Get Carlos first, then . . .

He pulled back the hammer on his gun and walked to the steps. The bedroom was silent. He tiptoed up the stairs. A tread squeaked.

He thought, if Carlos is up there, he has to know I'm here. He'd have heard me outside anyway. No time to wait for those other men to arrive, I have to go, keep moving.

Chalky concentrated on looking off to the side when he got to the top to let his eyes absorb any peripheral movement.

Still nothing. He edged up onto the landing, then along the hallway wall as he glanced around constantly. Chalky avoided staring at the light coming from the room. Even though it was dim, it could destroy his night vision. If Carlos was still here and going to attack, he'd be in the dark waiting somewhere, not standing in the light.

Flickering came from the open master bedroom door. When he passed the second bedroom door, he stopped and listened. Chalky heard a mewling sound. Scooter. The dog must be hiding in there. He stepped through the door and flipped on his flashlight and quickly followed the walls, then the bed, then the floor. Scooter lay on her towels, and her dark eyes shined in the dark. Chalky flipped off the light and waited a couple of seconds to let his eyes readjust to the dark again. He shuffled to the lit doorway of the master bedroom suite and leaned in. . . .

The bed was centered on the far wall with two white candles burning on either side of it. Their waxy smell was heavy in the chilled air.

On the bed, a figure covered head to toe with blankets—

His throat closed; his mouth worked.

"Peggy, oh, Peggy—I'm too late," he whispered.

Moving into the room, he let his gaze follow the wall. A chair, a dresser, a floor lamp. A closet with the door closed.

Nothing in the room but the bed—

And Peggy's figure under the blankets.

He shut the door, sealing off his exposure from that direction. Frozen snow tapped the window and the wind alternately gusted—the only interruptions of the deathly silence in the room. Peggy was still under the blanket.

Did she have her arms . . . or is she dead like the cop in the truck and Carrie? If she's dead, I don't care what happens to me, it won't matter. If her arms are gone, I'll still love her, take care of her, he thought.

Chalky approached the bed with an odd mixture of terror, tenderness, and love. No matter what had happened to her, she would always be his Peggy.

When he reached for the top of the blanket—

The figure was still motionless—

Peggy, I love you, don't be dead . . . don't be . . .

He put his gun in its holster, gripped the top of the blanket with both hands—and pulled—

Chalky froze in place—

Carlos leapt up and slashed him in the shoulder with a long-bladed knife while he screamed unintelligible sounds and flailed—

The pain was hot, shrieking through his system—

Chalky yelled—fell backward—

Carlos was on him like a wild animal with one intent—to cut and tear him to shreds—the smell of his hot breath was the smell of death—of insanity—

Carlos's arm arced back for another thrust with the knife and Chalky's hand followed it instinctively—

He got Carlos by the wrist—

They fell and rolled toward the door—

Carlos tried to force the knife to Chalky's throat—

Chalky struggled to hold Carlos off—

"You son of a bitch!" Chalky shouted, trying to push his hand away. Carlos was on top of him, and Chalky brought his knee up hard into Carlos's groin. Carlos crashed into the wall—dented the plaster with his head—but was on his feet like a cat and charged Chalky who had managed to scramble up too.

Chalky reached for his gun with his right hand. Carlos slammed into him again, knocking him backward. Chalky felt a sharp pain and warmth on his side, and he knew he'd taken another slash. He turned and hit Carlos hard across the face with his right elbow and Carlos went down stunned, and the knife clattered on the hardwood floor.

In a quick movement his gun was out and pointed at Carlos. Carlos crouched, shook his head, and looked up into the barrel of the gun.

Carlos hissed, then smiled as the blood trickled down his jaw.

"You're dead, gringo, you're all dead. Nobody can stop me, I'll kill you all!"

Chalky could feel his finger use up four pounds of the six-pound trigger pull. Peggy. I've got to know what happened to Peggy.

"Where's Peggy, you piece of human garbage?"

Carlos's eyes wavered and he leered, his face a mask of evil and hatred—

"Done know no Peggy, man—no Peggy—"

"The doctor, you bastard—the lady doctor!"

"Oh! The *puta*—the bitch!" Carlos smiled wider.

"Tell me where she is right now or I'll blow your fucking head off!"

"I screwed her, then cut off her arms, man, she's all fucked up . . . yeah . . . but I screwed her good . . . she loved it, man, she loved it . . . she begged for more . . . but I put her to sleep, man, I fucked her, then I fucked her up good!" He laughed shrilly and his eyes flashed with insanity. A chill went up Chalky's back at his words. Chalky's hand shook with the hunger to kill him, but he had to find Peggy. She could be anywhere . . . out in the snow . . . anywhere. . . .

In an overpowering rush of disgust, Chalky roared his hate and slashed the butt of the gun across Carlos's head. Carlos slammed forward on his face, moaning. Chalky straddled him and withdrew his handcuffs with his free hand. He snapped one end on Carlos's left wrist and was straining to reach his other wrist when Carlos raised up—

With a howl, Carlos rolled over and threw the weakened Chalky on the floor.

Carlos was up and running before Chalky could recover. Chalky righted himself and fired his gun and missed; the slug thudded into the wall. Carlos was out the door as Chalky jumped up and followed. At the doorway, Chalky could hear him pounding toward the stairs—Chalky braced to fire again when he heard the frightened cry of Scooter, then stumbling steps and a crashing sound. It was followed instantly by another loud smashing noise and a scream from Carlos.

Chalky dashed down the hallway, trying to adjust his eyes to the darkness.

Carlos had gone through the railing at the top of the stairs—

Scooter pulled herself into the bedroom, frightened, but not injured. Son of a bitch tripped over the dog, he thought.

Chalky cautiously looked over the edge to the living-room floor—

As his eyes conformed again to the darkness, he could see Carlos lying faceup in the middle of a wood-framed glass-topped coffee table—the glass smashed—

Chalky edged down the stairs and across to the table . . . still aiming his gun at Carlos all the time—

"Son of a bitch!" Chalky said as he wavered back and forth from the shock of his wounds.

"Help me, help me," Carlos said weakly. He was lying faceup on the floor, his feet and one arm still hanging in the frame of the glass-topped table he'd crashed through.

"Holy shit," Chalky said. Carlos's left arm was severed at the shoulder and was just hanging by a shred. Blood spurted from the ripped arteries in an uncontrolled stream onto the floor.

"Help me, please," Carlos begged, his voice getting weaker.

"Tell me where the lady doctor is, you bastard, then I'll help you," Chalky demanded. Looking at the arm, he knew there was nothing he could do. The wound was beyond simple first aid. Carlos's only chance was if the paramedics got here in time.

"Help me, you have to, you have to."

"Where is she, tell me!"

"Please, I'm getting dizzy, help me, help me." Carlos's voice was thin now. "Mama! Help me, Mama!" he screamed in a last effort. "Mama! See the sun . . . it's coming . . . so hot . . . hot . . . I'm sorry, I'm sorry I left you . . . help me . . . help meeeee. . . ." His voice trailed off, then his breath rattled and he was still.

Chalky collapsed in a chair and held his hand to his shoulder. It was warm, and he was getting dizzy either from shock or the loss of blood.

Outside, he could hear a door slam.

The police have arrived finally. I'll just sit here . . . until they come in . . . they can . . .

A groan from upstairs—

"Peggy!" Chalky yelled, then was up and moving for the stairs—

"Help. . . ."

A weak cry from the bedroom—

Chalky ran up the stairs, down the hall, and stumbled into the bedroom—

"Help . . . please. . . ." Her voice, soft and feeble.

The closet. Chalky ran to the bed and grabbed one of the candles, then turned to the closet door. Outside, more car doors slammed. The flickering light from the gumballs on the police cars came through the windows.

"Peggy!" Chalky cried.

Fearing the worst, he grabbed the handle and flung the door open—

Peggy lay on her side on the floor of the closet, wrapped tightly in a bloodied sheet. He looked desperately at her sides trying to locate her arms.

"Oh, God!" He was overcome with emotion. He knelt down and held the candle high, almost afraid to touch her, terrified at what he'd find. Her eyes opened as her head moved toward him. Recognition lit her face.

"Chalky, help me, please. Help, help . . . the pain . . ." Her voice choked with emotion or agony.

Chalky reached out and gently unwound the tight sheet from around her neck. "I killed a policeman, I didn't know . . . I didn't know . . ." she mumbled.

"He's alive, Pegs. He'll live," he said in a consoling tone. Chalky slowly unwrapped the sheet and remembered that the other victim was so out of it she had to be told her arms were removed. He clamped his teeth together trying to prepare himself for the worst. As horrible as it would be if she was mutilated, he loved her and was pathetically grateful she was alive.

Chalky gently unwrapped the last layer of cloth.

Shakily, she stretched to touch him. He choked with tenderness as he leaned forward and pulled her arms around his neck.

"Thanks, God," he said.

"So dizzy. What happened . . . where is he?" She was slowly realizing what had occurred. "He was injecting me when he heard the noise downstairs."

"It's okay," he whispered as he kissed her neck and hair. "He won't ever bother anyone again."

"Must not have given me a full shot, or I'd still be unconscious."

"Shhhh—shhhh," he comforted. "Don't talk now." He leaned back and inspected her as well as he could in the flickering flame—other than bruises on her arms, she appeared to be unharmed— "God, I love you, kid. Can you stand yet?"

Still heavily drugged, she looked up through unfocused eyes, put her hands on the floor, and wobbled on her weak arms. He grabbed her again and hugged her tightly. Tears of gratitude ran down his cheeks as he kissed her hair, her face, her neck. Peggy made soft moaning sounds and grasped for him, still unable to mentally assemble what had happened.

"Chalky . . . Chalky . . . is that you?" she asked.

He chuckled into her neck. It was going to be a while before she could find her feet and know exactly where she was. Chalky kissed her face gently and then her lips.

A crashing sound came from downstairs as the policemen kicked in the front door, then he could hear heavy running footsteps in the lower hall.

The lights in the house came on with a pop and a hum as the officers flipped on the main switch.

Two policemen broke into the room, glanced at them, then the bed and candles. One pointed his gun at Chalky and said, "Don't move, fellow, stand up and take your hands off that woman."

Chalky said softly, "The bad guy's in the living room, fellows. I'm a cop too—"

He hesitated.

"And as far as she's concerned," Chalky continued as he smiled down on Peggy—

"She's mine . . . get your own girl."

"SANDFORD GRABS YOU BY THE THROAT AND WON'T LET GO!"
—ROBERT B. PARKER

NEW YORK TIMES BESTSELLING AUTHOR

JOHN SANDFORD

__SILENT PREY 0-425-13756-2/$5.99

Davenport's ex-lover Lily Rothenburg of the NYPD wants him
to help her track down a group of rogue cops responsible for
three dozen murders. The cases couldn't be more clear-
cut—until they merge in unexpected and terrifying ways . . .

__EYES OF PREY   0-425-13204-8/$5.99

They're killers working in concert. One terribly scarred. The
other strikingly handsome, a master manipulator fascinated
with all aspects of death. Lieutenant Lucas Davenport knows
he's dealing with the most terrifying showdown of his career.

__SHADOW PREY   0-425-12606-4/$5.99

A slumlord butchered in Minneapolis. A politician executed in
Manhattan. A judge slain in Oklahoma City. This time, the
assassin is no ordinary serial killer...But Lieutenant Lucas
Davenport is no ordinary cop.

__RULES OF PREY   0-425-12163-1/$5.99

The killer is mad but brilliant. He kills victims for the sheer contest
of it and leaves notes with each body, rules of murder: "Never
have a motive." "Never kill anyone you know." Lucas Davenport
is the clever detective who's out to get him, and this cop plays by
his own set of rules.

For Visa, MasterCard and American Express orders ($15 minimum) call: 1-800-631-8571

FOR MAIL ORDERS: CHECK BOOK(S). FILL OUT COUPON. SEND TO:	POSTAGE AND HANDLING: $1.75 for one book, 75¢ for each additional. Do not exceed $5.50.
BERKLEY PUBLISHING GROUP 390 Murray Hill Pkwy., Dept. B East Rutherford, NJ 07073	**BOOK TOTAL** $ _____
NAME_____	**POSTAGE & HANDLING** $ _____
ADDRESS_____	**APPLICABLE SALES TAX** $ _____ (CA, NJ, NY, PA)
CITY_____	**TOTAL AMOUNT DUE** $ _____
STATE_____ ZIP_____	**PAYABLE IN US FUNDS.** (No cash orders accepted.)
PLEASE ALLOW 6 WEEKS FOR DELIVERY. PRICES ARE SUBJECT TO CHANGE WITHOUT NOTICE.	303b